"Fong knows his stuff and delivers it. *Fragmented* is taut, tense and terrifying."

—Don Winslow

Deftly plotted, lightning paced and immensely readable, *Fragmented* is a stellar debut from a talented newcomer. We will be hearing much more from this new author. Highly recommended."

—Sheldon Siegel

"Clean, vivid, and gripping, a knowing crime story written at street level. George Fong distills a twenty-seven year FBI career and his talent shines through."

—Kirk Russell

"Every page of George Fong's haunting debut, *Fragmented,* bears the imprint of real-life experience. Here is a writer with the dark, magnetic wisdom of a man who's seen the best and worst of the human species, and who possesses an intimate understanding of those who enforce the law, those who defy it, and the innocent lives caught in between. The story doesn't seem just plausible or likely – it rings true, it feels lived. It will not just surprise and entertain, it will shock and disturb. Prepare yourself for some late night reading – and a nightmare or two."

—David Corbett

FRAGMENTED

GEORGE FONG

Out Of The
GUTTER
AN IMPRINT OF GUTTER BOOKS
www.gutterbooks.com

To my wife, Rebecca, my children, Kyle and Rachel . . . and Sparky, the town greeter.

Acknowledgements

Many thanks to:

Author Robin Burcell, for taking a moment back in 2004 when, during a difficult time in my life, I sent her an email asking about the art of writing. And she answered! From that point on, I was introduced to the world's best people: mystery writers. Thank you, Sheldon Siegel, for letting me be a part of the Book Passage's Mystery Writer's Conference every year, which gave me the opportunity to learn from published authors and help me be part of their club. To Elaine and Bill Petrocelli, owners of one of the world's finest independent bookstores, Book Passage—for hosting the annual conference and their continued support and encouragement.

To the writers who've spent countless hours with me—talking, reading, editing, (not to mention drinking!), and of course pushing me forward in this wonderful endeavor: Michael Connelly, Lee Child, Don Winslow, David Corbett, Kirk Russell, Cornelia Read, and PF Chang's Platinum member customer, Tim Maleeny.

To the wonderful Kimberley Cameron of the Kimberley Cameron Literary Agency. Thank you for your patience and tireless advocacy. To my editor Joe Clifford, a phenomenal writer in his own right, who spent many days making me understand the meaning of "less is more."(Read his books. It will make you hug your child.)

To all the law enforcement officers I had the great pleasure of working with over my twenty-seven years as a federal agent. What I learned from these interactions gave me the stories and life experiences I will always remember (and wish upon no other person).

And to my family. To my beautiful wife, Rebecca, for letting me work, write, and (sometimes) pass on taking out the garbage. To my children, Kyle and Rachel, who have survived listening to my war stories. Without their patience, support, and understanding, I never would have made it.

FRAGMENTED

1

Chico Police Department
October 1999 – 2:44 a.m.

The smell was a combination of smoke and charred skin.

Detective Jeff Iverson remembered the first time he was exposed to it. He was a rookie cop, responding to a warehouse fire. Pulling up to the scene, he could hear the crying sound of a frantic dog over the yelping police sirens. By the time the fire department put out the massive blaze, the poor animal was smoldering and blackened stiff. It had a sharp odor, like bad meat left too long on the broiler. He couldn't take his eyes off the charred remains; sad to think just how horribly the dog must have suffered.

Today was different. It wasn't a dog that burned.

As soon as Alvin Cooper walked into the small interview room at the Chico Police Department, the odor hit Iverson immediately. He pushed the back of his hand against the front of his nose to stave off the acrid smell, but it did little to help. He couldn't stop himself from coughing up the foul air that invaded his lungs from the soot floating around Cooper, the only survivor of a devastating fire.

Cooper was slouched low in a hard, plastic chair inside the interview room. It was only hours past midnight, the sun far from rising. An EMS blanket draped across Cooper's shoulders, the dark blue wool still matted with broken twigs and fallen leaves that came

13

from his front lawn. His short, blond hair tangled above his head like loose hay. The splash of coffee left at the bottom of the Styrofoam cup perched in front of Cooper had gone cold, almost three hours old. Cooper rarely made a movement, his stare fixated on some invisible spot on the table. It's what people do when they've lost everything.

Iverson kept his eyes on his notebook, not wanting to stare at Cooper. It's never comfortable, two people sitting in a small room, void of conversation, having the only thing in common being a tragic event. He could tell Cooper was aware of his presence because every so often he would look up and give Iverson a look that said, Why are we still here? There were still a few facts he needed to gather. He had already collected the basics but knew his task force partner would have additional questions before calling it a night.

"You said you couldn't sleep?" Iverson asked.

Cooper nodded, his head hanging low over the table. "I tried but everything kept me awake." Cooper reached up and massaged his face with both hands without realizing he was smearing black soot deep into his skin. "I remember hearing a dog bark and the wind rustling through the trees."

"You had a lot on your mind?"

Cooper again nodded. "Work. Of all the nights to think about something so unimportant."

Iverson grunted, trying to sound empathetic. "When did you first notice the fire?" Iverson started flipping back a few pages in his notebook, scanning for something Cooper had said earlier in the interview. "You said you were already downstairs when you saw the flames. Do you remember how long?"

Cooper paused for a moment, as if running the series of events through his head. He was tired and distraught. In a matter of minutes, his whole life went up in flames and now he was trying to account for each and every detail as if this were a test. He dug his fingers into his forehead as if he could tear out the memory of what had just happened. A tear slid down his cheek and fell to the Formica top, marking it with a dark droplet the color of gray ink. "I went downstairs to pour myself something to drink."

Iverson interrupted. "You told me you went downstairs to watch TV."

"Yeah, both."

"Sorry. Go on."

"I walked into the kitchen, opened up the refrigerator and grabbed the milk. Then I remember walking to the living room and sitting down in my chair."

"The smoke, Mr. Cooper. How long were you watching TV before you noticed the smoke?"

Cooper's head rocked side to side. "I don't remember. I only remember the flames. Bright flames all around me. I could have fallen asleep and then woke up to the flames. I just can't remember. I didn't know what to do. I panicked."

Iverson reached over and patted Cooper on the arm. "Take it easy, it will be all right. I'm sorry we have to go through this but we want to get all the facts while it's still fresh in your mind."

Cooper's head slid out of his hand. He folded his arms on top of the table and buried his face in them. His body jerked in spasms as tears started to form a puddle of black below his face. "Two for one," he said to himself. "God I'd do it. Two for one."

"I don't understand."

He lifted his head and used his blanket to wipe his bloodshot eyes. Cooper reached across the table, grabbing a hold of Iverson's arm desperately. "As the saying goes," he confessed. "Two for one."

Iverson remained quiet, keeping his stare on Cooper.

"I would trade my life for my wife's and my daughter's, right now."

Iverson's eyes sagged. The wife was trapped upstairs in the bedroom. His daughter never woke up. They found his wife's body crumpled up by the bedroom door, his daughter's still in her bed.

Cooper buried his face in both hands. "Take me, God. Take me in trade."

"Everything's going to be okay."

Cooper's gaze drifted slowly above his hands, in Iverson's direction. "You think everything's going to be okay?"

Iverson felt the pang of guilt. "I didn't mean it that way."

"My wife and daughter were burned alive. They burned, for God's sake." Cooper's hands fell hard onto the table. The Styrofoam cup took a hop then tipped over, the remnants spilling, mixing with the soot and tears. "And I did nothing to save them."

"I'm so sorry, Mr. Cooper."

That's all Iverson could think to say. Alvin Cooper's entire world died four hours ago in a tragic accident. From what Iverson could surmise, it was probably the main gas line. Broke, leaked. The gas stove pilot set it off. It wouldn't be the first time in these older homes. Cooper woke after falling asleep in front of the television, became confused and disoriented. He stumbled out the front door, choking on the thick smoke and passed out, far enough away so that he wasn't consumed by the fire, unlike his family. Lucky him.

"I would trade places with them, I swear I would."

"I know," Iverson replied.

The minute hand on the clock rolled straight up. Three in the morning. Iverson fought back a yawn. The buzzing sound coming from the florescent lights in the ceiling was disrupted by the clank of the door hinge. Iverson sat up. Cooper remained lost in his own thoughts.

Iverson didn't get a chance to reach for the door handle before FBI Special Agent Jack Paris entered the small room. He had a manila folder in one hand and a small plastic bag in the other. Jack looked over at Cooper then over at Iverson.

"Okay to join in?"

Iverson nodded, adding a sigh of relief that his partner had finally arrived, hopefully bringing this day to an end.

Jack pushed the empty chair away from the table and then slid into the seat, shifting his position in order to face Cooper directly. He opened the folder, exposing a report from the on-scene fire investigator, and placed the plastic bag gently next to the folder. Inside the bag was a very small flat box with a picture imprinted on top.

Jack looked over at Iverson. "You get all the details?"

Iverson nodded and tapped at his notebook with his pen.

"Good."

Jack sat back in his chair but kept his stare on Cooper. It took a minute of silence before Cooper looked up at Jack, letting go of a deep sigh.

Cooper said, "What more do you want from me?"

Jack raised a hand, like he didn't mean to upset him. "I know it's late. I'm sorry for keeping you here so long but I want to cover a few facts before we stop. It won't take long."

Cooper's eyes fell shut as he discriminantly waved a hand. "Fine, I've got no place to go."

"You told Detective Iverson you got out of bed because you couldn't sleep?"

Cooper kept his gaze on the table. "Yes."

"And so you went downstairs . . . to pour yourself a drink."

"Yes, yes, a glass of milk."

"Then, turned on the TV."

Cooper lifted his head and looked at Jack. "That's right. Why are we going over this again? I told you all of this already."

"Bear with me." Jack picked up the folder, flipped through a few pages and then let the folder drop back onto the table. "The fire. You said the first thing you saw when you awoke were the flames."

"Yes." Cooper's voice was becoming agitated.

"Along the stairs, is that correct?"

Pause. "I think so. They were all around me. I can't be sure if they were in front of the stairs or not. I just know the whole house was on fire."

"You told Detective Iverson the stairs. That's why you couldn't go up to get your wife and child." Jack turned his head and looked over at Iverson.

Iverson flipped back a few pages and read from the notes he took a few hours earlier: "I couldn't get up the stairs. They were totally engulfed. I couldn't go up to save my family."

"That's right," Cooper responded. "The stairs were on fire. The whole fucking house was on fire."

"No, I don't think that's what you originally said. You said the stairs were on fire."

"The stairs, the living room, the hallway. The whole place."

"But if the whole place was on fire, how did you get out without even a burn mark?" Jack stood and walked over to Cooper, pushed back the blanket to expose Cooper's pajamas. "Those are cotton. They're covered in soot but not a singe. How do you explain that?"

Cooper's jaw tightened. He slammed the table with his fist. "I don't know. Why does this matter?"

"Because it doesn't make sense. Conflicting statements, no burn marks…." Before Cooper had a chance to respond, Jack continued. "This is the fire investigator's report. It's only preliminary but according to them, the fire started from outside, along a row of Japanese boxwood." Jack leaned forward. "That would be right in front next to the entryway door."

Cooper remained silent.

"The fire went hot and fast. That means there had to be an accelerant used. Your garage. There were three empty gas containers in there." Jack paused a moment to study Cooper's reaction. There was none. "The fire then made its way into the house, starting in the living room, then moving toward the back. Toward the stairway, as you stated."

Again, Cooper remained silent.

"How were you able to make it out the door when that's where the fire originated from? I mean, at that point, the whole front of the house would have been totally engulfed. You would have turned to charcoal trying to get through there."

"Maybe I didn't go out the front door," Cooper said. "I was confused. Maybe I went out the back?"

"No, that's not what you said. You said the front door. You were very clear about that."

Iverson remembered Cooper's original statement: "Front door, that's what he said."

"Front door, back door, I just got out." More tears welled up in his eyes. "My family. My family died."

"Then there was this." Jack picked up the plastic bag. He held it up in front of Cooper's face, close enough to read the markings. "It's a matchbook."

"So?"

"Look familiar?" The matchbook was unique. The cover depicted an airbrush painting of a naked woman in a seductive pose. The words "Black and Brown Club, Budapest, Hungary" were stenciled across the naked woman's legs. "Not something you would find in every household."

"What are you saying?"

"I'm saying the fire investigators found it outside on your lawn. Didn't you tell Detective Iverson earlier that you had traveled to Budapest after graduating from high school?"

"That was years ago. Thousands of people travel there."

"Yes," Jack remarked. "Thousands. But it was *your* house that burned down." Jack looked down at the plastic bag, studying the small item it held. "And this box of matches started it all." Jack tossed the bag back on the table.

Cooper sat up straight, his stare sharpened. "It's not mine."

"Crime Scene Investigators were able to lift prints from the box. Did you know we can lift prints from a paper surface? It's the oil that allows us to get them. From your fingers." Jack lifted a hand, flashing five fingers at Cooper.

"Why are you doing this? I told you the truth, I couldn't sleep, I went downstairs and poured myself a drink and turned on the TV. I fell asleep and woke to the fire. The fire that killed my family. The fire killed them. Not me."

Jack slid closer to Cooper.

Iverson followed Jack's lead and leaned in, giving Cooper little room to move. He took out his pen, knowing he needed to document whatever Cooper had to say, verbatim.

Jack let the moment settle. He had Cooper's attention. "I know what you did."

Cooper's face wrinkled. "What are you talking about?"

"You said you fell asleep in front of the TV?"

Cooper leaned forward, his face inches from Jack's. "That's what I said, Goddammit!"

You sit there very long?"

"I said I couldn't sleep."

"What was on?"

"What?"

"What were you watching?"

Cooper froze. He slowly fell back into his chair; his eyelids formed half-moons but his stare never left Jack's. "I want a lawyer."

"They burned to death, Mr. Cooper. You trapped them inside your house and let them burn. What kind of animal are you?"

Cooper turned away, averting his face from Jack's accusations. His anger drained from his expression, now taking on the rigidity of stone.

Jack stood up and pulled out a pair of handcuffs. He reached under Cooper's left arm and yanked him up, hard. Iverson made his way around to the other side, keeping Cooper from falling over.

Jack Paris ratcheted the cuff tightly on Cooper's wrists, enough to make Cooper wince. Cooper's head dipped toward the table, the air in his lungs slowly escaping through his nostrils.

"You were right, Mr. Cooper," Jack said. "Two for one."

As he heard Jack say the words, Iverson saw darkness build in Cooper's eyes. Cooper was never the victim; he was the predator.

Iverson got on his radio and within seconds two uniforms entered the room. They led Cooper out the door to a holding cell down the hall. Jack gathered up his things, dropping papers into open folders. Iverson leaned against the table, staring at the empty chair where Cooper sat and thinking how quickly things had turned.

"Why do you think he did it?"

Jack shrugged. "I can't say."

"Geez, Jack. You're accusing a man of killing his family."

Jack raised an eyebrow and gave Iverson a quiet stare. "Maybe she knew something he didn't want others to find out about."

"Are you telling me he couldn't think of a better way to keep things quiet?"

"Jeff," Jack replied. "There's only one way for two people to keep a secret."

"How's that?"

"One kills the other."

"What are you, the dark side of a lounge act?"

Jack didn't offer a reply, just continued collecting his papers.

Jeff Iverson began tapping his pen on the top of his notebook, wondering how Cooper could think killing was a rational answer to his problems—let alone his own family. "You think that's it? A secret?"

"I don't know," Jack said. "I just know he did it."

2

Five Years Later
Butte County, California
Monday – 7:15 a.m.

"**It was** the damnedest thing," Paul Baker said to his secretary, Rose, after pushing away from his desk at the Diamond County Bank.

"What was?" Rose asked, not really focused on the conversation, but rather sifting through a handful of loan files.

Baker paused a moment, thinking about the past fifteen minutes.

"Did you see his eyes?"

Rose murmured something, her attention still attached to the stacks of files cradled in her arms.

"I said did you notice his eyes?"

Rose finally stopped sifting and looked over at Baker. "Eyes? What about them?"

Baker thought for a beat, trying to formulate his jumbled, maybe irrational thoughts to describe what he was feeling, but couldn't come up with the right words.

Rose placed the folders on Baker's desk, and gave a curious look as she pulled back one of the chairs and sat down.

"What?" she asked.

"The customer you just brought over, Hampton Carter."

Rose paused a moment, wondering where Baker was going with his remark.

"Strange bird, don't you think?" he said.

Rose shrugged.

"He reminds me of that guy, from that movie, *Fargo*." Baker made a motion, circling his hands around his eyes.

Rose raised an eyebrow. "You mean Steve Buscemi?"

Baker tapped the top of his desk like he was dotting an i. "That's the one."

Rose nodded and smiled, looking like she was pleased with herself, guessing correctly on the first try. "What about him?"

Baker began to describe the short meeting he just had with the walk-in customer. "It just didn't feel right."

Baker was recently appointed the position of senior loan officer. His job was to evaluate all loans and—more importantly—the people asking for them. He had to determine not only their ability to repay but the willingness to do so.

Hampton Carter had been his first walk-in of the day, just some guy looking for a small loan. Rose had brought Carter over to his desk where he stood still for a moment, allowing Baker the opportunity to give him a good look-over. He was average in height, slender, wearing a blue-gray windbreaker, dark slacks. His hair was blond and short, combed straight back with gel that Baker could smell, even from a distance. But it was Carter's eyes that drew Baker's attention. His pupils were pinpoint, like periods on a page. And steely. Even when Carter smiled his greeting, his eyes betrayed a contradictory meaning, almost predacious.

Carter nodded and maneuvered himself between two large chairs that were in front of Baker's Rosewood desk. They spoke briefly, Carter telling Baker he was interested in a car loan for his wife but Baker found it odd the man wasn't wearing a wedding ring. Baker started explaining the requirements for the loan, all the while, Carter gazed straight and steady as if watching a movie.

"Are you married?" Carter asked.

The question caught Baker by surprise.

"Yes," he answered but then hesitated, not feeling inclined to elaborate. His voice stumbled before refocusing back on the loan.

Carter smiled.

Baker handed Carter a loan application, along with a handful of glossy bank brochures. "Mr. Carter, do you have an account with us?"

"No," was Carter's reply. One word. Baker wondered why a person wanting money from a bank where he was not a customer didn't offer more of an explanation.

Baker slid a small card forward. An information card. With a pencil, Baker pointed at a string of lines needing to be filled in: home address, telephone number, Social Security number. Throughout his entire instruction, Carter never looked down at the card, his stare locked on Baker.

"Children?" Carter asked.

Baker paused, confused. "Excuse me?"

"Children? Do you have any children?"

Baker backed his chair away from his desk. Without realizing it, he felt the need to put some distance between him and Carter.

"Yes. A daughter," Baker answered as he offered Carter the pencil. Trying to be polite, he asked, "How about you?"

Carter kept his smile but didn't respond. He simply took the pencil and started writing. He kept pausing, erasing and re-writing, as if he didn't know his own personal information. After a minute, Carter said, "Would you mind if I took the forms home, so that my wife could help me out?"

"That's fine." Baker reached out, retrieved the old information card, and placed it on the corner of his desk. He added a new one to the application forms, dropped both into a large yellow envelope, and handed it over.

"Here's a clean set," he said to Carter. He held them out but Carter's attention was elsewhere, focused on a framed photograph prominently displayed on Baker's desk. A portrait of his family.

Carter turned his head and looked at Baker. A smile stretched across his lips. "What's her name?"

Baker straightened up in his seat, feeling the hair on his neck tingle. "Who?" Baker knew who he was referring to; he just didn't want to answer.

"I assume the lovely girl in the photo is your daughter?"

For the second time during this short meeting, Baker hesitated, but felt forced to respond. "Yes."

A long silence followed as Carter waited for an answer to his original question.

"Jessica," Baker finally said. "That's my daughter, Jessica."

Carter grinned, exposing a set of bright white teeth. He picked up the framed portrait, gazing deep into the picture, and repeated her name: "Jessica."

Baker started feeling flush, hot and cold rushing through his body at the same time. He felt anxious but didn't really know why. One thing Baker was certain of: he didn't appreciate Carter's interest in his daughter and he wanted him to leave. "She's home with the flu." Baker pulled the picture from Carter's hand and returned it to its place. It was an uncomfortable moment as Baker stuck out a hand, thanking Carter for coming while shoving the envelope at him with his other. "Come back soon," he said but didn't really mean it.

Carter accepted the handshake and took the packet. He didn't speak, maintaining his smile before turning and walking away, out the lobby doors.

"We get a lot of crazies," Rose said after listening to Baker describe his meet with Carter.

Baker nodded, wondering if he was just being paranoid. He rested his hands on top of his desk and felt the coolness of the large plate glass. Fog formed around his fingers. He lifted his hands and realized his palms were sweaty. He pulled a tissue from his desk drawer and wiped his hands dry. That's when he noticed they were trembling. Why? He met strange people all the time in this line of work.

Baker caught sight of Carter's old information card and gave it one last look. What he had filled out was barely legible.

"Crazies," he said to himself.

Rose had stepped away for a second but returned with another file folder, sticking it out for him to take. Consumed in his thoughts, Baker didn't even notice the folder.

"Are you okay?" Rose asked.

Baker sat quietly for a moment, trying to place logic into his meeting with Hampton Carter—his inquiry for a loan that he didn't seem to want, interest in his family portrait, interest in his daughter, Jessica. Baker looked up. "No, Rose. I don't think so."

3

Yolo County, California
Monday – 8:00 a.m.

FBI Special Agent Jack Paris watched the temperature display in his Bureau car climb. It was a typical summer morning in the Central Valley, sweltering and getting worse. He slid two fingers under his collar and gave it a gentle yank. Sweat had formed a moist ring around his neck, making him not only uncomfortable but irritable as well. Chatter came over the Bureau radio. Already, there was a silent alarm going off at the Bank of America in South Sacramento. Two FBI agents were sent to respond. Too early in the morning to be legit. Jack turned down the volume but kept an ear tuned to the communication with dispatch, waiting for the agents to confirm a false alarm, just in case. Traffic was light but he found himself maneuvering around slow-moving cars crawling in the left lane. He cranked the air conditioner and held an arm in front of the vent, letting the cold air flow up his sleeve.

He made his way off the freeway and down several surface streets, eventually pulling his Crown Vic up to the gate of the Sacramento Field Office. Jack waved his photo ID badge across the Hirsch keypad—an electronic card reader—as he punched in his private code. Several seconds passed before green lights flashed. The 3,000-pound black, steel gate lumbered open. A security guard on the other side stood at attention.

Jack found an open space, exited, and entered the building. More keypads, double-locks and man-traps. He made his way to the squad bay and fell into his chair, greeted only by the glowing red bulb of his telephone message indicator. Jack Paris hated messages. They were mostly electronic packets of bad news. His eyes drifted away from the phone, to the right, resting on a copy of *The Investigator,* a monthly newsletter about things happening throughout the Bureau. It was opened to a page with the heading "Anniversaries." Jack glanced nonchalantly through the rows of credential photos filling the page, each with the employee's name, years of service and their current office assignment. There, just above center, was Jack's picture. Someone—presumably whoever left the newsletter for Jack to see—had given the photo a make-over by penciling in Groucho Marx glasses along with the standard comedy mustache and an Alfred E. Neumann missing front tooth. Classy. Below the photo: Jack Paris, Twenty Years, Sacramento.

He studied the picture. With a Caucasian father and Asian mother, Jack didn't look like your typical agent. He took on his father's height at six feet and his strong jaw line. From his mother, her olive skin. He also inherited a good part of her tenacity. From the day he first became an agent with the FBI, he never thought of himself as different in any way. Agents were all the same, everyone equally abused by the Bureau. Today, however, he looked at the photo and finally saw a difference, but in a good way. He recognized his heritage from both sides and what it brought to his life as an agent. He was an amalgam of his parents. What they had ingrained in his character stared clearly back at him, even if it had taken twenty years to see it.

"Nice, eh?" The question came from behind him, steep in a Boston accent. Jack craned back and found Special Agent Sean Patrick Dooley, or Dools as he preferred, puffing his chest out, proclaiming himself king of the cartoon doodle.

Jack pointed at the drawing. "Nice artwork."

"Congratulations," Dools said.

"For what?"

"Twenty years. That's a big accomplishment."

"I guess."

"Your ex can now start collecting your retirement benefits."

"We're separated, not divorced."

"Yet," Dools added.

Jack stretched forward and tapped at a photo on the bottom right. It was Dools'. They were classmates at Quantico, both reaching the twenty-year mark together, both ending up in Sacramento, Jack by choice, Dools not so much.

"Speak for yourself." Dools was recently divorced.

"Touché."

Dools stuck out a hand, rocked it from side to side. "Not one of my best." He reached around and tapped a pudgy finger just to the right of Jack's. He laughed. "Look at that. Dale Cortavin."

Jack had slouched back in his chair, his eyes zeroed in on Cortavin's photo.

"Yup," Dools said with bite in his tone. "Cortavin with twenty and already an SAC." As in Special Agent in Charge.

"You got twenty," Jack said, reminding him that in the eyes of seniority they were all equal.

"Yeah, but I never aspired to rise to the top."

"You mean like a turd in a punch bowl?"

Dools pressed his finger on Cortavin's photo like he could smash the smile off his face. "Yep." Then he shook his head. "A real piece of shit."

Jack remained silent.

"You know I'm referring to Cortavin?" Dools said.

Jack nodded.

"You got to be a dick to be an SAC."

Jack knew Dools was just blowing off steam.

"Cortavin," Dools continued, "thinks he's the best thing that came to the Bureau since J. Edgar, himself."

"Don't think much of him, do you?"

Dools shook a finger at Cortavin's photo. "From the words of Senator Lloyd Bentsen, 'He's no Jack Kennedy.'"

That made Jack smile.

"You speak to Emily lately?" Dools asked.

The smile evaporated.

"You tell her about that job offer?"

Jack looked away.

"You should."

His response was polite. "Back off."

Dools opened his mouth but stopped short, deciding it was best not to venture forward in this conversation. He gave Jack two pats on the back, turned and walked down the hall to the file room.

Jack looked back at the telephone.

Lots of messages.

He took a deep breath and, with his notebook in hand, started cycling through a weekend's worth of calls.

"You have . . . ten . . . new messages and . . . twelve . . . old messages," the automated system informed him.

Jack didn't wait for instructions, punching in the proper codes. He began logging those that were important and dumping the rest into the electronic trash can.

One message caught his attention. "Jack, this is Ray Sizemore out of Seattle. I was told to call you specifically." There was a pause and the sound of shuffling papers. "I've got an old homicide that goes back about fifteen years. I may have new information pointing at a suspect in your territory. Give me a call and let's talk."

Jack cycled through the rest. Messages from defense counselors wanting time to cut a deal for their clients, news reporters wanting an interview. Jack jotted their numbers but already decided he had more important things to do. He came to the last message and a familiar voice.

"Jack, Border Collins."

There was a long silence as if Collins was hoping Jack would pick up the line.

"The Board met today. They'd like you to come in for a second interview."

Jack took a deep breath and held still.

"They were thinking this Friday, around ten o'clock. Listen, Jack, I know leaving the Bureau is a tough choice to make. It was hard for me, too. But you'll get use to it. I think you're going to be a great addition to our staff. Give me a call."

The message stopped and Jack let the call soak in. He looked back over at *The Investigator*, pulled it closer and stared at his twenty-year photo. Too many years had passed unnoticed, and somewhere during that time, he'd lost what he'd wanted most. His home life. The twenty gave him an out. The ability to start a new career and maybe find a way back to Emily. The job offer made him anxious and nervous at the same time. Maybe Dools was right. Maybe he should tell Emily. Twenty years was a long time, maybe long enough to now make a change. He knew he had to do something. He just didn't know what. Jack reached over and pressed a button on the keypad, hearing an automated response: *"Message Saved."*

Right now he needed coffee. Jack wandered to the kitchen, waited for a pot to brew, filled his office mug with what looked more like brown water and returned to his desk. He dialed Agent Sizemore, who he had heard good things about. The phone rang once before Sizemore answered. With a quick greeting, Jack opened up a fresh page in his notebook. "You said in your message you're working on a cold case?"

"An old one that's been sitting on the shelf for a while. Let me tell you what I got." Sizemore sucked in a breath, like this was going to take a while. Jack's curiosity was piqued.

"A little over fourteen years ago King County Sheriff's responded to a suspicious activity report at an abandoned church in a town outside of Renton. Neighbors kept seeing a van coming and going. Thought it had to do with drugs. Every once in a while they overheard strange noises late at night. The van stopped coming and the noise went away. The neighbors talked, decided to call the cops, you get the idea. When the locals got out there and went inside, they found a girl who had been reported missing."

"Dead?" Jack knew the answer but had to ask.

"Deputies found her body in a crawl space. She was fifteen-years-old. Based on the decomp, forensics estimated she'd been dead for a week by the time they arrived. They found her tied up, gagged and abandoned. The pathologist said she most likely died from dehydration. Whoever did this left her to die a slow death."

"I remember reading about that one. Hard to forget a case like that."

"It stayed in the news for months. Renton PD was able to I.D. the vic. Grace Holloway. Came up as an MP out of Seattle, Capitol Hill District, originally classified as a runaway. County ran an all out search for her killer without any luck. The crime scene yielded some evidence but it never panned out to much of anything."

"DNA?"

"That's the good news," Sizemore said with a bit more enthusiasm. "Luckily, the crime scene analysts took everything at the time of the search—paper bags, water glasses, old clothing. They had no idea if they were related. The stuff was worthless fifteen years ago, but recently they were able to pull the DNA from a couple of specs. Real small but enough."

"And?"

"They got a hit."

Jack smiled.

"Three months ago, I pulled the evidence and sent all the swabs to our DNA lab. They came back today with a hit in CODIS. The guy is a fine, upstanding citizen in your territory. Alvin Franklin Cooper. Get this, Jack, according to his criminal history, Mr. Cooper was convicted five years ago for torching his house with his wife and eight-year-old daughter sleeping inside. Burned to death while the asshole watched. It looks like killing is a hobby for Mr. Cooper."

Memories rushed back. "I remember Cooper. I worked the case with Chico PD."

"Then you know what happened to him."

"No, not really. I was just assisting with our evidence response team, did the follow-up interview when the fire call came in. After the initial interrogation, I was done." Jack paused for a second. "I was never called to testify. I think he took a plea deal."

"He did. To manslaughter."

"That doesn't seem right."

"I was told the DA made an offer and Cooper's attorney jumped on it."

Jack asked, "Does he know you're on to him?"

"Not yet. His record shows he's incarcerated at the Butte County Jail under a work furlough program."

Jack couldn't believe what he had just heard. "Work furlough? He murdered his entire family?"

"Apparently, part of the plea deal was that Cooper was deemed mentally unstable when he killed his family. He was ordered to County treatment. I spoke to a friend of mine at the California Department of Corrections who found out Cooper was going to therapy and has been a model prisoner ever since."

Jack tapped his pencil hard on his notepad, breaking the tip. "I had no idea."

"I need to learn more about Cooper to lock him down on this murder. I need a hold placed on him immediately. Get him off work furlough and in segregation."

"I'll get right on it."

"Could use your help interviewing him if you got the time." Sizemore's voice hardened, expressing the harsh realities of life. "I've been working these kind of guys for decades. You know just as well as I do, their stripes don't change. I'd check your unsolved files. From what I know about Cooper, I'll bet you a steak dinner and a cold beer at Morton's he's good for more."

Jack winced at Sizemore's contention and his stomach started to knot. "Get down here. I'll make sure our Mr. Cooper is safely tucked away until your arrival."

When the conversation ended, Jack looked up the number for his contact at the Butte County Jail. The call went through to Sergeant Dennis Warfield, the daytime watch commander. Over the years, Jack had dealt with Warfield on a number of homicide cases. Common acquaintances, Jack would always say.

"Tell me, Jack, which offender are you looking for?"

"Alvin Franklin Cooper."

There was a pause before Dennis responded. "I guess the Feds really are watching everything you do."

"What do you mean?"

"Alvin Cooper, model prisoner of the State for nearly five years, granted work furlough status for the past three months with no problems?"

Jack had a bad feeling where this was going.

"Three days ago, Mr. Cooper failed to return from work furlough. Between you and me, the guard gave Cooper the evening to report back, trying not to get him in trouble. Thought he was just running late. That evening's bed count came up one short and the guard knew he was screwed. Cooper's on the lam."

Jack slouched down in his chair and shook his head. "Just my luck."

"I don't get it. Cooper had less than a couple years left. He lucked into a work furlough program. He was low maintenance here."

"What are you doing to find him?"

"I got the state fugitive team out looking for him. It's not that unusual; we get walkaways like this. In the end they usually get caught."

Jack sighed.

"Why you looking for him anyway?" Dennis asked.

"Nothing significant. We just found out that Mr. Cooper may be a serial killer."

4

The man in the blue-gray windbreaker sat low in the driver's seat of his car as he watched Paul Baker unlock and enter a Chrysler 300 sedan parked in the driveway. The man had been watching the Baker house from a few houses down the street since yesterday evening when he followed Paul Baker home from the bank. From where he was parked, he could see anyone coming and going. That morning, Paul Baker was the first to leave.

He reached for his binoculars and leveled them up to his eyes, watching the Chrysler back down the driveway. A small digital camera rested next to his leg. He one-handed the camera, aimed it out the window, pointing it in Paul Baker's direction and snapped off a few shots. His gazed followed the Chrysler as it coasted to a stop, then lurched forward accelerating past him. When the car crested the top of the street and fell out of sight, the man let out a deep sigh and stretched.

After following him home, the man had contemplated all night how he was going to get in and get out of the house without any trouble.

He lifted the binoculars back to his eyes. The house fell into focus but the windows were nothing more than black squares. He couldn't see what was going on inside. He wished Mrs. Baker would leave. Maybe run some errands, go grocery shopping. Go to the store to get her sick daughter cough medicine. By his calculations, he needed ten minutes—fifteen tops—to get in and do what he needed to do.

The early morning sun crawled high into the sky. The inside of the car was starting to heat up. His body was pressed snuggly against his vinyl seats, causing beads of sweat to form and roll down his back, dripping around his waistline. The mixture of heat and perspiration made the interior of his vehicle feel like a sauna. The man cracked the window, felt a puff of air gently slap him across the face; it wasn't any cooler than inside his car. He dragged a shirtsleeve across his face to clear the sweat from his eyes, then forced himself to find a comfortable position. This was not the first time he had sat in front of a house, watching, observing, stalking. It was the waiting part he disliked the most. But in the end, it always paid off.

By ten in the morning, he saw the front door open. Mrs. Baker stepped out of the house with a purse swinging from her arm and a set of car keys rattling in her hand. He recognized her from the photo. A tiny woman, slender. He instinctively raised the camera again and clicked off another series of shots. She was in a hurry. Mrs. Baker glanced momentarily toward the man's car, shading her eyes from the bright summer sun, then turned her attention back toward her own car. He watched Mrs. Baker point her keys like a laser gun. The car chirped and the brake lights blinked. She pulled on the car door, tossed her purse inside, and settled herself in behind the steering wheel. With a quick look over her shoulder, Mrs. Baker backed the car down the driveway and drove out along the quiet, empty street. The man's stare returned to the house. The girl was alone.

Exiting the car, he was careful not to make any noise that might draw the attention of a neighbor. He meandered toward the side of the residence, like he was an expected guest, crossing over the well-manicured lawn. He ran his fingers through his short, bristly hair, clearing the salty sweat that dripped into his eyes. He crept along the edge of the house, peering into windows, looking for a glimpse of the young, sick daughter of Mr. and Mrs. Baker. He cleared a row of Italian Cypresses and stepped into a walkway between the tall, thin trunks and the stucco wall. An opened window behind the row of cypresses led to a bedroom with painted yellow walls and a floral print chair positioned against the corner and covered in stuffed animals. A large mirror hung on the wall facing the window. He could see himself in its reflection, a stranger looking into the room of a young girl. He craned his neck, trying to see as deep into the room as possible. He pressed his head slightly on the nylon screen and caught a glimpse of the ruffled bed skirt. He pressed just a little harder and the screen bowed inward. His heart started to run at a higher speed, thumping in his chest after each breath. Then he heard a moan. Jessica.

He made his way around the side of the house and found the backyard gate. He turned the corner to neatly arranged terracotta pots with colorful flower arrangements dotting an Arizona flagstone patio that ran to the edge of a free-formed swimming pool. The dark blue color of the pool gave him a sense of cool even though the outside temperature felt hot enough to melt steel. He pulled on the sliding glass door and found it locked, but the latch was old, something he had no issues overcoming. He pulled out a screwdriver from his back pocket, forced it between the lock and the frame. The latch popped.

He stepped inside to a dark living room. The shade from the trees and the patio cover kept the air in the living room cool until the late afternoon sun had a chance to bake through the back windows. Quietly he stepped down the hallway, gauging which room was Jessica's. The walls were lined with framed photos of the family. Annual portraits, each one aging Jessica one year at a time.

It was as if he had the opportunity of watching her grow up before his eyes.

He paused at a closed door to his left, gently placing a hand on it. This one.

He pressed his ear against the white cathedral-style design, straining to hear any signs of breathing or movement. With a gentle twist, he turned the doorknob and slowly pushed the door until he caught sight of a young girl asleep on the bed. He stared, waiting for his eyes to adjust to the darkened room. Finally he could see her face clearly. It was her. Just like in the portrait on her father's desk.

The comforter and sheets were kicked down to the end of the bed. Her pajama top was bunched high above her waist, exposing her belly. The legs of her pants were pushed above her calves. Her skin silky white and arms soft. Her hair splayed across her pillow, moistened from a night of fighting a fever. The man was stunned for a moment, caught in an overwhelming wave of astonishment at Jessica's youthfulness. Unspoiled beauty. For just a moment, the man wanted to reach out and touch her soft skin, but he knew that would not serve him well. Not yet.

It would only be a matter of time before Mrs. Baker would return from running her errands. Timing was everything. If she showed up before he had a chance to finish what he started, he would have no choice but to take drastic measures. He would not go back to prison. He wouldn't allow Mrs. Baker to be responsible for sending him back to green walls and steel bars, bad food and the smell of urine. No lights off at nine and wake up calls at five. The man pulled his hand back and re-focused on what he came here to do.

He reached into his pocket and retrieved a syringe. He popped off the plastic safety cap with a flick of his thumb and carefully squeezed out all the air in the tube until a small amount of clear fluid spat from the end of the needle. His head slowly rotated, focusing his stare at Jessica.

"You belong to me now," he said.

It was a swift move. He plunged the syringe into Jessica's hip, pushing the fluid instantly through her body. Jessica gave a quick raspy gasp and then became still. Her eyes shot open for a split second before falling shut. Jessica Baker drifted back into a fog, never having the opportunity to comprehend what had just happened. He pulled the bed sheet loose and wrapped it tightly around her, mummy style. He slipped both arms under her small frame and lifted, carrying her toward the door. He stepped into the hallway, picking up speed on his way to the front door before hearing a noise coming from outside. A familiar sound. A key being inserted into the front door lock.

5

Jack tried not to make too much noise as Special Agent Lucille Marquez steadily rocked in a cushy office chair and stared at a flat screen monitor. She had been doing this for the past two hours. Jack waited patiently, hoping to spot a break in her concentration so he could ask for help in tracking Cooper. Help was scarce. Jack had worked with Marquez in the past and he knew she was good. More importantly, she owed him.

Marquez had been hunched over the computer in her covert warehouse space in an unincorporated area of Sacramento, strolling through a maze of chat rooms and transient websites in search of child pornography. Commercial-grade or homegrown—your basic smut. The front window of the undercover location was blacked-out with a sign displaying the business name: "Captain America Garage Doors – Installations and Repairs." The door was perpetually locked and there was no receptionist to answer the phones.

Jack stared quietly at Marquez, watching her eyes shift from left to right, scanning the monitor inches from her nose. Marquez was assigned to the Bureau's Cyber Squad as an undercover agent in search of child predators and purveyors of kiddie porn, the cyber version of a street corner prostitution sting. The only difference

41

being the Internet was a street corner that circled the globe. Dubbed Operation Viewing Glass, this program was tailor-made for Marquez. Posing as a twelve-year-old girl or boy, whichever worked for the occasion, Marquez would helplessly fall prey to someone wanting to trade pictures of child pornography or, worse, meet at a motel for a quick romp in bed. The cesspool that she angled from was filled with society's bottom feeders as well as the community's big fish. It was a fine line determining if the chat was purely fantasy or one of intent. Marquez was good at making those determinations.

Just north of thirty, Marquez was trim, athletic, and still ran a 5K every other day. A lot of agents—male agents to be specific—would describe Marquez as having *natural beauty*. That's what guys always say when they can't think of another way to describe a woman like Marquez. She kept her blonde hair pulled back in a scrunchie, and she looked stunning in a pair of jeans. Jack knew more about Marquez than most. She had more than just looks. He thought of her as the total package but preferred describing her as simply a great agent. One who just happened to look stunning in a pair of jeans.

Marquez also had a Master's in clinical psychology. The first time Jack's seventeen-year old-son met Marquez, he later told Jack she was a hot chick with a gun. Kids.

"I can tell you're onto something," Jack said. "You're starting to talk to the monitor."

Marquez didn't turn her attention away from the screen, just cracked a half smile.

Jack scooted his chair next to hers and watched as she clicked through a series of webpages filled with .JPEGs and .GIFs ready for download if you had the password and the stomach. She had both. Colorful pictures flashed on her 42-inch flat-screen, raunchy, offensive images reflecting off her rimless glasses.

"I just got this set of kiddie porn pictures." Marquez pointed at the screen. Photos of young girls. "The guy I got them from goes by the moniker of Horny John."

"No hidden agenda there," Jack replied.

"Homer got me this guy."

Homer was Marquez's informant. Previously arrested for distribution of child porn, Homer sat behind them, smiling. He had become—albeit with the threat of ten years in a federal prison—a member of the FBI's intelligence base in the area of child exploitation. Or as Jack liked to call him: a cyber snitch.

"Okay, Homer, you sure he's the right guy?" Marquez didn't bother turning around when she asked the question.

"I told you, that's him. A real A-hole."

A week ago, Homer was dutiful in advising Marquez of a clandestine website where individuals were trading kiddie porn. His attention had been piqued when one of the members spoke about plans to seduce young girls. The person never told Homer that he had had sex with a child, but the conversation certainly alluded to his involvement with children. Homer decided that Agent Marquez would be interested in this one.

"I know you got a lot to do," Marquez said, "but if Homer is right and this guy is molesting little kids, I think we need to put the clamps on him right away."

Jack nodded as he lifted a consoling hand. "I'm fine with it. After this one, I'm calling in a favor anyway. That's why I'm here."

"Fair enough, tell me what you need."

"Got a guy ID'd on a cold case murder up in Washington State. I helped do the guy five years ago for killing his wife and kid. Took a plea and got a sweetheart deal. Come to find out, he's done this before." Jack blew out an exasperated breath. "Wish we would have known that before he was offered a plea. Maybe instead of manslaughter, he'd be convicted on murder charges. Anyway, he was housed here in Butte County."

Marquez paused, waiting for Jack to finish. "What do you mean was?"

"He escaped."

Marquez shook her head. "Figures."

"Three days have already gone by. Trail's cold. Chasing him right now or later isn't going to make a difference. I got Dools working with Cal DOJ's fugitive unit. Hopefully, they'll have something by the time we're ready to join them.

"If you say so."

"So, you'll help me after we're through here?"

Marquez raised her right hand and smiled. "Promise."

Jack returned his attention to Marquez's case, swung around to another computer and pounded out an administrative subpoena on the Internet Service Provider—the ISP—used by Horny John to locate his address. After getting a response, it only took Jack thirty minutes to draft a search warrant on the residence of Horny John, an apartment located in Modesto.

"The apartment's rented to an Andre Burke," Jack said. "Who knows if that's his real name or not."

Marquez leaned back in her chair, holding onto the affidavit in one hand while tapping a pencil to her head with the other. "Ah, yes, the lovely town of Molest-o."

Jack nodded. Too often, Jack found the home of another child predator in the Central Valley town. "Homer, you've done your duty for God and Director and earned a day's pay. Go home and we'll call you tomorrow."

Homer beamed a wide grin. He threw a short wave, grabbed his Member's Only jacket and headed out the door, his polyester pants sounding like a cat on a scratching post.

An hour later, Lucy Marquez walked the warrant through the system. The two left the magistrate's office and were heading out the door to their cars.

"You ready?" Marquez sounded anxious.

Jack nodded. "Couldn't be more ready."

"Let's go get Mr. Burke and see if he's having sex with little kids."

The two split in different directions in the parking lot, and caravanned south on their way to Modesto.

6

As the haze of a deep sleep faded, Jessica Baker looked for the clock on her nightstand or the moonlight shining through her bedroom window. She couldn't see either. This wasn't her room. There was no nightstand, no clock. Then she remembered the man and the prick of a needle.

She tried to sit up but couldn't. Her hands or legs were tied down. She tugged harder but every attempt felt like razorblades dragging across her skin. Jessica tried to blink her eyes clear of the blackness. But they were covered. Heavy tape wrapped around her head and over her eyes, the tape yanking her hair every time she moved, sending a sharp stinging pain across her scalp. Adrenalin flooded the core of her body and Jessica felt a wave of panic overwhelm her. She struggled, pushing and pulling, but the ties held fast.

Her head was trapped in a fog, making it difficult to formulate words, let alone sentences. What words did spill from her lips sounded sloppy and drunk. But her body sensed it was vulnerable. Unable to see, unable to move, Jessica Baker was petrified.

She felt the touch of a person's hand on her head, straightening the pillow that was positioned too high. The touch made her jerk.

45

She gasped a short breath that was stuck tight in her chest. She couldn't breathe fast enough; every nerve ending felt like it was on fire.

"That should make you more comfortable, Jessica," a man's voice said.

"Who are you? How do you know me?"

"Not now, we'll talk later. You need your rest. You're sick and need to get better."

His calm words made Jessica shiver. Her heart thumped hard in her chest and throat.

The foul smell of her captor's breath wafted past her cheek, his face next to hers. She pushed herself deep into the pillow, trying to retreat from his touch best she could. The metal posts of the bed frame squealed as she twisted her fastened arms. She felt the man leaning closer; the stench of sweat and pungent odor of his breath became stronger.

"Shh. Don't bother screaming. There's no one to hear you."

Even through the stranger's stink, she could smell stale dust, like a cabin after it's been boarded up for the winter.

"Listen, Jessica, if you're good, I'll think about taking the tape off your eyes."

Jessica shifted uncomfortably under her bindings. "Please, untie my hands. They hurt."

The man mumbled something, then said, "No."

"Please. You're scaring me."

"Sometimes, fear is what a parent needs to get a child to behave."

The man touched her face, sliding his fingers down the side of her arm. It made her skin burn. "You remind me of someone I once knew."

The words "once knew" sent electricity down her spine.

She heard rustling, a slight pause and then the clicking of something mechanical. "What are you doing?"

Another pause, then the man said, "I'm taking pictures."

Jessica heard his walking, pacing around her. Her head swiveled from side to side, trying to track his movement. The floor creaked when he walked past. Then he stopped and she heard the clicking of the camera shutter snapping photo after photo.

"That's good, Jessica, that's good," the man said, his tone trying to sound calming.

But Jessica was far from calm. Her body was breaking down into an uncontrollable shudder. With every click of the camera, Jessica's face flinched. Tears welled up in her eyes, held back by the tape across her face.

"No, don't cry," the man said. "You'll ruin the pictures."

He reached out to stroke her arm. As he leaned closer, her whimpering turned into uncontrollable sobbing.

The man withdrew and walked away. She struggled to hear what he was doing. A zipping sound, like thick tape being pulled from a roll, a tear. The man scurried back to the bed and sat down beside her. His hands pressed against her face, her eyes. He was putting on more tape. The man pressed the edges down firm, making sure she couldn't see anything. She didn't want to see anything, especially him. She knew if she did, he would never let her go. Not alive.

The man backed away, his steps slowed and became distant. She heard the creak of a chair straining under his weight. Then silence.

Over the next ten minutes, Jessica remained still, hearing nothing but the occasional squeak of the chair, letting her know he was still there. The silence was numbing. Soon, her body surrendered to exhaustion. Her mouth gaped open, sucking in air as if she had just completed a marathon.

As she succumbed to fatigue, Jessica heard the camera whirl back to life. This time, Jessica Baker didn't move, didn't cry, didn't beg. She just lay there, waiting for the man to finish.

Jessica's breathing became shorter, shallow and quick. She could only imagine what might happen to her. What she had already experienced was horrifying and the lack of not knowing what was to come only made it worse. Five minutes after it had started, the camera noise stopped. Her body shivered. For the first time in her life, Jessica Baker understood the real meaning of fear.

7

The outside temperature hovered at 105 degrees as Jack stepped out of his Crown Vic. The air conditioner was running full blast and the contrast in temperatures caused a puff of cool to escape when the door pulled wide. A ball of dust exploded under his shoe as it landed on the edge of Highway 99, where he was instructed to meet the other agents. He stared out at the vast expanse of arid soil that surrounded him. The Central Valley was the world's largest grower of fruits and vegetables, the land that feeds the world. To Jack, it was a large dirt clod. It was like standing on Mercury—only hotter.

The entry team met near the Modesto Airport, in preparation of executing Marquez's search warrant for Andre Burke's home. Three agents stood beside a blacked-out Suburban, adjusting their ballistic vests. Their pistols were slung low on their leg, SWAT style. The rest stood ready but looked antsy. Marquez, on her radio, checked with dispatch to ensure a clear channel during the operation. A dark green Impala was parked under a tall oak tree on the edge of the lot. An agent sat on the driver's side, door opened, his legs hanging outside of the car. He was checking his holster and yanking on his ballistic vest, trying to find a comfortable position.

It was Tom Cannon, a new agent fresh out of Quantico. Cannon fumbled with his gear, looking nervous. He gazed toward the rest of the crowd, then at Jack. Even from a distance, Jack saw Cannon's face was pale. Jack returned a nod, then pulled his gear from the trunk and got ready.

It was almost two by the time the team crowded into the Suburbans and drove up to the side of the apartment. They bailed out and formed a straight line, six deep. Marquez moved forward. She had the team stack up along the apartment building wall. With a wave of her arm, Marquez commanded the team to advance. Jack fell in close behind the lead agent, who was carrying a ballistic shield. Jack unholstered his 40-caliber Glock, trigger finger resting on the side of the frame, muzzle down. An agent trailed closely behind toting a mono-shock battering ram with the words *Knock Knock* painted on the side in white letters. As the three stood by the front door, the rest of the crew circled around and surrounded the perimeter. With a green and go signal from Marquez, Jack walked around the shield and pounded an authoritative fist on the front door. He waited a few seconds, listening for any sound coming from within. Hearing nothing but the rubbing of Velcro and click of agent firing pin safeties being released, Jack shouted out into the afternoon air, "Andre Burke! FBI, we have a search warrant for the premise. Open the door, now." Jack listened for a response. Nothing. He checked his watch. Knowing the Supreme Court's latest decision on the issue of knock and announce, he counted. "Ten, nine, eight . . . screw it . . . two, one. Break it down!"

An agent stepped forward and, in a single motion, slammed the heavy metal ram into the door handle. The frame splintered and the lock shattered as if made of glass. The door flailed loosely on its broken hinges and the team poured into the apartment, guided by the muzzles of their MP-5s, searching for threats. Jack rolled in and to the right, lighting up the area with his compact Surefire flashlight. The drapes were pulled closed, making the room as black as night. A crash came from the back bedroom and someone shuffled out trying to find his way in the dark. Jack focused his light on a young man wearing boxer shorts with skinny legs, stumbling in the darkened hallway. He held a pasty, white arm over his eyes, protecting them from the glaring searchlights. His hair was long and stringy, tussled from being roused from a deep sleep. The suspect was pencil thin with colorless skin, like Play-Doh over bone. He matched the driver's license description of Andre Burke.

As if still in a fog, he began babbling, the words stumbling over his tongue. "What's going on? Who are you guys?"

Before Burke could get an answer, Jack and another agent grabbed him by his neck and took him to the ground. They had him pinned in the prone position, his hands being securely fastened together with a pair of flex-cuffs.

"Hey, man, take the drugs, just don't hurt me!"

Jack grunted as he pulled Burke up into a sitting position. "Relax, Romeo. We're not here to rip off your drugs. We're here to search your place."

"For what, man? I ain't got nothing."

"Didn't you just say you had drugs in the house?"

Burke gave a deer-in-the-headlights look, pausing quietly for a second, before letting out an exasperated sigh. "Oh, right."

It took Marquez fifteen minutes to explain to Burke the reason for the unexpected visit. She provided him with a copy of the warrant, tossing it onto a dusty coffee table. As a goodwill gesture, Marquez had removed the flex-cuffs from behind Burke's back and refastened a new set in front. Burke sat quietly, listening to Marquez's spiel, unable to comprehend why the FBI was interested in searching his computer for pictures of pornography.

"That's illegal?" Burke asked, his head cocked to one side like a dog hearing a silent whistle.

"Yes, Andre, it's illegal. Can get you five to ten in federal prison."

"Shit, that's serious time, right?"

Marquez rolled her eyes.

Two FBI examiners from the Computer Analysis and Response Team, CART, began to unpack their specialized gear that would mirror the hard-drive of Burke's computer. With the use of EnCase forensic software, the information stored on the hard-drive could be searched and reviewed without damage or destruction. Jack knew purveyors of child porn often set destruction codes on their systems if accessed incorrectly to wipe out any evidence in event of a raid. Jack looked over at Burke and studied him for a beat. He concluded Burke did not possess enough brain cells to devise such a proactive plan.

Within fifteen minutes, the examiners had the computer disassembled, and it wasn't much longer before the drive was mirrored, with a detailed search of the system flashing on the portable monitor. They scanned rows of commercially manufactured porn in search of anything resembling pictures of minors.

"Hey, Jack," one of the examiners called out. "I think you better take a look at this."

As Jack walked toward the kitchen table covered in electronic search equipment, Burke shouted, "Hey, man, maybe I want my lawyer."

"Shut up, Burke!" Marquez said, continuing to fill out paperwork for the items she planned on taking.

Jack stared at the monitor. Burke's computer case was opened with colorful bands of cable streaming out and into the Bureau's hardware, the data in Burke's computer pumped like water through a hose into the FBI's storage space. The computer monitor flashed snapshots from Burke's hard drive. Mostly commercial grade porn, the stuff Jack had seen floating around for years.

"What have you got?" Jack asked.

"Mostly Eastern European crap," replied the CART examiner.

"We peeked at a couple of files and came across some unusual ones. Take a look at these." The examiner tapped on the keyboard, moving through a maze of files and sub-files before going into Burke's trash can. He clicked on it and a series of pictures materialized.

"What the hell is this?" Jack whispered.

"Pretty disturbing," replied the CART examiner.

The first picture was a grainy color shot of a young girl, tape covering her eyes, lying on a bare mattress. The room was dark but Jack could make out cardboard boxes and several pieces of broken furniture scattered randomly around the room. A single overhead lamp was the only source of light, harshly illuminating the unknown girl. Sharp lines and stark features. The girl in the picture wore pajamas, bunched and disheveled. Jack studied the image and a rush of dread filled his body. Jack spoke, his words soft and careful: "This isn't porn, boys."

The CART examiner nodded. "I think you're right."

The picture was clearly not intended for pornography. She was not erotically dressed; she performed no sexual acts, showed no seductive poses. As much as those types of pictorials sickened Jack, this photo was worse.

Marquez stood from the sofa, left Burke alone and walked over to Jack's side.

Jack's tapped a finger on the screen. "Lucy, that's not a picture of smut."

She studied the picture, nodding the entire time. "You're right," she said. "That's a kidnapping."

8

"I don't know the guy, I swear!" Burke pleaded, the realization that he was in deep shit becoming more evident. After viewing the photo of the tied and bound child, Jack and Marquez surrounded Burke like two hungry wolves standing over an antelope with a busted leg. It was time Burke came clean on his relationship with who sent those pictures.

"Look, that shit arrived this morning before I crashed. Man, I'd been up all night. Dude sent it to me and I told him it was too freaky, so I canned it. I swear."

"Jack," the examiner called out, "I got more for you to look at."

Jack and Marquez walked over to the monitor. Burke's body went limp as he sunk deep into the cheap sofa.

The examiner had pieced together another series of photos from deleted fragments. They were similar to the first, same girl, same position.

"I checked the hash marks on the photos," the examiner said, "to determine if they were modified at any time. No alterations. What you see is what you get. I also pulled up the internal clock to determine the time and date the pictures were taken. If the camera clock is accurate, they're from today, probably as early as late morning."

Jack turned toward Burke, whose eyes sagged, his posture limp. Jack jabbed a finger into Burke's boney chest. "Who is he?"

Burke's jaw slacked and his head shook back and forth. "Just some guy, some guy that wanted to trade pictures."

Jack knelt next to the couch, invading Burke's personal space. "You better come up with some answers soon, because if I can't find out who that girl is and she dies, you'll be going down as a conspirator."

"Bullshit!" Burke tried to jump up but Jack slammed a hand against Burke's chest, sending him sprawling back to the couch.

"You're wasting time, Burke."

Burke started to ramble; the words spat out fast and flustered. "It's like I said, a bunch of us were just talking trash. Someone sends me pictures, I send some back. Then this guy logs on sometime this morning and starts to talk about child discipline and punishment."

The room grew quiet.

"I thought he was talking about kinky stuff. Then he sends out these pictures and we all look. I think, this guy's a sick fuck, what does this have to do with porn?"

"What's his name?"

Burke squeezed his eyes tight and cocked his head, struggling to remember. "Jure. He said his name was Jure. Goes by the screen name of JPetroski."

"How long have you two been chatting?" Jack asked.

"I don't know. A couple weeks at most. He just showed up one day. Didn't seem like anyone knew him that well."

Jack shook his head, letting Burke know it wasn't enough.

"Look, guys, I didn't know what those photos were. I thought they were staged and that this guy's just into that sort of stuff."

"What kind of *stuff*?"

"S&M. You know, kinky."

"With children?" Jack said.

Burke frowned. "Whatever."

By this time, Marquez was on the phone with the office, instructing an agent to issue an administrative subpoena to the server of the chat room. She hoped the trail of JPetroski's past messages would help pinpoint his whereabouts.

"The subpoena has been faxed to the ISP server," she said. "Should have an answer in fifteen."

"In the meantime," Jack said, "I think it's time to do a little hunting ourselves."

He and Marquez looked over at Burke, who sat quietly, trying to figure out what Jack meant. Then, the light bulb flashed in his head. "You want to see if he's on now?"

"Yeah. And we want to go on as you."

"You can go on as me?"

"Is that a question or consent?" Jack asked.

"Whatever, man."

The examiners disconnected their forensic equipment from Burke's computer and signed on to the chat room, searching for Jure Petroski.

"Go get 'em, Marquez," Jack said. "See if Mr. Petroski is out hunting for more pictures."

"He's not a picture kind of guy," Burke interjected.

Everyone looked at Burke.

Spittle started to build around the corners of his mouth. "Look, this guy, he was into talking about family and children. We all thought he was going somewhere with the conversation. You know, getting into child discipline." Burke's face turned white. "It's talk. Fantasy. Anyway, everyone in the chat room starts joking about it, but Jure, he gets angry. You can see it in his messaging. He starts scolding everyone for not taking him seriously and all of the sudden, everyone starts signing out."

"How did you leave it with him?"

Burke shrugged. "Okay, I guess. Didn't really get too deep into his tirade. Just kind of listened."

"Listened to what?" Marquez asked.

"To him talk about starting over."

"Starting what over?" Marquez's voice sounded irritated.

"I don't know, with a new family, new kids, almost like he got rid of the old one and started a new one." Burke snapped his fingers, still handcuffed. "I tell you what. This guy either lives in or has lived in California. He talked about the summer heat and the winter cold of the Central Valley. I remember him saying that his previous family hated the heat."

"Previous?"

"His words not mine. I just took it in. It wasn't something I thought I needed to psychoanalyze." Burke said the word psycho-analyze like he knew what it meant.

Marquez's cell phone rang. The agent on the other end had just gotten the information from the ISP search. Marquez put her phone on speaker so everyone could hear.

"Your sender's name is listed as Jure Petroski," the agent informed. "Occupation, electrical engineer. Get this, home address is Budapest, Hungary. Nothing in California. Looks like you've got a long drive ahead of you."

"That's not good," Marquez said.

"They're still trying to determine the origination point of the user. It got a little complicated. Looks like he may have routed his communication through a number of servers that includes an overseas connection. We're also checking for DMV records and criminal history. I'll let you know as soon as I find out."

Marquez ended the call. She returned her attention to the monitor. Her fingers clattered on the keyboard, linking her to a maze of websites known to attract sexual deviants. The first five sites yielded nothing other than the standard perverts and curious newcomers to child smut. Marquez deflected their requests in her hunt for bigger fish. They'll be around tomorrow, she contended. The next four sites were empty and the last two were already shut down, discovered by the server to be illegal porn sites.

Marquez crossed her arms and glared at the monitor. "Where oh where can he be," she sang. She cocked her head toward Burke. "Got any suggestions?"

Burke stood up and walked over to his computer. Even though his hands were cuffed, he was still able to maneuver the mouse and tap the keyboard. Through a series of links and secret websites, Burke landed on an occupied chat room. Burke stopped for a moment and looked over at Marquez. "You want me to see if he's here?"

Marquez waved her hand, giving Burke the green light to go fishing.

Burke placed the keyboard on his lap and started to type.

looking for jure. any 1 hear from him?

Silence.

Burke typed more: *i got pictures for him.*

More silence.

family pictures

Marquez looked over at Burke. "Let's not be too obvious."

"Can't lure a rat without cheese," Burke replied.

A message flashed up: *he was here earlier. talking crazy shit again*

Jack moved closer to the table where everyone stood watching the exchange.

"Let's see if we can make this more interesting," Jack said. He took the keyboard from Burke and started typing a message to everyone in the chat room. *Jure sent some strange pics today. i want more. anyone got any new?*

As quickly as Jack hit the send button, a message returned: *do i know you?*

"It's him." Burke yelled, "That's Jure."

The name Jpetroski blipped at the top of website where the chat room names posted.

Jack responded. *chatted this morning. u sent me pics. nice. got more? Y?*

just interested. who is she?

There was a pause. *she is mine.*

r they real?

yes.

Jack's heart started to pound. "We may have stumbled onto a legit kidnapping." He handed the keyboard to Marquez and dialed the office. The call was routed to Special Agent Chris Hoskin, Sacramento's team leader for the Evidence Response Team. "Chris, need your help."

"Go ahead."

"Check NLETS for any suspicious situations where a kid has come up missing." NLETS was the National Law Enforcement Telecommunication System, the hub for all criminal justice information in the world. "Also, check with the local agencies. Include the RA territories. I'm looking for any unreporteds."

"What do you got?"

"Photos over the Internet of a guy with a bound and gagged child. Pics are eerie enough to be real."

Hoskin went quiet, pondering. "He could be anywhere in the world."

"Marquez's chatting with the perp online. There's some past conversations about the Central Valley, like he knows the area. If he's around here, I want to know."

"We'll give it a run. I'll ring you if I come up with anything." They ended the call and Jack returned to where Marquez was sitting, trying to lure Petroski into a face-to-face meeting.

lets meet for an exchange, Marquez typed.

what do you have for me?

children. Marquez looked up at Jack with a raised lip. "Sick fucks need sick responses."

Before getting a response, Marquez fired off another message.

*Im in sacramento, california. know the place? where r u?
north.*

"We're getting warmer," Marquez said.

She continued typing. *how far north?*

A message broke in from another listener in the chat room. *what
r u? a cop?*

"Great, just what I need." Marquez slapped the keyboard and
said, "I should have moved to a private chat room so we could have
conversed without others nosing in." She sat for a moment,
contemplating whether to send out a response message or wait for
a response from Jure Petroski. Then, just as the opportunity had
come, it vanished. On the corner of the screen, Jpetroski disappeared. He left the chat room, gone from Marquez's reach.

"Dammit!" Marquez screamed and slammed her fist on the table.

A CART examiner called out. "I think I got 'em. I'm online with
the server. We were tracing back while you were chatting. He's close
by all right. Couple towns away. Chico." He provided the address
and the crew started tossing gear into bags. They could be out of
Modesto in five minutes.

Jack looked over at Marquez. "Pack it up, Lucy. On the drive
up, call and educate Chris as to what we've got here and have him
pound out a warrant for Petroski's house in Chico. By the time we
get there, he should have it signed by a judge." Jack glanced back
at Marquez and confessed, "Warrant or not, we're going in."

Marquez nodded. She was busy lifting Burke up by his armpit
and handing him off to another agent for transport.

"Your lucky day, Burke. You get an all-expense paid vacation in
Sacramento County lock-up. Tomorrow, if everything goes well
tonight, I'll make sure your bail is low enough for you to post," she
said.

Burke's jaw fell. "What do you mean low enough? Can't I just
stay here for the night?"

Jack and Marquez responded in unison. "Shut up, Burke!"

9

The highway reader board flashed between the afternoon sun and Jack's eyes for a microsecond, like a single frame from a running motion picture. He gunned the gas and cranked the wheel right, speeding toward the Woodbridge exit, a small street that he had marked in his Thomas Guide, where Jure Petroski had sat and chatted with Marquez less than two hours prior. The area northeast of Chico was extremely rural, older bungalow style homes scattered between large clumps of trees, dirt roads the only connection between neighbors. Orange plastic mailboxes sprouted from bushes along the main streets.

Sergeant Doug Blackwell from the Chico Police Department met Jack at the start of a long dirt path. He leaned on Jack's driver's side window and pointed toward a three-bedroom house with a detached garage one hundred yards away.

"I've sent two officers around to an adjacent lot to get a better look at the property. They reported back there's a light on inside but can't see if anyone's home. No dogs or other people in the area. Your call if you want us to go ahead and enter."

Jack shook his head. "Let's give it a minute." He worried if Petroski was not in there, entering would show their hand, giving

Petroski the opportunity to run. Jack had sent three agents of his own around the back and over a graveled levy, where a creek ran behind the residence, keeping an eye out for any movement.

Thirty minutes passed, everyone getting antsy. Dusk had settled, making it increasingly difficult to see very far. The sergeant was fidgeting and checking his watch, wondering why they needed to wait. Marquez drove up and came to an abrupt stop next to Jack's car.

"Got the warrant." She stuck her head out the car window and pointed her chin toward the house. "You think he's in there?"

Jack shook his head. "Don't know, haven't seen any movement since we've been here. There's a small light on inside but no telling if anyone's home. I don't think we can wait much longer, Marquez. If there's a kid in there, we got to move."

"Let's kick in the door and see how many cockroaches fall out."

Jack waved the sergeant over. Within a minute, they rallied the team together and Jack led four FBI agents and six Chico officers to the front of the house. The two officers bringing up the rear peeled away to the right, raising their rifles toward the side windows. A third continued around the edge, knelt down and covered the back porch.

The rest of the team slid across the front porch, cloaked under the shade of dusk. The agent behind Jack placed a heavy metal crowbar known as the pick between the frame of the house and the flimsy door, and the second agent wedged a battering ram—the key. Jack signaled with a pump of his arm and then speared forward. No knocking this time. Marquez had requested a no-knock warrant because of the possible victim held inside. Judges hate to see children hurt. Authority granted.

The agent swung the large black cylinder back like a pendulum before ramming it forward, slamming it squarely on the head of the pick. A huge clang echoed as the doorframe splintered into kindling. The handle shattered and the door flew wide open, allowing the stream of agents and officers to pour into a dark living room.

They flared side to side inside the cramped quarters, flashlight beams searching the area. The forward team quickly advanced through the front room, pushing down a narrow hallway. Doors kicked open, the entry repeated. Penetrate, clear, move on. Penetrate, clear, move on.

Five minutes later, the house was thoroughly swept and declared secure. Jack flipped on the light switches as he walked from room to room, studying the layout and scouring for any indication of a kidnap victim. Trash cluttered everywhere but nothing overt to indicate there was a hostage held here.

The officers holstered their weapons. Photographs were taken to document the condition of the rooms. The house, a single story bungalow, included three bedrooms, one bath, with a detached single car garage. Whoever lived here must have liked beige because that was the color of the entire house. Cheap, seventies-style carpeting covered the floors and hallways. The swamp cooler on the roof strained against the stifling heat from outside. The entire house was stuffy and smelled heavily of mildew.

"No one inside, Jack," the sergeant called out.

Jack nodded, unable to hide his disappointment. He pointed down the hall with his Maglite. "Let's start searching the back. That one looks like our guy's room."

Two agents and a Chico detective proceeded down the hall carrying large evidence bags and latent print kits.

Jack headed into the kitchen. White walls, yellowing from age and bordered in a black and white porcelain tile countertop. The Formica dinette table was small with a gray and white marble swirl pattern. Leftover Chinese food containers sat opened on the counter next to the sink. He walked over to the table and studied a paper plate with a slop of mixed vegetables and rice. There was no steam rising but the plate was still warm. A Styrofoam cup sweated droplets into a puddle beside it. Jack peered into the cup. Half-filled with fizzless soda, a small chunk of ice bobbing in the center like a drifting iceberg. It was well above eighty degrees inside the house. In this heat, the ice should have been history.

"Marquez, keep an eye out. Petroski's been here recently."

Marquez looked around the room then pushed back one of the thin sheers on the front window, scanning the wooded area outside.

In the living room, Jack spotted a laptop computer propped open on a dark green sofa, whose cover was well worn and stank of body odor, the couch most likely doubling for his suspect's bed. Summer heat and sweat. Jack opted against sitting and instead slid on a pair of latex gloves. He picked up the laptop and carried it to the kitchen table, craning and looking for any detectable fingerprints on the keyboard or screen. He peered over the monitor and hooked a thumb to one of the evidence technicians.

"Scan this for prints."

A technician dressed in a blue one-piece coverall placed a large black plastic case next to the kitchen table. He popped the locks and removed a small periscope with an attached pistol grip. This was the Reflected Ultraviolet Imaging System, or RUVIS, designed to detect latent prints on surfaces without the use of powder or ninhydrate. Peering through the periscope while shining a florescent light bar onto the keyboard, the technician scanned the area for any possible prints.

The technician groaned like a doctor peering down a patient's throat. He stood straight, pursed his lips and shook his head. "Got nothing."

Jack scoffed. "A million dollars in high-tech equipment and I can't get shit."

The technician shrugged.

Marquez followed Jack down the hallway toward the bedroom door. A heavy wooden bed sat directly under a large picture window covered by a dark green, heavy curtain. The agents who entered first had drawn open the curtains to let in the evening light, and a stream of moonlit dust floated aimlessly about. A cheap wood paneled highboy and chest of drawers boxed the room, the smell of musty clothes wafting from the half opened closet. The place was a shit-hole, Jack thought, even by Modesto standards.

Jack walked over to the bed, careful not to touch anything. He knelt low to the front posts and studied the straps securely tied around the legs. The ends were bunched and frayed, obviously used. Jack stood slowly, keeping his hands pressed against his thighs. By the time his eyes fell level with the bed sheets, Jack could smell the odor of urine. Small dark stains of dried blood spotted the linen.

Marquez stared at the bed from over Jack's right side. "Looks like he may have had a guest."

Jack grunted an acknowledgement.

The sound of the front door slamming against the outside wall yanked Jack out of his concentration. A police officer shouted "halt" outside and Jack's instinct took over as he bolted for the front door.

Before Jack could make it there, Marquez had already drawn her weapon and rounded the front entryway. An agent screamed, "He's into the trees! He's getting away!" Then the agent called out the word that sent everyone's pulse racing.

"Gun!"

Jack drew his pistol, bounding out the front door. His focus narrowed on agents and uniformed officers darting toward an opening through a row of tall trees twenty feet from the side of the garage. An FBI agent standing in the driveway stabbed a finger toward a thicket of trees and tall bushes. "He cut right. That way."

Jack pushed off to the right, bolting down a dirt path that cut through a thick overgrowth of hedges. Dust swirled wildly in the air. He didn't know the direction or the exact description of the person he was chasing. Right now, it didn't matter. The first person he came across running away would be the target of a hard tackle and a hit to the head.

Deeper into the woods, Jack slowed, straining to hear crunching leaves or breaking branches. Footsteps sounded to his right. Jack crouched, raised his pistol and pointed it in the direction of the noise. The sound grew near. Jack watched the thick branches along the row of hedges start to rustle. The hot summer evening provided no breeze, no noise. The movement was from something other than wind. Someone was fast approaching, cutting from inside. Jack took a bead with his front sights, aimed at the heart of the shuddering branches. He focused on the spot where he calculated the exit point for his approaching suspect to be. The limbs shook and the sound of stomping feet grew louder. Jack placed his finger on the trigger and began to apply pressure. From the edge of the forest, his target leaped in his direction. A frightened deer, escaping the commotion of a police manhunt. Jack blew out a tense breath and lowered his weapon. He stood up and tried to shake out the tension. Then came the concussion of a gunshot. Then another.

Quickly, he moved in the direction of the firefight. Two deputies appeared to his left rushing forward. Jack followed. The sharp crack of more rounds exploded in the air but he couldn't determine the direction of the gunfire. He cut again hard to the right, caught sight of a dirt path. He took off up the trail, dust kicking up from every stride. Suddenly, he heard the staccato thud of running boots. Not his agents. Not another deer. He quickened his pace. It was dark, too dark to get a clear view of anything other than the slashing branches that banged against his face while he raced in full sprint. As Jack climbed a high ridge, the moonlight illuminated a levy road ahead. Thirty yards downwind, Jack spotted a pickup canted at an angle along the road, rumbling a low idle from the other side of the embankment. A footbridge forged the narrow waterway to the other side. Early model Chevy, light color, short bed with a camper shell. Jack squinted, trying to make out the license plate.

"Four, Lincoln, six. Maybe eight." He struggled to read but the license plate was too far away, the night too dark to make out the rest.

A blurred figure jumped into the driver's seat and the engine roared. The tires squealed and the truck disappeared in a thick cloud of dust as it slid from side to side in an attempt to find traction. The truck chirped into high gear and faded away down the trail, out of sight. Jack could only stand and watch as his suspect elude capture. Jack kicked the ground, growling like an angry dog, a blanket of dirt rising above his head.

This close, only to lose him.

"Fuck!"

Sergeant Blackwell paced by the kitchen table with his cell phone pressed to his head. He had put out an APB but, so far, no luck finding the truck or their runner. Helicopters hovered overhead with their spotlights searching along the levy road. They spotted lots of trucks but not the one they were looking for.

Jack stood in the doorway to the living room watching two agents turn over furniture and pull out vent hoods. The sergeant made his way into the room, his face flushed and twisted. He glared at one of his officers standing in the background, watching the agents tossing the living room furniture. He pointed a finger. "Get in there and find out everything about this son-of-a-bitch!" Then he turned to Jack. "I've issued an all-western-states BOLO for this guy Petroski."

BOLO, be on the look out.

Unfortunately Jack did not get a clear look at the person who had returned to the house to shoot it out before running. A search agent brought Jack a crumpled sheet of paper, pressed it flat for Jack to read.

"The house utility bill," the agent said. "Account belongs to Petroski."

Another agent holding onto a cell phone called out from the behind. "I got a previous address for Petroski. It's in Citrus Heights."

The sergeant chimed in. "I'll send two detectives down there now."

Jack turned and pointed at the first agent he saw. "Get on the phone and call Hoskin, find out if he's heard back from anyone on a missing kid. I'm chasing someone and we have no idea who he's got."

The agent turned away and went straight to his phone.

Jack looked around again for more help. Tom Cannon was squatting next to another agent, scanning through the unopened mail left on the living room floor.

"Tom," Jack called out.

Cannon looked up.

"Go with the two detectives to the Citrus Heights address. Do a neighborhood, find someone that knows him. Maybe someone will remember this guy and have some idea where we can find him."

Cannon nodded and quickly stood up, gathered up his notebook and car keys.

"And, Tom, be careful. Nothing says he's not back there hiding with an old friend."

Cannon forced a nervous smile and waved a two-finger salute before heading out the door with the two detectives.

10

Jack walked into the forensic lab at the Sacramento office. Calling it a "lab" was giving the area more credit than it deserved. It looked more like a converted storage closet in a Tokyo electronics store. Jack stared at the rows of blinking lights and monitors scrolling as if they had a life of their own, and wondered how the world of criminal investigation had changed so quickly. Back in the day, investigations meant talking to people and digging through papers, even garbage. Now everything revolved around hard drives, the Internet and thousands of electronic databases. If you wanted to know anything about anyone, go to their computer. It's everyone's personal diary, everyone's identity, warts and all.

Special Agent James Harrington's face was buried deep in the guts of Petroski's seized computer, deep enough to occasionally bump the aluminum cover of the computer's hard-drive, gouging a scratch on the tip of his nose. Jack watched from a seat beside Harrington, who was too engrossed in his work to even notice Jack's presence.

Harrington pulled strands of multi-colored cables from his bag, plugging them into ports and sockets inside Petroski's computer. He had already spent an hour making an exact copy of the computer's hard drive so that the investigators could manipulate the data in search of pictures, text, and anything else that would help them locate the whereabouts of the bound and gagged child. The mirrored copy was plugged into a Bureau computer and immediately rows of data streamed onto the large monitor.

"What do think? Anything of value?" Jack asked.

Harrington tilted his head toward Jack, obviously annoyed at the disruption. He pulled off his glasses and tossed them on the computer bench, then scratched his head causing the thin, short hair on top of his head to tangle like fine strands of blond cotton. "The good news is I found your photo."

"And the bad?"

"It's encrypted. A safety precaution. Without going through the right protocol, the system will start to destroy its contents. Every time it's turned back on, the system starts to eat itself alive. I was able to terminate the destruction sequence but the data is scattered all over the hard drive. Right now it's difficult to know if the good stuff has been overwritten. I also determined that a large chunk of data had been deleted. I'm guessing to get rid of incriminating evidence."

"Can you get them back?"

Harrington puffed out his chest. "If I can't get it, nobody can."

"Then you can get it?"

Harrington shook his head. "Nobody can."

Everyone wants to be a comic.

Jack rolled his eyes. "What *can* you get?"

"There are things I might be able to retrieve." Harrington began tapping on the computer keyboard as layers of codes flashed on the screen. After a series of pages, Harrington stopped and pointed at a row of hash values. "Look here. This tells me the photo of the girl was the last in a series taken yesterday, which we already knew, but this information tells us that the picture is number two-fifty nine."

"Where are one through two-fifty-eight?"

"More than likely recently deleted."

"Great."

Harrington turned and shook a finger. "Not to worry. I think I can at least retrieve most of those photos. This stuff may have been taken out as recently as today, which means the area where the information was stored has not been over-written. If I'm lucky, I should be able to retrieve most of the data and piece it back together."

"What do you mean, piece it back?"

"Just that. Find the pieces and put them back together. Data isn't stored on a computer all in one spot. If you could see what is written on a hard drive, you would see bits and pieces of data scattered, separated by specific types of values. This allows for efficient use and speed of data retrieval by the CPU. How they all come together is through software. It's like gathering pieces of a shattered mirror and putting it back together. Your data is fragmented."

Jack thought about the explanation. Fragmented.

"Sounds malignant," Jack said.

"Would it be easier if I just say it's all magic?" Harrington cleared his throat. "The data is up and running on our system right now. I'm going to try and retrieve as much as I can and reassemble it. Fragmented or not, I should be able to get you something."

"How long is this going to take?"

"Maybe a day. But I can't guarantee success."

Jack didn't like his answer but had to accept it. "Thanks."

Harrington gave an empathetic shrug of his shoulders, indicating he was doing all he could, then turned back to continue his hunt for slivers of electronic shavings. His mouse pad had a picture of the Star Trek Enterprise soaring through space at warp speed. That's how fast he continued his search, filtering through folders, which were both empty—as well as crammed full—of pornographic images. Bit by bit, Harrington began the slow process of piecing together fragments of information in hopes of finding out just who was the girl in picture two fifty-nine.

11

Tom Cannon approached the dingy white house with blue trim in the middle of a cul-de-sac on Redburn Road, followed closely by two Chico detectives, Manny Salazar and Jay McGuire. The front porch light was on but Tom saw no other light coming from inside. He pointed to one of the detectives, indicating for him to circle around back.

A black, steel-bar gate protected the front door of the house. Most of the residences in the neighborhood had the same bars. A telling sign about their crime problem. Tom pulled on the grate and it swung open. The screen was not locked.

"Not very protective," he said to the detective.

McGuire leaned to the right of the door and peered into the house through the front window. The back of a couch, an old high-back chair, a fireplace and console TV. Several cheap, framed pictures hung on the walls. He could make out a walkway leading to a kitchen nook but could not see how far back the house went. The evening rendered the unlit area completely black, blurring the shapes of the furniture and appliances. He raised a flashlight up to the window looking for movement from within. Nothing.

Tom pulled open the heavy steel gate and pounded on the front door. He waited for any sound while McGuire kept close watch through the front window. Still no movement.

"I guess no one's home," Tom whispered.

Salazar returned from the back of the house.

"No movement around back. I looked through the patio slider. Doesn't look like anyone's inside."

"Agent Paris said Petroski listed this as his address of record not more than a week ago," McGuire stated. "Judging by the way the inside looks, I can't believe someone moved in and settled that quickly."

Tom turned away and walked back to the street.

"I guess we can do a neighborhood search to see if anyone has seen this guy Petroski. Maybe we'll get lucky."

The two detectives shook their heads.

Salazar said, "Don't think that's a good idea. It could alert the asshole we're on to him before we can get a chance to find him."

McGuire nodded in agreement.

"What do you suggest?" Tom asked.

The two detectives looked at each other.

"Did you hear that Agent Cannon?" McGuire said.

Tom raised an eyebrow, confused.

Salazar looked over at Tom. "Sounds like a child crying. It's coming from inside that house." Salazar pointed toward the front door.

Tom creased his forehead. There was no noise, no baby crying. Then suddenly he caught on to their scheme. *So this is how it's done.*

He strolled back up the walkway, followed by the detectives, all three pulling their weapons from their holsters. Upon reaching the front door, Tom paused and silently prayed for forgiveness from the law enforcement gods. He reached down and twisted the doorknob. Just like the security gate, the door was unlocked. Salazar smiled at McGuire, who in turn slapped Tom on the back. "Let's go save that crying baby."

Tom pushed open the door and shined his flashlight while the two detectives split to each side, one heading left toward a hallway, the other to the right and the kitchen. The air was hot and stuffy, indicating the house had been buttoned shut for a while. Tom swatted away flies dancing around his face. He scanned the room with his flashlight, weapon drawn, before trailing McGuire down the hallway. The detective cleared two opened rooms to the left, while Tom kept his flashlight aimed at a closed door straight down the hall.

The first door led to a bedroom filled with boxes stacked around a small, wooden table and chair. A day bed was shoved in the corner under a window. Stacks of old clothes covered the bed. No one had used it for some time. McGuire backed out of the room and continued down the hallway. They approached the second door to the left. McGuire fixed his flashlight into the darkened room.

"Police," he called out, waiting for a response. As he swept his flashlight across the room, something disturbed the silence.

"Movement," the detective shouted. "Police, show your hands!"

Tom pivoted, steadying his light and the muzzle of his pistol. Two glowing green dots emerged from the depths. A house cat walked out of the dark toward the two officers. The detectives lowered their weapons and exhaled a sigh of relief. The gray tabby sauntered out of the room and rubbed against Tom's leg, purring, before prancing down the hall toward the last room. The hair on the cat was twisted and matted, wafting a cloud of stink.

Tom grinned. "Cats like me."

Salazar smiled. "Maybe the cat just wants to rub its shit off on your pants."

Tom looked down, checking for skid marks on his neatly pressed trousers before shadowing the cat with his flashlight.

The cat strolled to the end of the hall and sat in front of a closed door, which had a towel stuffed under it. The one officer let out a groan. That's a bad sign. Tom reached down and yanked the towel away. A foul odor engulfed the hallway. Tom bit down hard, fighting off the urge to hurl his lunch, and carefully opened the door. With the room partially exposed, Tom saw it was a bathroom. A white porcelain bathtub and a cock-eyed curtain rod fell into view, the curtain covered in fuzzy mold thick as a fur rug. The vile stench poured out in waves.

Tom's cheeks ballooned as he forced back the feeling of bile coming up his throat. "Oh, Christ, that smells bad." He choked out a dry cough then pressed his shirtsleeve tight over his mouth.

Having never been privy to a murder crime scene, Tom Cannon was unfamiliar with the smell of a rotting corpse. But Salazar knew it well.

The two entered the bathroom, crisscrossing streams of light illuminating the cramped space. Tom held his free hand over his nose and mouth.

Inside the bathtub lay a contorted body, its fluids puddled in the basin. The body had turned purple with an almost black tint, the elevated extremities hardened to a crusty yellow and orange. The face had sunken into the skull, with portions of the face scavenged from blowfly activity. Areas of the body not inflicted with rotting ooze were covered in maggots. Hardened brown shells littered in and around the chest and open orifices indicated advanced larvae colonization. Blowflies swirled around the body, disturbed by the intruders. The first time viewing a dead body, coupled with the pungent smell, continued to churn Tom's stomach, making him nauseated. McGuire pointed out the door with his chin, ushering the rookie out before he could contaminate whatever evidence might be in the room. Tom took advantage of the offer, bolting out the door and down the hall.

The acrid smell hung in Tom's nose as he sat outside on the front concrete steps with his head between his legs. He could feel his stomach grinding. With his elbows planted deeply into his thighs with his fingers weaved into his hair, Tom struggled to take slow, even breaths. The detectives exited the front and each gave a consoling pat on Tom's shoulder, Salazar maintaining a look of empathy while McGuire went to retrieve the car.

"It's never easy coming up on a dead body." Salazar knelt down. "You going to be all right?"

Tom took in several deep breaths. "I'm okay." He stood up and straightened out his clothes. "Any idea who's the unfortunate bastard in the bathtub is . . . was?"

The detective nodded. "He's pretty rotted but based on what I can tell, same guy in the pictures on the wall. Also found his wallet in one of the bedrooms. No license or credit cards. Library card, Costco, couple other photo I.D.s"

"Guy have a name?"

Again Salazar nodded. "Yeah. Jure Petroski."

12

By the time Alvin Cooper found his way back to the secluded single story bungalow house, the sun had already fallen behind the hills and the sky was as dark as a raisin. He tapped a nervous finger on the steering wheel, unhappy with his current situation. His world had again become a dilemma.

The air was balmy and the dust that kicked up from his truck's tires clung to the hairs on his arm. Cooper glided the truck down the gravel road that led to a detached garage hidden alongside the L-shaped house. The old wooden structure was scarcely sound, the door held into place by rusty hinges and a large rock placed strategically in front to prevent it from slamming shut. He parked under a large oak tree, which swallowed up the truck in its dark shadow.

Cooper exited the driver's side door, grabbing a brown paper sack from the passenger's seat. His breathing labored, he had a sour taste in his mouth, angry with himself for allowing the cops to find him so easily. He got away this time, having found a new place to stay, but maybe next time, he wouldn't be so lucky. He was also upset that he had been unable to delete everything on his computer before getting the hell out.

He approached the front door to the two-bedroom house. Cooper pulled a silver key from his pocket and inserted it into the lock. He jiggled the key and pushed hard on the flimsy front door. The frame was so misshapen Cooper needed to punt the bottom of the door to get it opened. The smell of mildew was overpowering. He walked into the living room where stacks of cardboard boxes formed multiple pyramids across the floor. He placed the paper sack on top of one of the stacks before flicking on a light switch, and a dim lamp illuminated the room in an off-white glow. Cooper collapsed onto a broken chair.

He reached over and grabbed the brown sack. It crunched onto his lap. He retrieved a bag of Doritos and a bottle of Jack Daniels. He stared at the whiskey's black and white label, tracing the scrolling calligraphy with his thumb, then unscrewed the top and took a swig. A sharp twinge rushed to his head as the snap of liquor hit his throat and swooshed down his gullet. He held his breath until the burn subsided. He let his body melt, closing his eyes and resting his head.

The house was recently rented but Cooper didn't know for how long. The renter was a new friend he had made on the Internet, Klaus Monroe. Trading porn can be interesting, but meeting people was far more intriguing.

Yesterday, Klaus Monroe had invited Cooper over for a meet-and-greet. Share a little drink, a little food, maybe more. It was all fine with Cooper until Monroe made the fatal mistake of misreading Cooper's intentions. Monroe, a former ward of the state, confessed to Cooper his arrest for child molestation. After endlessly bragging about his escapades, his conquests, Cooper grew tired and wanted him to shut up.

Throughout that night, Monroe laughed incessantly at events that led to his incarceration. After draining a cheap bottle of bourbon, Monroe's words became an endless string of incoherent sentences, nonsensical bullshit. Finally, Cooper had enough. A lull in the conversation and Cooper took the opportunity to slip away from the room. Standing outside smoking a cigarette, Cooper found a metal pipe lying in the dirt near the front of the house. Scraping off the dirt, he measured the weight and heft of the steel. He returned to find Monroe slumped low in an overstuffed chair, the empty bottle of bourbon cradled by his side. With a gentle hand, Cooper tilted Monroe's head to one side, then swung the pipe, striking Monroe across the left temporal lobe. A heavy thud resonated a low-sounding thump, like a watermelon rolling off a kitchen counter onto the floor. He struck again, this time the distinct sound of crushing bone. Monroe never opened his eyes. He slumped to the right as his head fell over the armrest. Droplets of blood dripped from Monroe's tongue onto the hardwood floor. If not for the blood, one might have thought Monroe had simply fallen asleep.

Cooper's eyes popped open. He was no longer recalling the past, back living in the present. His haze evaporated, returning him to reality, to the spot where he had killed someone twelve hours earlier. Although killed was hardly the correct word. More like liberated. Yes, the world was liberated from the likes of Klaus Monroe.

He stood from the chair and brushed off his pants as though trying to rid his clothes of the stench of Mr. Monroe. He was feeling agitated, especially after a very disturbing conversation earlier in the afternoon. A cop had been trolling the Internet, trying to bait him. Which is what forced Cooper to leave and move into Monroe's home.

He placed the bottle of Jack on the wooden floor and pushed himself out of the chair. He yawned, the alcohol taking hold of his senses. He blinked his eyelids hard, shaking off the fatigue before heading out the front door. He made his way to the back of the truck. The rear window of the camper shell was smoked, prohibiting anyone from looking in. He took out his keys and tried a number of them before finding the one that unlocked the back lift-gate. He pulled it opened and dug around in the dark for his suitcase. The back end was full of junk. It took a few minutes of randomly swishing his arm through the piles of loose bags and boxes before he found the handle. He yanked hard. As the suitcase fell from the heap, so did an arm protruding out of a burlap sack. Cooper took a hard look at Monroe's limp appendage lying across the lift-gate, the rest of him still stuffed under the burlap fruit sack. Cooper pushed the cold limb inside the truck as if stuffing an overhead compartment aboard a crowded airplane. By early tomorrow, the summer heat would certainly engulf the truck in blowflies. Cooper needed to dispose of the body tonight, even with cops swarming around. The truck would be useless if it stank like a corpse.

Cooper carried the suitcase into the house and placed it on the living room floor. He unzipped the bag and pulled opened the flap, exposing neatly folded clothes, several pieces of electronic equipment and a number of CDs and floppy disks. He stacked them by the side of the chair and then dragged the suitcase to the back bedroom, placing it on top of an unmade bed.

He headed out the front door, turning on the porch light as he passed through the entryway. With the light on, no one would be suspicious that anything was wrong, that Klaus Monroe was no longer living here. That Klaus Monroe was no longer living. Cooper hopped behind the wheel of the Chevy and fired up the engine, grinding the gears into reverse. Already the smell of decomposing flesh began to seep into the cabin. A blowfly landed on the truck's steering wheel. Cooper flicked a finger at the lone parasite. It smacked against the windshield before flying off. He backed the truck out, made a two-point turn and headed up the dirt trail toward the highway. Cooper intended to find a commercial dumpster to deposit the remains of Klaus Monroe. By the time someone found his body, he would be a John Doe, just another transient who succumbed to an illness or drugs. That gave Cooper more time to find an answer to his predicament.

The truck crawled forward under the shade of oak trees. Before coming to the end of the dirt road, Cooper felt his cell phone vibrate in his pants' pocket. He pulled it out, flipped opened the cover and scanned the caller ID. Cooper smiled and pushed the green answer button. "Well, hello."

"Where are you?" the caller said through a cloud of background street noise.

"At Monroe's. Where the hell are you?"

"Close." The caller hesitated for a beat. "Where is he?"

"In the back." Cooper chuckled, then added, "Asleep."

"You mean he's dead."

It saddened him his friend wasn't in the mood to play games. "Yes, dead." Cooper paused, took in a deep breath, catching a whiff of the decaying Monroe in the warm, moist air. "You coming?"

The caller again hesitated before answering. "Yeah. I'll meet you and give you a hand."

"I'll call you when I find a spot for my friend." Cooper didn't wait for a response. He closed the phone and shoved it back into his pocket. He glanced at his watch before gazing back toward the camper. "Sorry, Klaus, don't have much time to dawdle." He turned his attention back to the road as he reached the end of the driveway. The truck lumbered up and onto the main stretch. Cooper cruised at the legal speed limit as he drove in search of a repository for Mr. Klaus Monroe.

13

Jack ended his phone call with Tom Cannon, and slouched in his office chair, staring at a copy of the photo taken from the computer of Petroski, or whatever his name really was. It had been less than twelve hours, according to Harrington, that the photo was taken and they were no closer to locating the girl. Marquez had taken a break from assisting Harrington. She grabbed an empty chair from another pod and rolled it next to Jack, where she plopped down and elevated her feet on his desk.

"Looks like our Petroski is nothing more than a borrowed name," Jack said.

Marquez raised an eyebrow. "Borrowed?"

"Tom went to the Redburn address and searched the residence. They found Mr. Petroski in the bathtub and—let me give you a hint—he wasn't taking a bath."

"So your suspect needed an identity and Mr. Petroski was the unfortunate volunteer."

"I'll bet our suspect met Petroski on the Internet trading smut. They meet face-to-face at some point in time, even become friends. Then, opportunity came a-knocking and Petroski finds himself the recipient of a chalk outline."

82

"You think our UNSUB knows we're on to him?"

"From what the detectives could tell, Petroski had been dead about a week. If we didn't find him, the locals most certainly would have. With this heat, I'm surprised the neighbors didn't already call the police about the smell." Jack sighed before continuing. "Our guy had enough time to rent the Chico residence, set up shop and kidnap a young girl. It's only a matter of time before he realizes we know the real Mr. Petroski is face down in a pool of sludge. He'll need another identity."

"That means—"

"That means," Jack interrupted, "he'll kill again."

"If he hasn't already."

His desk phone rang. The front switchboard operator.

"Agent Paris, I just got a call from the Chico PD. They're responding to a homicide and possibly a missing sixteen-year-old."

"We were just with Chico. They didn't mention any reported kidnappings. How long ago did this happen?"

"Don't know. I just got the call." The switchboard operator gave Jack the name and number of the detective who called.

Jack immediately started dialing. While it rang, Jack looked over at Marquez and said in a low voice, "Looks like we may have just found out who our kidnapped child is."

The phone call connected to the Chico Police Department dispatch center and was routed to Detective Mark Colfax. Jack made a quick introduction and jumped into the pertinent questions.

"We got the call around 6:30 p.m.," Colfax said, "from the 911 operator advising that a Mr. Paul Baker had called in screaming that his wife had been murdered. We dispatched two units to the location but they couldn't get Mr. Baker to come to the door. The officers were concerned he was armed. It took another hour and a half just to convince him to come out of the house with his hands raised. By the time we got the whole story out of him, it was nearly nine. Said his daughter was missing. We posted a TRAK flyer to all western states, put out a BOLO on NLETS. Name's Jessica Baker. No car or suspect, so no Amber Alert."

"What does she look like?" Jack asked.

"Five feet, ninety pounds, slender, athletic, dark hair, shoulder length."

Jack stared at the photo while Colfax described his kidnapped victim. Without confirmation Jack was only guessing, but his inclination told him it was the same girl. Jessica Baker. Jack informed Colfax on their investigations, their search and the photo. Even without seeing the photo, Colfax believed they were the same girl.

"What happened to the mother?"

Colfax's voice lowered as he cleared his throat. "Pretty ugly. Husband came home and found her in the bathtub. Head bashed in, throat slit ear to ear. It's amazing her head wasn't detached. The husband told me when he returned from work, wife's car was in the drive. He went to the refrigerator, grabbed a beer, went through the mail. Daughter had stayed home sick with the flu. Thought she was still asleep and didn't want to disturb her. When the wife didn't appear, he started searching the house. That's when he came across her body."

"Forensic sweep the place?"

"We're just getting started. I had a difficult time locating all our crime scene examiners this late at night."

"What about blood and DNA?"

"No shortage there. There's blood everywhere. CSI should be able to find something in that mess."

"I can send our ERT crew if you're short-handed," Jack offered.

"Could use the help."

"I'll contact our team leader to give you a call and get you whatever help you may need at the scene. Detective, I think it would be beneficial to both our agencies if we meet to coordinate the investigation. Better chances of locating our killer and finding Jessica Baker if we work together."

"That's fine with me," Colfax replied. "When?"

Jack paused for only a beat. "How about now?"

14

Jack retrieved the TRAK flyer of Jessica Baker that came across the Bureau's fax machine. TRAK, which stood for Technology to Recover Abducted Kids, had sent this flyer to every law enforcement agency on the West Coast. The picture showed Jessica's high school portrait. Based on the hair and Colfax's description of her build, Jack had little doubt that this was the kidnapped girl from the photo. An uneasy feeling ran through him as he thought about Jessica Baker, the trail of murders, the killer's need for new identities. There was certainly more to this case than what they knew. Their suspect had taken a child but had not asked for a ransom, and in Jack's mind that was as bad as it could get. Marquez looked over, watched Jack rubbing his forehead between two fingers, tension surfacing through his temples.

"Tell me what you're thinking," she said.

Jack glanced over at Marquez. "Four parts to a kidnapping, Lucy."

Marquez nodded, and held up a single finger. "The abduction, being grabbed. Big mistake. *Go without a fight, won't live through the night.*"

Jack nodded.

"The transport to another location." Marquez held up two fingers.

"A very bad one," Jack replied. "And...."

"Three, the ritual. Rape, molest, hurt." Three fingers straight up.

"And four?" Jack's voice grew edgy.

Marquez's lips thinned as she looked at the TRAK flyer photo of Jessica. "Without a ransom—the disposal." Her hand fell flat on Jack's desk, and she rubbed a small spot in a slow circular motion.

Jack tapped a nervous finger on the face of his watch and stood from his chair. "Four hours, that's the average length of time a kidnapped victim is kept alive. Based on the time and date of the photo image, if she is alive, Jessica Baker's on borrowed time."

No ransom, no demands. Nothing in exchange for her safe return. That only meant whoever had her was not intending on letting her go.

"Let's see what Jim has put together from the computer." Jack slipped on a sport coat and reached in his desk drawer for his pistol. Marquez stood and slipped on her jacket. Marquez's pistol was already on her side.

The two hurried down a long green hallway to the CART examination room, where James Harrington's back was still to the door. Hunched over an opened computer tower like he was conducting surgery, Harrington straightened up and let out a guttural sigh. Pain was radiating up his back after being bent over for an hour. As he twisted his stocky frame to relieve the tension, he caught sight of Jack and Marquez watching his exercise routine.

"Got something for you," Harrington said.

They walked over and peered at the monitor on the examination table. Numbers, icons and squiggly lines spanned the length of the monitor. Harrington maneuvered through a maze of computer words and commands until small segments of images appeared. He pasted them together, overlaying parts onto the screen, refreshing and doing it all over again. Finally, Harrington clicked on an icon, a second rolled by before a full screen image materialized. Grainy at first, then the process started to bring the image into focus. A photo of a house, single story, tree-lined street. A large, light-colored sedan parked in the driveway. Jack recognized it as a late model Chrysler. The photo was taken from inside a car parked on the other side of the street, a reflection in the side view mirror. Jack stared sharply.

"You can see an image of the person taking the picture in the side-view," he said, pointing at the fuzzy mirror.

"Not enough detail for an identification," replied Harrington, who continued punching at the keyboard, drawing up additional images. "Look at the next set. I think this may answer some questions."

The second and third images began to appear. Another picture of the house, this time a man making his way to the car. A blurry shot of the vehicle driving past. Another of a woman walking from the front door, garage opened. The next, a woman backing an SUV down the driveway.

"Looks like surveillance photos," Jack said,

"More like stalking photos," Marquez replied.

"Here comes the creepy ones," Harrington said.

The screen scrolled down revealing a blurry, off-centered photo of a house window, as if the photographer was jogging toward it as he shot the digital frame. The next picture was through the window into a bedroom. The next showed the backyard slider.

"We're watching a break-in," Marquez said.

Jack turned to Harrington. "How much more were you able to retrieve?"

"There are several missing between this one and the next, but it's one that will help identify your victim. It's still a bit fragmented, but I think it serves its purpose."

A partial photo appeared of a bed with a young girl lying asleep and facing away from the camera. She was unaware that she was being photographed. Her hair partially covered her face, her pajamas bunched at the waist and calves.

"It's not the best," Harrington said, "but it's something to go by."

Jack hit the print button and a photo-quality copy of the image spat out the printer. Jack picked it up, careful not to damage or smudge the glossy photo. He'd bring the picture to the Chico Police Department and show it to Paul Baker, depending on his state of mind. If Jack was right, whoever took the photo was the same person Marquez conversed with last night over the Internet. The man who had kidnapped a young girl, murdered the mother, and taken the identity of Jure Petroski before hacking him into a slurry mess inside a bathtub. Whoever this man was, he was on a mission.

15

Tuesday 11:45 p.m.

Jack stood behind a one-way mirror, observing Paul Baker sitting in the interview room at the Chico Police Department, staring at a blank table. Jack had been here before, five years ago, watching a victim turn suspect. Baker's eyes moved back and forth, left to right. He was reliving the events of the past five and a half hours in his head like a movie projected on the Formica surface. It was all too familiar but this one felt different.

Detective Mark Colfax walked up behind Jack with a mug bearing the Chico PD logo on its side. He didn't say a word, just handed the mug of coffee to Jack. He tapped his mug against the side of Jack's.

"Salud."

Jack forced a smile.

"We got the initial information, but I'd like to get some details," Colfax said. "Care to join me?"

Jack pulled the grainy photo of the unidentified girl and stared at it for a moment. "How do I show him this?"

Colfax shook his head. "Don't have a choice. We've got to know."

The two entered the interview room. Baker quickly looked up. His eyes said it all. The cup of coffee that he was given earlier remained full at his side. Jack sat in front of Baker, Colfax taking a chair to his right.

"Mr. Baker, my name is Jack Paris." He reached out and gave Baker's arm a gentle touch to get his attention. "I'm with the FBI. I want to help you."

Baker looked directly into Jack's eyes. "Help me? My wife was murdered and my daughter's gone. How can you help me?"

Jack chose his words carefully. "By bringing your daughter back to you. Help me find her."

Baker shook his head, flashing both palms forward. "Just tell me how."

Jack pulled the photo out from a file folder and gave it a moment before sliding it forward on the table. As much as he needed to get confirmation, showing a photo like this to a father was going to hurt.

Baker appeared puzzled at first, then his eyes focused, horrified. Without a word, his face gave away the answer. Baker broke down and sobbed.

"Do you have any idea who may have done this?"

"No!" Baker slammed a fist hard on the table. "Who would do such a thing?"

"Let's talk about the past several days. Was there was anything you may have noticed that was out of the ordinary?"

He again shook his head, threading his fingers though his hair. "No, I can't think of anything."

"How about your daughter, Jessica? Any problem at school, with a boyfriend?"

Baker never stopped shaking his head. "No, nothing."

Jack worked his way through all the possible scenarios, with the same answer coming from a distraught man.

"You're a loan officer at the Diamond County Bank in Chico. Can you think of any customers that may be upset with you or the bank?"

"I just became the new senior loan officer."

"Anything out of the ordinary? Something unusual?"

Baker was silent, his eyes closed in concentration. Suddenly, his eyes thrust wide and his mouth fell open. "Carter, Hampton Carter!"

The room grew uncomfortably quiet, and for the next few seconds, Jack studied Paul Baker. His moves, his words. There was no question this was a man filled with grief, desperate for answers. Jack knew right away, Paul Baker was a victim. He wasn't anything like the person Jack interrogated five years earlier. That man was a killer.

16

After a dozen phone calls, Jack was able to locate the Diamond County bank manager, convincing him to meet in the branch lobby. A check on Paul Baker's loan files could not wait until morning. Jack pulled into the parking lot to find the manager waiting at the front door, keys in hand. He looked as if he was wearing pajamas under a lightweight jacket. Jack pulled up next to the front entry and exited his car.

"Mr. Nelson?" Jack removed his credentials from his jacket pocket and held them up. "Sorry to get you up this late at night."

"Technically, it's morning." The branch manager shrugged his shoulders. "You said this had to do with Mr. Baker? I hope everything is all right." His voice had the tone of someone annoyed, like maybe Paul Baker had done something wrong and the FBI was there to prove it. He unlocked the bank doors and entered a code on the security keypad.

"Actually, it's not. Mr. Baker's wife was murdered last night and his daughter has been kidnapped."

Nelson froze, then muttered what sounded like a sloppy apology.

"We're trying to determine who might be involved."

While Jack talked, Nelson switched on the lights. Florescent bulbs high above flickered before illuminating the dark wood tables and marble counters inside of the branch in a commercial gray tone.

"I spoke to Mr. Baker and he mentioned he had a customer yesterday morning. Hampton Carter. Said he was applying for an auto loan. Can we check to see if there's anything in his file?"

"Paul is extremely organized. If Mr. Carter came to him, there's documentation of that." The two walked toward Baker's desk, which looked like a shrine to anal retentiveness.

"We keep information cards on every customer, contact information." Nelson bent low, staring at the rows of neatly arranged folders, alphabetized, slotted between chrome metal bands. He reached for the first file. Jack grabbed Nelson's wrist and waved a scornful finger.

"Let's not add more prints to the papers if we don't have to."

Nelson nodded. Jack removed a pair of latex gloves from his pocket and offered them to Nelson, who strained to get them over his sweaty hands. Jack slid on a pair of his own.

It took only ten minutes for the two to review the files on Baker's desk, flipping open the covers, checking the names, scanning the applicant's background. No Hampton Carter.

"Maybe Paul got the name wrong," Nelson said. "I can't believe he would forget to create a file."

Jack took one last look around Baker's desk, then peered under the large, dark redwood table, where he found a separate, free-standing set of stacked bins, papers neatly arranged and stapled. A slim folder lay on the top of the stack with a routing slip paper-clipped to the outside. Jack picked it up and found what he was looking for: Mr. Hampton Carter. Will return with completed application and, 1.) VOE, 2.) W-2s, 3.) Tax Returns.

Flipping open the folder, Jack found a half-completed information card with an address written in the margins. He figured the address was bogus, but made note of it, saying a silent prayer he'd get lucky on this one. It was the best lead he had on Carter.

He placed the folder into a plastic sleeve. Maybe they'd pull latent prints. Out the corner of his eye, Jack caught sight of the gold-framed portrait of Baker's family on the edge of the desk. During the interview, Baker said Carter had seen the portrait and was asking questions about his daughter. Jack bent over and studied the photograph closely. Several smudges on the covered glass and frame, something he knew would have driven neatnick Paul Baker into a coma. Filthy fingerprints from someone's curious hands.

Jack said, "We got a winner."

Thirty minutes later, Jack was back at the office with Special Agent Chris Hoskin, team leader for the Evidence Response Team. He had given Hoskin the picture frame to lift the prints for review. On his way in, Jack called in the address information. Colfax immediately sent two detectives to check it out. If it was legit, they would have an answer within the hour.

Hoskin placed four plastic, pyramid-shaped cones inside a cardboard box. As if on table legs, the glass from the picture frame was balanced at each corner. In the center, Hoskin placed a can of Sterno, heating a small tin of cyanoacrylate ester—a fancy name for superglue.

Hoskin nodded and straightened his glasses. "Cyanoacrylate-developed latent prints really should be allowed to sit overnight before I apply dye stain."

"We don't have time," Jack said.

Hoskin lit the Sterno and seconds later the superglue bubbled into a fizz.

Harrington walked over and watched Hoskin working on the plate glass. He smacked a wad of chewing gum and shook his head waiting for Hoskin to take notice. "How technologically advanced, Chris. Cardboard box, sterno, superglue...."

Hoskin kept his focus. "What works, works."

Harrington harrumphed. "Not like inventing the Internet."

"No. This one actually has value."

Harrington chuckled sarcastically before turning around and walking out the door.

Several minutes passed and the box filled with a toxic fog. It would take about an hour before Hoskin would be able to remove the piece of glass from the cardboard box. Glue takes time to adhere and dry. By then, those invisible prints left behind would turn purple, permanently affixed to the glass, giving Hoskin something to study.

"Call me when you've got something," Jack said.

Hoskin gave a thumbs up and returned to his work.

17

Wednesday – 2:41 a.m.

Jack held a photo of the latent print inches from his face, as his eyes followed the twists and turns of the loops and whirls, the tented arches. A thumb and three fingers is what Hoskin had been able to successfully lift. Jack carefully placed the card on his desk, his fingers rounding its edges. "Are they being checked in IAFIS?" The Integrated Automated Fingerprint Identification System comprised the database for all prints on file.

Hoskin nodded. "Already submitted. We put a rush on the card. Hope to have an answer back within a couple of hours."

"That's too long."

"I'll go push."

"You do that. Tell them the SAC has ordered you to be pushy."

"You know he's out of town."

Jack lifted one eyebrow.

"Works for me." Hoskin walked out of the bullpen.

Jack picked up his briefcase and looked over at Marquez who was tapping a pen on a notepad.

"Let's go, Lucy."

"Where to?"

"ERT's still at Baker's house. Let's see what they turned up."

There was little else they could do and waiting was something Marquez despised. She grabbed up her jacket, and the two headed out the door. Jack yelled at Hoskin as they passed him down the hallway. "Call me the moment you get a hit on those prints."

Hoskin gave two quick pumps with his right hand, turned and disappeared into the radio room.

They arrived an hour later. Two SUVs blocked the entrance to Baker's driveway, and yellow evidence tape circled the perimeter. Several neighbors stood in bathrobes outside, wondering what horrible thing had happened inside the Baker home. Jack maneuvered his vehicle between an ERT Suburban and a patrol car. The lights in the house were all on and Jack could see agents milling around inside, a photographer's camera flashing every few seconds and large brown paper sacks being carried out to the evidence van. Jack looked down at his watch. 3:44 a.m. He rubbed his tired eyes. "You ready?" he asked.

"Like a race horse," Marquez answered.

As they made their way toward the front door, a uniformed officer gave them a hard stare before throwing a casual salute and stepping aside. A dozen agents roamed the hallways in latex gloves and Tyvek containment suits. Green light beams from the RUVIS illuminated a small monitor screen as the agent panned the equipment over the glassy surface of the back slider looking for fingerprints. Jack turned the corner and found his way into the living room. A half-empty beer bottle sat on the coffee table in a small pool of water, moisture from the sweating glass. Jack imagined Paul Baker sitting on the couch, scanning the mail while his wife lay dead in the bathtub down the hall. The thought of coming home to find his own wife, Emily, murdered gave him a chill. He paused to regain his focus. He needed to get back on track, back to finding Jessica Baker.

He turned to see three agents conferring down the hall next to a doorway, and headed in their direction. Marquez followed. An agent, Sheldon Stewart, exited the room right where the three stood, holding plastic evidence bags, which he handed over to Brad Houston, who placed them in a large box already filled with other pieces of evidence. Hoskin had designated Houston team leader for this search.

Houston reached in his jacket pocket and pulled out a pair of wire-rimmed glasses, slipping them on and carefully jotting down notes in a log.

"What do you have, Brad?" Jack asked.

Houston looked over. "I see the cavalry has arrived." He shook Jack's hand before waving the crew to follow down the hallway and into the master bedroom, where more evidence bags were neatly stacked on the corner of a crimson-stained mattress. A bedroom chair lay on its side and a glass lamp was smashed against the wall. Droplets of blood dribbled across the carpet, followed by larger, smeared bloodstains, denoting something heavy dragged into the master bathroom. Jack maneuvered around the evidence and into the room.

"The place has been gone over already. Samples taken, items photographed, hairs and fibers vacuumed. Nothing else of value for you to look at."

Jack pointed at the blood smeared across the carpet. "Looks like there was a struggle."

Houston nodded. "A pretty bad one. Mrs. Baker must've put up a helluva fight. There's handprints in blood over the broken lamp and streaked across the bed sheets. My guess is the assailant killed her here." Houston pointed to a spot next to the bed where a dry, dark stain crusted on the carpet. "This is where she bled out before being dragged into the bathtub."

"How was she killed?" Marquez asked.

Houston pointed toward the ceiling and a long splatter of blood trailing across it, dripping down the walls. "Hit her with something hard, over and over." Houston swung his arm up and down, mimicking the motion. "Her head took a good beating." Houston dragged a thumb across his neck. "To add insult to injury, he sliced her throat open for good measure."

Jack shook his head in disgust. "What about the daughter?"

"No sign of a second struggle, and we found nothing to lead us to believe she was killed."

Jack already knew she was alive based on the photo. Still, it was reassuring to hear Houston affirm it.

"I guess that could be good news," Marquez said.

Houston shook his head. "I'm not so sure. If this guy wanted money, he wouldn't have killed the wife." He pointed at the blood soaked floor. "This asks for cops to be involved."

"No ransom note found, I take it?"

Houston shook his head. "Her bed sheet is missing. I'm guessing her kidnapper wrapped her in it to conceal her as he carried her out. I think the daughter was drugged."

"How did you reach that conclusion?" Marquez asked.

Stewart held up a plastic evidence bag with a spent syringe. A tag dangled from the bag. Jack reached down and took the bag, reading the tag. "Ketamine?"

Houston tipped his reading glasses below eye level. "Not just for horses. It's used to quiet cranky patients. Like inmates."

Jack paused and Marquez chimed in. "Inmates?"

"Yeah, wouldn't have figured it out without some good old-fashion luck." Houston pointed further in the bag. "We found it under the bed sheets. Probably fell out when he was struggling with the wife." Inside, a smaller clear plastic bag, torn open at one end, with white typed lettering: 150 mg dose of Ketamine from Butte County. "That's Butte County Jail Infirmary," Houston continued. "My sister worked as a nurse at a lock-up in Minnesota. Said they used Ketamine to calm inmates when they get all spooled up. We could be looking for someone with access to the drug vault in Butte. Possibly an employee."

Jack paused for a moment, the pieces coming together in his head. There were too many coincidences. Drugs from Butte County Jail, where a child killer recently escaped. And now, suddenly a child is missing.

Alvin Franklin Cooper. He had come back into Jack's life, and he was picking up where he left off.

Marquez glanced over, curiously. "What?"

"You know that case I needed your help with after this one was over?"

"Yeah."

"Forget about it. We're already on it."

18

The man sounded out of breath when he walked through the creaky door that separated Jessica from the outside world. Thick tape was still over her eyes and a rag tightly knotted around her mouth. She didn't know how long she had been struggling to breathe as the quietness voided all sense of time. Between the summer heat and fever, Jessica felt nauseated, fighting off the urge to throw up.

A sharp sting raced across her face as the tape over her eyes was ripped away; she cried out a muffled shriek. A second later, bright lights and blurry images swirled in front of her. She blinked hard, trying to get everything in focus. Suddenly, she could see. See him. Jessica dropped her stare, forcing herself not to look directly at her captor.

From the corner of her eye, she watched the man walk over to an old wooden table and shove sacks of groceries to the center. Dusty and cramped, the room looked exactly liked it smelled. The man reached into the bags, pulling out a two-liter plastic bottle of Pepsi, white bread, salami, and something that looked like cheese. He removed toilet paper and coloring books from the other bag.

"Hello." The man spoke in a low soft voice. "Thought you might be hungry."

Jessica twitched her head from side to side, still refraining from looking into his eyes. She winced, the tape that bound her hands cutting deep into her wrists every time she moved. She fought against the bindings but it didn't matter. Even if she was able to break free, she was too weak to escape.

"I'll make you a sandwich. Do you like cheese?" He spoke like she was a guest in his home. "I like cheese," he added. "Grilled cheese, but I don't have a stove. Still, it'll be good." The calmness in his voice rattled Jessica's nerves. She bit down hard on the rag, trying to force herself steady.

As the man prepared the sandwich, Jessica's body started to tingle, her mouth dry and scratchy. Her head began to pound and she started to cough through the gag. Sweat beaded across her forehead, her pajamas soaked in perspiration. The man stopped what he was doing and walked over to her, placing a hand on her forehead. She jerked back from his touch.

"You still have a fever," he said. "You're sick."

Jessica's coughing advanced into spasms. The man pulled the gag from her mouth, and immediately she sucked in a mouthful of air, the ability to breathe freely relieving some of her stress.

"There, there. You need to rest," the man said. "You're as sick as a dog. Luckily, I have a microwave. I'll heat you up some soup."

Jessica cleared her throat. "Please, please untie me and let me go. I won't tell anyone about you. I don't even know what you look like."

The man placed a hand over Jessica's lips. "Shhh, it's all right. I'm not going to hurt you."

Jessica took several rapid breaths that made her cough. "Why? Why me?"

The man stood still, gave it a moment of thought. Then rolled his shoulders. "Why not?"

"What do you want from me?"

"In time, we will get to know each other better."

The microwave beeped. The idea of soup on a hot day in a stuffy room made her feel even sicker.

"I'm not hungry," she said. "Meds, I need my meds."

"You'll be fine. It's just the flu."

Jessica felt the tingle intensify, her head swimming into a deep fog. "My meds. Please, I need them now."

The man leaned close to Jessica face, this time staring right into her eyes. There was no way she could avoid the details of his features. She slowly allowed the weight of her eyelids to fall shut, but she knew it was too late. She felt the man place an ear next to her mouth.

"What do you need?" he asked.

Her head rocked, her eyes remained closed. She licked her lips and said in a soft, hushed tone, "My insulin."

19

This was Jack's third try at calling Ray Sizemore on his cell phone. Jack knew Sizemore would be boarding a flight to Sacramento that morning but didn't know exactly when. He wanted to fill him in on what they had learned over the past twenty-four hours. Jack tapped the tip of his pen on a note pad impatiently, waiting for the call to connect. After five rings, Sizemore finally picked up.

"This is Sizemore.

"It's Paris. Got some information. You may want to reconsider coming."

Sizemore let out a long groan. "Shit."

Jack summarized the chronology of events about Cooper being on the lam. Then he told Sizemore about the Baker kidnapping, the murder and the stolen drugs from the Butte County infirmary.

"If I called you three days earlier, maybe none of this would have happened."

"Not your fault," Jack replied. "Had we known more about Cooper five years ago, we wouldn't even be talking."

Sizemore remained silent.

"I had sent two agents out to check out Cooper's place of employment. No one had seen him for a couple of days, knew nothing about where he goes or whom he sees. Most didn't even know he was on work furlough. They said he was a loner. We've got the prints from the crime scene, which matches Cooper's. That makes Cooper our Mr. Hampton Carter, who is also your killer and my kidnapper. And I'm guessing he's our Mr. Jure Petroski, as well."

There was a long pause before Sizemore spoke. "What do you want me to do?"

Jack thought for a moment. There were a thousand things to do, but right now, the rescue of Jessica Baker took priority. Ray's knowledge of Cooper may help him find her, and he could use an extra hand. But his response came out sounding more like a plea for help than a suggestion. "Why don't you come on down."

"Flight leaves in an hour."

Jack drove back to the Chico Police Department, where a command post was set up, task force hastily being thrown together. Before the morning broke, agents from the California Department of Justice's Sex Predators Task Force arrived to assist. Their access to the State lab was vital, allowing evidence to be analyzed immediately. Although the FBI lab in Quantico, Virginia, was more than willing to make this a top priority, it would have been time consuming for Jack to fly every piece of evidence across the country. In the packed command post, Jack caught sight of an officer pushing his way through the crowd. Cal DOJ Special Agent John Allison made his way to Jack and handed him an inch-thick file containing the results from the searches.

"Here's the report. I also got the investigative notes from the Washington State laboratory on the Grace Holloway kidnap/murder investigation. I compared their latents to the ones taken from the Baker house, gave it a complete review." Agent Allison's head bobbed. "You got a match. Mr. Cooper is definitely your man. He doesn't seem to care who knows he's a killer."

Jack perused the report, reading the things he had already knew, but he couldn't understand why Cooper was so careless about leaving evidence of his guilt. "He kills a person and takes their identity. He kills a girl in Washington, kills his family, then kidnaps a young girl. I don't get it. What the hell is setting him off?"

Allison responded. "Here's the scientific answer about your guy: He's fucked-up in the head."

Jack could only agree. He thanked Agent Allison for the report and headed down the hall to Colfax's office. He entered the detective's room and took a seat. Colfax was hunched over the telephone, jotting onto a note pad, nodding continually in agreement with the caller on the other end of the line. He hung up the phone and looked at Jack.

"Anything new develop since last night?" Jack asked.

Colfax leaned back and placed a finger on his note pad. "Got the toxicology report. It's confirmed the ketamine was stolen from the Butte County infirmary. Everything is pointing to Cooper."

The evidence was piling up and the confirmation that the drugs came from Butte County made Jack cringe. The arrest of Cooper five years ago, the sweetheart deal he got, and the opportunity to walk into the bank and invade another person's life was all too much to believe. Baker must have felt victimized for the third time when he was shown the photo of his daughter. Jack couldn't help but feel he was to blame.

"I think it's time to plaster Cooper's face across everyone's TV screen. The clock's ticking and the longer she's out there, the higher the chance we won't find her alive."

"There's more," Colfax said.

Jack kept silent.

"Baker tells me Jessica's a diabetic. She's on insulin."

Jack's sharpened his stare. "How critical?"

"Says she needs it daily."

"Can it get any worse?"

Colfax shrugged. "Doctors say that if we don't find her soon, they can't guarantee she won't fall into a coma."

"Great."

"We sent two officers out to the address listed on his loan application." Colfax shook his head. "It's a church."

"Did they do a canvass?"

"No, they were waiting for us to give them the go-ahead. Didn't want to spook anyone if Cooper was still in the area."

"Let's get out there."

The two pushed themselves out of their chairs and grabbed their briefcases. Colfax reached in his top desk drawer and removed his pistol, snapping it into his holster. Jack had sent Marquez back to Sacramento to continue her hunt on the Internet in hopes of finding Cooper on-line. Cooper probably wouldn't use the moniker of JPetroski in any chat room anymore, but maybe his personality would give him away no matter what he called himself. Hoskin had been working throughout the night with the forensics team and Harrington continued to dig through Cooper's computer. Fragmented.

"You ready?" Colfax said, eyes puffy and voice rough.

He thought about Marquez's response to the same question. "Like a race horse."

Colfax nodded. "Let's get him."

They stepped out of the station and the bright sun caused them both to squint. Jack slipped on his Ray-bans. It took only seconds for sweat to pool and start to drizzle down his back. The temperature was soaring and so was their frustration. They hopped into Jack's vehicle and cranked the air conditioner. The heat made the pavement appear to squiggle. But Jack didn't lose his focus. This morning, Jack knew finding Jessica Baker was his priority and Cooper the target of his investigation. Nothing would change that.

20

"**The address** he listed is 5521 South Brandon," Colfax said, "in an unincorporated area of Butte County. We're about fifteen away. So tell me, what do you know about this guy, Cooper?"

Jack rattled off everything he knew about Cooper's history. "Alvin Franklin Cooper, born to an unwed mother in Shafter, California. No other siblings. Mother died when he was in high school. Records showed cause of death to be natural; I have my doubts. He makes his way through high school alone, saves his money, travels outside the U.S., before returning to California. Where he goes and what he does at this point is still a mystery. Next time we see him, he's married and has a child. The rest you know."

"Seems strange a guy like Cooper doesn't have a rap sheet a mile long."

"For all we know, he could have left a trail of dead bodies from here to bum-fuck Egypt. Just haven't been solved."

"If you ask me, this guy broke a gear sometime during his youth. After he killed his wife and kid, they should have plugged him into a wall socket and lit him up like a Christmas tree."

Jack couldn't argue.

The traffic was light, and ten minutes later they exited the 99 Freeway and headed east, toward South Brandon. The neighborhoods started to thin, turning mostly into rural farmhouses and pocketed communities of older, L-shaped homes, streets filled with old trucks and tall, established trees. They turned onto South Brandon, and drove directly to a two-story building with a brick walkway. At first, Jack thought it was a converted home. Then he caught sight of the large cross that was part of the front wall façade. A place of worship. The lawn was neatly mowed and thick shrubbery filled the areas surrounding the building. Big umbrella trees offered shade, keeping the blistering summer heat down during services. The windows were all opened, as was the front door. Parking in the adjacent lot, they exited the car and approached the opened door. Jack peeked into the building, whose interior smelled of old wood and dust. A registry was opened on a brass stand for guests to sign. Jack was flipping through the pages when he heard a voice from outside.

"Can I help you?"

The two turned around to see a slender man wearing a straw hat, a clean white shirt and jeans. He was holding onto a water hose, the spray nozzle dripping from a faulty seal. Jack wasn't sure if the shirt was wet from sweat or the leaky hose. He appeared to be in his seventies. A little old to be the gardener, Jack thought.

Jack introduced himself. "We're looking for the pastor of this church."

The old man's head slightly bobbed but his eyes didn't move. "That would be me," he finally said. "I'm Pastor Joel."

Colfax motioned at Pastor Joel with his notebook. "You caught us off guard, not being in uniform."

"I could say the same about you," Pastor Joel said with a smile. He dropped the hose and pulled off the glove on his right hand, which he extended, greeting Jack with a comforting shake.

"In this church, I double as the grounds' crew too. What is it I can do for you both?"

"We're investigating the kidnapping of a young girl that occurred yesterday."

"And what does that have to do with my church?"

"We're not sure. The person we believe responsible listed this address as his residence. Hampton Carter."

The Reverend pondered the name, rubbing his chin before responding. "Doesn't sound familiar. Of course, we get a lot of people, mostly migrant workers, passing through, looking for Sunday services, that kind of thing."

"How about the name of Alvin Franklin Cooper," Jack asked.

Pastor Joel shook his head no.

Jack pursed his lips and reached over to take the case file out of Colfax's hands. He sifted through the reports and removed Cooper's prisoner inmate photo. Jack never liked showing a single photo as opposed to a six-pack. Defense counselors like to exploit the opportunity, contending the investigator prompted the witness to pick their client as the suspect. Time was short and Jack didn't have much choice. "Does this man look familiar?"

The pastor took the photo from Jack. Recognition immediately lit across his face.

"You're putting me in a bad situation," the pastor said. "I know this man but my conversations with him are protected by privilege."

"Look," Colfax interrupted. "Privilege or not, this guy may be responsible for the murder of at least four individuals, two of whom are children. He's holding a child as we speak and she may not last much longer."

Pastor Joel's mouth fell slack and Jack could see the conflict in his face. He took off his straw hat and removed a handkerchief from his rear pocket. Moisture pooled around his thinning hairline. "This man," the priest began, "he came to me a couple of weeks ago. Walked into my church, spoke with my assistant. Said he wanted to speak to the pastor, wanted to confess."

Jack asked, "Confess what?"

"I can't say. Privileged, you understand."

"Reverend, if you don't tell me what you know, God is going to have another guest very soon."

Pastor Joel's hands started to shake as he continued to wipe the sweat from his brow. "You said he's kidnapped a young girl, is that right?"

Jack nodded, "She's sixteen."

The pastor pressed two fingers to his lips as his stare drifted toward the ground. "That's what he was talking about."

"What was he talking about?"

Pastor Joel fumbled with the weaving of his hat, then said, "This conversation never happened."

"I forgot it already," Jack replied.

"A girl. A young girl. He dreamt of a young girl becoming his daughter. A new daughter. He told me he lost his own daughter years ago and was feeling depressed. He feared his dream at first, then said he realized it was a sign. From God. I told him he was just going through the stages of grief. Depressed at his loss and that, in time, this too shall pass." Pastor Joel swallowed hard. "I had no idea he was talking about taking a child."

Jack placed a hand on the pastor's shoulder. "Did he say where he was living?"

"No. He just comes and goes."

"When was the last time you saw him?"

He thought for a moment. "Yesterday. He came by to say he had done something bad. He said he made someone apologize for doing wrong. He said that person promised never to do wrong again."

"Was he driving?"

"I don't know. I never see him arrive. I would never see him leave."

"Anything. A name, a friend, a telephone number. Something to help us find him."

Pastor Joel grabbed his head, shaking it as if some tidbit of memory would fall out. "Nothing, nothing. He wouldn't even tell me his name until yesterday."

"What name did he use?"

"Klaus. I remember now. It was Klaus, a good German name." He paused before his memory found the answer he was looking for. "Klaus Monroe."

21

Dispatch operator Mike Escobar stared intensely at the monitor, ignoring the sound of the radio calls that filled the overhead speakers. The agents in the office nicknamed him Batman because he primarily worked at night. He was pulling a back-to-back shift at the FBI's Sacramento office. Although he preferred the quietness of the midnight hours, the bustling action during the daylight was a nice change of pace.

The dispatch room was full of life. Along with the FBI channels, dispatch monitored the local Police Departments as well. The PD radio dispatch operator boomed over the loudspeaker. *211 Silent . . . Man reporting shots fired in the vicinity of Stockton and Fruitridge.* One after another. It never stopped. After listening to the handful of dispatch centers calling in at the same time—an event nothing short of a calamity—Batman had attained a Zen level of tuned-out, unless an officer was in need of help.

After a few expletives, he continued to check and then re-check each function on his computer. Agent Hoskin called only fifteen minutes ago, requesting a run through every database he could muster to locate Klaus Monroe. Should be an easy task, he thought. How many Klauses can there be? Giving an age span of thirty to forty years old, he focused his attention as the system began spewing DMV checks. After an electronic sputter, the California Law Enforcement Terminal System, also known as CLETS, returned with its results: 125 Matched Criteria on L/N F/N.

Batman slid his hand through his hair, shaking his head in disbelief.

He ran it a second time, just to make sure. Same information. 125 matched by last name and first name. Since CLETS only supplies the amount without giving up any details, the only option was to have all 125 pulled and forwarded to the office for review.

"Screw this," he shouted from inside the closed room, which was separated from the rest of the dispatch center. He knew the request would take too long for a response. He decided to take matters into his own hands. Start limiting the field. New DOBs, middle initials, cities of origin. Anything that would get him a list. It would then be up to him to take those names and filter them himself. He ran through the alphabet, guessing at ages, three years up, three years down. Potential cities Agent Hoskin had provided. Streams of responses, "No Match for this Criteria" and "Invalid" popped up, making his anxiety soar higher than the outside temperature. A bead of sweat slowly trailed down his brow, meandering to the bridge of his wire-rimmed glasses. He continued to punch at the keys, now on a mission. He crammed the next series of commands and slammed the Enter key. The hourglass tumbled for a second before a license appeared. Batman's eyes widened and his jaw jutted toward the screen. He raised a brow and said through a broad grin, "Yeah, baby, that's what I'm talking 'bout!"

With a push of his foot, his chair sped backwards across the floor on squealing rollers toward the radio board. He made a fist and thumped the bottom of the telephone receiver, launching it into the air, catching it in mid flight. His fingers danced on the dial pad as he elevated his feet onto the consul. It took several rings before the person on the other end answered the call.

"Yeah, it's me," he sang. "I got your man."

Jack stood by the side of his vehicle, the engine running with the air conditioner blasting. Jack had called Hoskin to run Monroe's name and was soon informed he got a hit. Still outside of the church, Jack took notes on the hood of his car, jotting down the information Hoskin provided.

"You said his last known address was in West Covina?"

"That's it," Hoskin replied. "At least that's where he was last registered. I'm guessing it's dated and he's moved on."

"What about his criminal history?"

"He's got a pretty extensive rap sheet." There was a pause as Hoskin scanned the report. "Got him a couple of years ago for kidnapping, assault. Most of the charges were dropped for lack of evidence. The only thing he was actually convicted of was possession of child pornography, a misdemeanor. For some reason, there's nothing indicating he had to register as a 290 sex offender."

"No registration means I am going to have a hard time finding him."

"Maybe not. Monroe was ticketed for a moving violation here in Butte County. Looks like he was cited last month on the twenty eighth."

"Does it show what vehicle he was cited in?"

"Commercial plate for a pickup." As he read the plate, Jack felt the eeriness of déjà vu. It was the truck plate he glimpsed fleeing Petroski's residence. He scribbled the citation report number and hung up.

Jack grabbed his papers and called out to Colfax, who stood in the middle of the street, hands on his hips, staring down the road at nothing. Colfax lumbered back toward the car.

Jack handed Colfax the note he wrote. "We might have a pretty good lead. CLETS shows Klaus Monroe was cited for a moving violation last month here in Butte County. My guess is he's left his former residence of West Covina for the good life in your county. Do you think we can find the officer who wrote the ticket to see what he remembers?"

"Yeah, I think we can find the guy." He grabbed his radio off his belt and called in to dispatch. It took a minute for dispatch to inform Colfax of the officer's name.

"Officer's name is Jessie Cambridge. I know the kid. We call him Jessie James. Young and eager to become a detective. Always looking to catch a big fish." He called back on the radio to find out Cambridge's shift and learned he was on duty. "He's in service, Jack."

"Let's get him back to the station. In the meantime, could you have your office pull up Monroe's DMV photo and criminal history? Find out the current registered owner of the truck."

"My guess is he paid cash for the truck and neglected to worry about re-registration. Probably still in the original seller's name."

Jack took a deep breath and held it for a moment. He knew Colfax was right. "Run it out anyway. It's just time and paper. Maybe we'll get lucky."

Jack made his way around to the driver's side and entered the cool interior, escaping the climbing outside heat. The blowing air conditioner gave Jack a quick shiver. Colfax climbed in and secured his seat belt. Jack threw the car into drive and pulled away from the curb, heading in the direction of the Chico Police Department, while Colfax called out on his radio for Officer Cambridge to be ordered back to the station. Time was precious.

22

Officer Cambridge sat in the conference room, staring at the DMV photo of Klaus Monroe. Next to the photo was Alvin Cooper's inmate photo. Placed next to each other, the pairing was a poster for birth control. Cambridge stared at each picture, his eyes darting between the two. Jack and Colfax sat on the other side of the table, patiently waiting for a response from the officer.

Cambridge tapped at the photo of Monroe with his right index finger. "Yeah, I remember this fellow. Nervous type."

"What do you remember about this guy?" Jack asked.

Cambridge looked up at the ceiling and sucked in air, his chest expanding and making the ballistic vest under his uniform creak. "I pulled this guy over for not coming to a complete stop at the intersection of Davenport and Main." He glanced over at his notepad and nodded. "Yeah, that's right. I get out, get his license and registration. R/O doesn't match his DL so he tells me he's borrowing the vehicle and then says he didn't realize he didn't come to a complete stop. Says he's visiting a friend in the area and that he's from SoCal. I remember that because he doesn't exactly fit the profile of a typical Southern California resident."

"Did he mention who—or where—his friend was?" Colfax asked.

118

"No, but in looking over my notes, I see I wrote down a phone number. Can't remember why, or if it's even his. I jot down a lot of stuff. Could be from another contact." Cambridge turned his notepad around and slid it in front of Jack.

Jack wrote down the number and returned the pad to Cambridge. "Why didn't you list Monroe's telephone number on the citation?"

"Said he didn't have a number. I think that one was to his friend's house. That's probably why I didn't list it on the ticket." Cambridge frowned and tipped his head down. "Guess I messed up."

The number had a 530 area code, which covered Butte County, not Southern California. "Don't worry about it, Jessie, you got a number and that may be a big help." Jack handed Cambridge his business card. "If you remember anything else or if you see the truck again, contact me right away."

"This guy kidnap a young girl?" Cambridge asked.

"Unsure at this time," Jack replied. "The kidnapper might actually be using Monroe's identity to conceal himself."

"This guy Monroe would let someone do that?"

Jack shook his head. He looked out the window at a park across the street. "Not voluntarily."

Harrington moved his index finger a bit to the right, pushing away a bundle of cables, which were blocking a port to plug into. A spark popped between his finger and the casing, causing Harrington to jolt out of his seat. His hand hit the casing hard enough for the entire computer to start rocking, ready to tumble onto its side.

"Damn it!" He stuck the shocked finger in his mouth and sucked on it. Harrington took a deep breath and slowly exhaled, trying to gather his composure. He grabbed the bundle, looped it over a parallel line and reached for the set connected to the Bureau's analysis unit, then twisted in his swivel chair and scooted back to the bench. His hands passed over the top of buzzing equipment and he could feel the temperature was at least four or five degrees hotter. He started to type on his keyboard, the same one that he used to draw up the chopped pictures of Jessica Baker. With Alvin Cooper identified as their main subject, Harrington continued typing, sending programs to attack the computer believed to belong to Cooper, gathering fragmented pieces that may consolidate into good leads.

The tumbling hourglass, now replaced with an icon of the Starship Enterprise, spun for a moment before a tree of folders materialized listing hundreds of files, more than likely filled with smut. Folder 127T5aa, 9978a, 5004.tha....

Harrington stared at the screen, studying the tree, following the branches with his eyes, like driving a car along a winding road. His eyes darted down a long branch that passed a known folder, the one with Jessica's picture. Further down, Harrington saw a hidden folder buried in a field of junk and system program files. The folder was marked "BTrip." He clicked on the folder, causing it to expand, listing a dozen subfolders. Harrington puckered his lips and rubbed his chin. He scrolled down the list, stopping on one marked "12251989." Harrington raised an eyebrow. "Christmas Day, 1989," he whispered. He clicked on the sub-folder finding fifty .JPG files listed in a neat row. He continued to slide the arrow down the list of files, launching randomly on the fifth one down. A second passed before a message popped up: *Error. Your viewer is unable to recognize this file.*

Harrington slammed his fist on the bench, a tech agent's way of throwing down the gauntlet. No doubt, the files were corrupted. Harrington would have to work for a finished product. He wondered why Cooper wanted these pictures destroyed more than the others. Images of bound and gagged children were bad enough, and yet several of them were left intact. Revealing photos of his last travels to the Baker residence were also retrievable. These images in BTrip, however, were intentionally placed on a higher priority for destruction. The images in this folder needed to be pieced back together. More software programs were called into play and Harrington started sifting through millions of bits trying to find the proper fit for each piece. Launching and re-launching, the programs gathered the fragmented data, placing them in a strand before attempting to view the finished product. Finally, the first set of images appeared in a row like a proof sheet from a roll of 35mm film. He scanned the small images before launching the first one. Rows of pixels scrolled across the screen, revealing thin slivers of the images riddled with black spots where data could not be found. More pixels coalesced until Harrington could make out two smiling faces of teenagers standing near a river by an old ornate bridge.

Two large squares partially covered one of the faces, leaving only one eye and the left side of his visage captured. The other one was complete. Harrington picked up a booking photo of Alvin Cooper and stared at it for a second, then back at the recovered photo. Even though one of the faces was partially blacked out, Harrington recognized him. He just imagined a few more years on that face and he knew who it was.

Harrington turned toward a laptop on a separate table. It was his Internet computer. He logged on and Googled bridges. He filtered through photos of bridges around the world, comparing them to the one recovered. It was only a few minutes before he landed on a match. Harrington looked back at the image on Cooper's computer and clicked his tongue. He stretched his arm out and grabbed the telephone receiver, dialing Jack Paris' cell phone number.

"I got something here you may want to see," Harrington said when Jack picked up.

"What is it?"

"A picture of your Alvin Cooper. He's with an UNSUB standing next to the Chain Bridge in Budapest, Hungary."

Jack paused. "As in over the Danube?"

"That's the one."

"I remember Cooper traveling to Hungary. Helped prove his role in his family's murder. The photo must have been taken when he was touring after high school. Any others?"

Harrington felt a little miffed, thinking that his quick identification of the Chain Bridge was significant enough to warrant a better response from Agent Paris, not to mention finding another person who might be able to provide information about Cooper. "I'm still working on the rest. Should have some results by the time you get here."

"I'll be there in fifteen."

By the time Jack got to the office, Harrington had already pieced together a series of photos contained within the fragmented folder. The photos were printed and lined on the workbench for Jack to review. Many were only partials, some better than others. Jack stood over the brightly lit table, scanning them for clues.

"Nice job, Jimmy."

Harrington smiled. "I think I can tell you where these photos were taken." Harrington punched his fingers on two partial photos.

Jack looked at the pictures. A young man stood next to a frail elderly lady, her eyes sad, her face without a smile. Another of the same man in front of a bar with a sign reading "Blackie's by the Beach." Overcast skies and a sandy beach, obviously near the ocean. In the background, motorcycles crowded the parking lot and men with large guts and leather vests stood by the entryway.

"That's in Newport Beach," Harrington said. "I was there a few years back with some friends."

Jack gave Harrington one of those inquisitive looks. He knew the place as well. "Doesn't seem like your kind of place."

Harrington leaned back, pointing a finger at himself. "I can be cool."

"My mistake."

"So, when do we go?" Harrington said.

"*We* aren't going anywhere."

Harrington's bottom lip folded in a classic display of disappointment.

"Look, Jimmy, I need you here to put those pictures back together. The more you find, the better our chances of finding our girl."

Harrington huffed. "Fine."

Jack pulled a pen and a Post-It from a desk drawer. He jotted down the directions, even though he knew the way. He worried how much time he would have to divert from his search but knew he had to go. The flight down and back would take maybe a day, hopefully less. With Hoskin working with Colfax, and Marquez searching the Internet, Jack knew that it was best to cover all bases.

Whoever this person was, a contact could lead to Cooper's whereabouts. Jack folded up his notes and stuffed them inside his coat pocket, then turned and shuffled backwards. He lifted a hand of gratitude to Harrington. "Keep building those files. I'm counting on you."

Harrington nodded and threw Jack a quick salute.

A second later, Jack was out the side door and in his car. The drive to the airport was about thirty minutes. Precious minutes, wasted.

23

United Express flight 328 touched down at John Wayne International in Orange County right on time. Before the wheels chirped on the tarmac, Jack's cell phone registered seven missed calls. The exit door was pushed open and passengers began shoving their way forward like a cattle round-up. Jack cycled through the calls as he shuffled in the middle of a tight pack, clearing the crowd at the terminal gate, hustling to the Hertz counter. He considered calling the Santa Ana Resident Agency for help but didn't want to wait for an agent to come out this late, never mind the time he'd lose having to brief them. By the time Jack explained everything, he could be back on the plane and on his way home. He knew this was not the proper protocol; he'd deal with the fallout later.

He handed the Hertz representative his Bureau credit card and she handed over the keys to a bronze-colored Pontiac Grand Prix. The shuttle shipped him to the Hertz lot and a sea of Grand Prixs—all bronze. He pointed his clicker, pressed the unlock button, and scanned the parking lot for blinking lights. It was the seventh car down.

The outside temperature was a comfortable 79 degrees and the smell of the ocean air gave Jack a moment of pause. He transferred out of the FBI office in Los Angeles for several reasons, one being the death of a partner, the other to salvage a trashed home life. Jack's world had taken a left turn when it should have taken a right. Three months ago, he'd moved out of the house, his wife Emily being the one who made the request—okay, more like a demand. Even though things were getting better, his work kept creeping in and taking control. Like an infectious disease. Aside from the prodding he got from Dools the day before, Jack hadn't thought of the separation, too preoccupied with the kidnapping, with work. Between the job and his train wreck of a personal life, Jack started to believe his existence was nothing but two choices: bad marriage and bad people. He took a deep breath and tried to clear his head, twisted the key in the ignition and the Grand Prix fired up with a low growl, idling like a racecar. He punched the gas pedal, quickly accelerating out of the lot, heading north onto PCH toward Blackie's.

The sky over the Pacific Ocean was crystal blue straight to the horizon line, what a true Californian would refer to as "SoCal blue."

Jack drove north along the Coast Highway. Traffic was light but he found himself darting through pockets of cars moving barely above a crawl. He pulled out the Post-it note from his breast coat pocket and glanced at the directions.

Fifteen minutes later, he was off the PCH and onto the 55 South, heading toward the beach. As he crossed the bridge that took him into the heart of Newport, Jack stared at the rows of sail boats, yachts and coastline cruisers whose values totaled more than a small country's GNP. Small shops neatly stacked along the main thoroughfare. Surf shops, trinket boutiques, and art studios were the primary attractions for the tourists. He entered the heart of the business center, nosed the Grand Prix to a stop at a four-way intersection, before pulling into a half-filled parking lot lined with rows of coin meters. In the nearest stall, Jack removed a small placard from his briefcase and tossed it on the dashboard: Department of Justice, Federal Bureau of Investigation, Official Business.

He started toward a strip of old wooden buildings with large glass windows facing the ocean.

It was a short walk before Jack saw a hand-painted wooden sign hung high above one building that simply read, "Blackie's." As Jack approached the bar, the music grew louder, the noise of clinking glasses and falling beer bottles becoming more prevalent. It all came rushing back to him, the evenings spent with his squad mates, draining more than a couple of tall beers at the counter, blending in with the SoCal crowd. Back when it felt good to be something other than a cop, back when he felt normal.

Entering, he was greeted by curious eyes. Blurry stares and glances by the patrons, before they turned back to the bartender, signaling for more to drink. Jack ordered an Amber on draft, pulled the photo from his jacket nonchalantly and glanced at the picture of Cooper with the unknown friend before placing it face down on the counter. The bartender brought over his beer and Jack tossed him a twenty. As the bartender reached for the bill, Jack pointed down at the photo. The bartender stopped, eyes drifting down toward the counter. Jack leaned forward, trying not to attract attention. He slid his creds from his coat pocket. "Listen, I don't want to disrupt your business but I was wondering if you know these individuals." Jack curled the end of the photo so only the bartender was able to see.

He studied it for a beat before shaking his head. "Nah, don't know them. Sorry." He wiped the counter in a quick swirling motion with a wet towel before walking away. Not a good start.

Jack turned around on his barstool and studied the customers, seeing if he could spot the regulars. Someone here had to be a frequent flyer. Maybe Jack would get lucky and find someone who knew Cooper, tell him who the other person in the photo was. The bartender returned with Jack's change. Jack gave it one more shot. "Keep it. Just tell me who here's a regular."

The bartender remained still, hesitant to respond.

"Look," Jack said, "I got a sixteen-year-old girl that's been kidnapped. I'm just trying to find her before something bad happens."

The bartender paused, giving him a hard once-over, then held up a finger and walked away, disappearing into a sea of bodies. Jack grabbed the photo and turned back around to watch the crowd. He caught sight of a woman bending over a jukebox, wearing a pair of tight jeans and a top resembling a small napkin.

"I hear you're looking for a man."

Jack turned to see a young woman with a drink tray shoved under her right arm. Thirties with long blonde hair and a look that would make any man hand over his wallet. Her breasts filled the low-cut white T-shirt she was wearing, the words, "Blackie's, Order by the Pair," stenciled across her bumpy parts.

"Yeah, that would be me. A couple as a matter of fact." He took the photo from his jacket.

She took the photo from Jack's hand and scanned the picture from all angles, before handing it back to him. "This one," she said pointing at the UNSUB. "I've seen this one."

"When was the last time?"

She shrugged. "Maybe six months, less than a year."

"You got a good memory."

"Only when I need it," she replied.

"What's your name?"

"My friends call me Whisper."

Figures.

"Well, Whisper, do you know his name?"

Whisper shook her head. "I did, but can't remember now. Nice guy. Was a regular, then kind of vanished."

"Got any idea where I might find him?"

Whisper pointed eastward, toward the Peninsula. "Lido Piers. He worked for a guy who owns one of those coastal cruisers. One of those really big-ass yachts."

"Got a name of the owner or the yacht?"

Whisper tilted her head and smiled. "Maybe."

Jack reached into his wallet and pulled out a fifty.

Whisper plucked it from his hands. "The guy's name is Peter Thibault, but his friends call him Skip. He owns a yacht called the Emerald Eyes."

"Thanks, Whisper."

"Why you looking for him anyway, detective?"

"That's Special Agent." Like it mattered. "And I'm looking for him because I'm trying to find a girl who was kidnapped. She's sixteen."

Whisper's eyes sharpened and her glossy red lips gaped slightly opened. Her teeth were model-perfect.

"Thanks for the help," he added. Jack stood from the barstool and started to walk away when Whisper placed a hand on his chest. He saw her take in a slight breath and her gaze fell toward the ground.

"Here," she said, placing her soft hand in Jack's, gently sliding the fifty into his palm. With her other, she gently patted him on the chest, grinned at no one in particular and walked away.

Jack stepped outside and immediately took in the smell and feel of the salt air. His gait was slow as he meandered his way though the lot to his car. Jack unlocked the rental and slid behind the wheel. A parking ticket was stuffed under a wiper blade.

Really?

He opened the door and reached around, grabbing the ticket by the corner, folded it in half and tossed it on the floorboard.

He entered back onto the 55 North over to the Lido Peninsula, along the coastline on Lido Park Drive until he saw the road sign that read Channel Place.

Million dollar yachts lined the harbor. Jack scanned the names looking for Emerald Eyes. He arrived at a dead end, flipped around and retraced his path, bending north from the southeast end. Then he spotted it, a large, majestic yacht, easily a hundred feet long. Large letters along the stern prominently displayed her name: Emerald Eyes. Emerald, Jack thought. Like the color of money.

Jack tapped his foot pedal hard looking for a place to pull off. He heard a chirp from squealing brakes. The car following closely behind Jack bounced in his rearview mirror, the driver slamming on his breaks to avoid a collision. The car pulled to the left and sped by, laying down a hard palm on his horn while flipping the finger to Jack, who simply waved back as he pulled to the side onto a patch of dirt.

The yacht was docked, sandwiched between two other large vessels, their masts raised high above the roofline of the adjacent buildings. A man stood on the deck of the ship wearing khaki shorts, Sperry Top-Siders shoes and an untucked shirt. He was coiling yellow nylon rope on the ship's deck. Fifty feet in front, Jack spotted a narrow road that led to the dock's entrance. He crept the rental past a black metal gate into a large parking area, and found a slot fifty yards from where the Emerald Eyes was moored.

The man was still working the rope when Jack approached. The worker caught sight of Jack and tipped his ball cap. Jack looked up and the brilliance of the sun backlighting the man caused him to shade his eyes.

"I'm Special Agent Jack Paris with the FBI," Jack called out, pulling out his creds and holding them up into the sunlight. "May I come aboard? I have a few questions. Won't take much of your time."

The man nodded and waved him up. Jack climbed the stairs, onto the deck.

The yacht was nothing short of pure elegance. Hardwood deck, slick fiberglass and chrome. Glass windows lined the entire length, smoked for privacy. A stairwell led to an upper deck where Jack could see two jet skis secured on a platform at the stern. He peered into the cabin as he walked past an open doorway. The interior walls were lined in deep burgundy wood and glass. A leather sectional spanned in front of a bar, flanked by velvet, covered winged chairs. Further inside a black lacquered table with a glass top adorned with a large decorative vase filled with brightly colored flowers. Real flowers. Jack estimated the furniture alone was more than his annual salary. He made his way to the stern of the ship.

The owner was about fifty, sporting a healthy tan with dark hair slightly graying at the temples under his ball cap. He was wearing a gray polo shirt with an embroidered emblem of a stallion. Ferrari Stallion. Go figure. He smiled and leaned against the port side railing.

"What can I do for you?"

"I'm investigating a possible child abduction."

The man's smile turned to a straight line. "How can I help?"

"Are you Peter Thibault?"

"That's right." He stuck out a hand and Jack took it.

"Nice ship."

Thibault smiled. "I like to call it home. It's a Burger."

"I take it we're not talking meat."

The man tilted his head and laughed. "If we were, we'd be talking pure Grade A, USDA prime. No, Burger Yachts. One of the finest made. One hundred twenty-one feet of pure luxury."

"It's a beauty." Jack pulled out the folded sheet of paper from his jacket and handed it to Thibault. "Do you recognize any one of these individuals?"

Thibault studied the picture a moment before his eyes fell heavy and his lips went tight. "Yeah, I know him," he pointed to the UNSUB. Thibault shook his head and looked up at Jack. "Pretty old photo, though. He's a lot older now. Worked aboard the Emerald Eyes for six months, about a year ago. Name's Eric Youngblood. Showed up one day looking for work, scrubbing decks, polishing railings, things like that. Looked eager, so I threw him a bone and gave him a job."

"Where is he now?"

"Said he had to move north, hook up with an old friend. Hated to let him go. He did a lot around here. I relied on him. He kind of left me hanging."

"You have an address for Mr. Youngblood?"

"No," Thibault responded. "I paid him his last week's wage and off he went." He paused, then snapped his fingers. "I do know that he's from around here, though. Grew up and went to high school in Newport Beach. Lived with an uncle up along PCH in Sunset Beach."

"You got a name for the uncle?"

Thibault nodded. "Hold on. I think I actually do."

He disappeared into the forward cabin and left Jack standing under the overhang of the upper deck. He returned after a few minutes.

"Here it is. I thought I had it." Thibault handed Jack a file folder containing the payment record for Youngblood. Along with the record sheet was a sheet of yellow legal paper with hand written notes. "Right here." Thibault pointed at a name and address scribbled on the bottom of the page. "That's his uncle, Bernard Russell. It was his emergency contact."

Jack took out a pen from his jacket and wrote down the information on the back of a piece of paper, then folded the paper and slid it into his jacket pocket. "Eric didn't by chance mention the name of the friend he was going to see up north, did he?"

Thibault shook his head. "No. Just said he heard from an old friend and wanted to reconnect. Eric never seemed the sort to put down roots. I guess he just got restless and needed to move on." He sighed. "Sorry I wasn't more help."

"You did fine."

Thibault paused for a second before asking. "Did Eric have anything to do with this kidnapping?"

"We're not sure yet."

Thibault nodded. "For whatever it's worth, Eric was a good kid. Got into trouble a while back. Drugs, mostly marijuana, nothing big. I told him if he wanted to stay working here, he had to clean up his act and he did. Never had any problems after that."

"Thanks for the insight." Jack looked around one last time, soaking in his surrounding. Working undercover, Jack had access to the undercover yacht, a Mercedes sport coupe, and a posh apartment overlooking the bright blue Pacific. The difference was it wasn't his. It was all pretend. This, as he looked out over the side of this multi-million dollar yacht, was something someone actually owned.

"Mr. Thibault, if you don't mind me asking, how did you come up with the name Emerald Eyes?"

Thibault looked at Jack and smiled. "My daughter, Mr. Paris. It was the color of my daughter's eyes."

"She must be very pretty."

His eyes glistened. "She was. Died five years ago. Auto accident."

"I'm sorry."

Thibault forced a thin smile as the two walked toward the gang plank.

"Agent Paris, do you have children?"

Jack nodded, feeling a slight bit guilty. His envy of Thibault's wealth was over-shadowed by something far worse than what money could fix. "I do. Two."

Thibault again smiled. "Don't wait until something bad happens to memorialize them." He took a hold of Jack's hand, a firm handshake.

"I'll do that."

"I hope you find the answers you're looking for."

The walk to the car was quiet. The pedestrian traffic grew thick as Jack found his way toward the parking lot. People lined the waterway, some walking their dogs, others out for an afternoon jog. Back behind the wheel of his rental car, Jack sat silently, staring at the Emerald Eyes, at its long sleek shape and the opulence of its stature. Some people measure success in dollars. But Jack knew that wasn't always the case.

He rubbed the cover of his cell phone cradled in the palm of his hand, then flipped it open and remembered he had seven missed calls. He started filtering through them as he stared out the window, not paying much attention to any one of them until he came to the last message.

"Jack, it's Border Collins." The job offer. "Haven't heard back from you. We're still on for Friday if you can make it. Give me a call as soon as possible." The call ended. Jack thought about Thibault, his daughter, his last remark. He pressed nine, saving the message.

Jack cycled through his phone address book, stopping at the number listed for home. He thought for a moment, considering calling Emily just to say hello, check on the kids, maybe mention the job offer. Jack wasn't sure he wanted to say anything until he'd made a decision. Their last call, over a week ago, ended badly. The idea soured. He shoved the phone in his pocket and tried to clear the last thirty seconds from his mind. Sliding the key into the ignition, Jack cranked the engine over and backed out of the parking slot. He stared down the road, looking for the on-ramp that would take him north on the Coast highway. Two hours and ten minutes had passed since landing at Orange County Airport. The ticking of a clock and the thought of Jessica Baker without her insulin was all he could think of, and it didn't make him feel any better.

24

The homes along the shoreline were long and thin, like books on a shelf, each paneled in shake siding with large glass windows facing the scenic Pacific Ocean. If the water wasn't moving, you'd think it was a postcard. Feeder roads cut between the rows of slender beach houses where people on bicycles and joggers filtered through on their way to the beach. The air was comfortably moist, filled with the conflicting sounds of crashing ocean waves and the rumbling of convertibles roaring by.

The houses had been around for decades. Most were rentals to families and college students during the summer months.

Jack slowed along PCH as he entered Seal Beach. Small businesses lined the major highway with gaps leading to the sandy coastline. Jack continued north, parallel to the coast, coming upon a row of older beach cottages, colorful nylon flags gently floating from their front porch decks. He parked in front of a deep, navy blue cottage sandwiched between one painted bright yellow and another weathered to a dingy brown. A white picket fence formed a rectangle around the front of the building.

An uneven brick walkway led to a hardwood door with a triangular glass window. Jack knocked and peered inside. Soon, a man appeared. Late sixties, maybe early seventies, thin white hair, clean-shaven, wearing jeans and a Hawaiian shirt. He peeked through the window and caught Jack staring back. The man returned a blank stare, like Jack was a salesman or worse, someone trying to enlighten him on the word of God. Jack pulled out his credentials and held them up to the glass. "Can I have a word with you, please?"

A metal latch pulled back and the door creaked opened.

"Mr. Russell?" Jack asked. "I'm Special Agent Jack Paris with the FBI. Can I come in?"

Russell hesitated for a moment, then shrugged and stepped aside.

Russell motioned with his hands, nervously. "Would you like some coffee?" he asked, making for the back of the home and the kitchen, which like the house itself was small and narrow, the walls canary yellow, the floors burgundy and white, checkerboard asphalt tiles. A bay view window looked out toward more rows of quaint homes. Russell pulled two mugs from a cupboard next to the stove and poured them each a cup.

Jack removed the photo from his jacket and pointed at Eric Youngblood. After Russell acknowledged their relationship, Jack's finger slid toward Cooper.

"Do you know the person standing next to your nephew?"

Russell glanced at the picture, eyes shifting down through his black plastic bifocals. "Yeah," he whispered as he shook his head. "That's Alvie. Alvin Cooper. Eric met him when we first moved into the neighborhood back in 1990." Russell raised his eyebrow. "He's in jail for murdering his family, you know?"

Jack nodded. "I know. We're looking into another matter."

"Is he in more trouble?"

"Could be."

"Is Eric all right?"

"I don't know. I spoke to his former employer, Peter Thibault. He said Eric took off about a year ago. I was hoping you could help me find him."

"Haven't heard from him since he left. Kind of his style, though." Russell stood from the table and walked to the counter, where a wire basket spilled over with unopened mail and folded correspondences. Russell plucked a small card. "Got this from him maybe a month after he split." He handed the card to Jack and sat back down at the kitchen table.

The postcard featured a picture of the Space Needle in Seattle. Two scribbled lines on back: *I'm doing fine. Thanks for everything. Eric.*

Russell rubbed his jaw. "Only thing I got from him. Far as I know, he's still up there."

"Any family or friends live in Seattle?"

"None. Eric's mother, Gayle, died back in the early '80s. Cancer. They lived in San Diego back then. Didn't know his father. Just some guy passing through town, a one night stand. Eric came to live with me after his mother died. Had no one else."

"How long have you been here?"

"Going on fifteen years. That's about when we met Alvie. We moved here at the end of '89. I got a refurbishing job here at a local boat shop. Rented this place and we had an extra room. Thought it would be good to have a tenant to help pay the bills."

"He would've been about nineteen," Jack said.

Russell nodded. "That's about right. Same age as Eric. He said he needed a place to stay. He graduated from Bolsa Chica High School, not too far from here. Said he took a couple of months traveling Europe, a graduation gift from his mother." Russell cleared his throat and his voice became sullen. "While he was away, his mother died of a heart attack. He didn't find out until he returned. Hell, when he told me that, I felt sorry for the guy. Took him in that afternoon, told him he could pay me when he got a job."

"How long did he stay?"

"Just under two years."

Jack thought about the timing. Two years put him right in line with a trip north and the killing of Grace Holloway in Renton.

"You know, Eric and Alvie traveled up and down the coast. Disappear for weeks. At first, I worried, but it brought a little life back into Eric, something that was missing since his mother died."

"Did they ever travel to Seattle together?"

Russell arched an eyebrow, nodding. "Kind of strange. I remember when they came back from one of their trips north, things were a little different."

Russell's response piqued Jack's interest, and he asked Russell to explain.

"I don't know, just different. They seemed edgy. It wasn't long after that, Alvie packed his bags late one night and just vanished. Didn't hear anything about him until years later when I learned he killed his wife and kid."

The room fell silent. Russell kept staring on his coffee. "Something happened when they took that trip up there, didn't it?"

"A fifteen-year-old girl was kidnapped and murdered," Jack said. Then as if reading the old man's thoughts, he added, "There's no evidence Eric was involved."

"What about Cooper?"

What about Cooper? Russell now referring to Alvin in the formal term, not the family friendly name he had been using.

"It looks like Cooper . . . contributed . . . to her disappearance."

"And her death?"

Jack nodded.

Russell's stare drifted downward, his forehead settling in his palm.

"Did Eric ever tell you he was heading up to Seattle to see Cooper?"

"No."

"I need to find Alvin Cooper. I'm thinking Eric can point me in the right direction."

"I thought Cooper's in jail?" Russell said.

Jack shook his head. "Escaped."

All color drained from Russell's face. "I wish I could help you, Agent Paris, but like I said, I haven't heard from Eric for almost a year."

"You said Cooper just up and vanished?"

"That's right."

"I'd like to see Cooper's room."

Russell hesitated a moment before relenting. "I guess that would be OK."

Jack stood and motioned for Russell to lead the way.

Upstairs, the rooms were divided between the front and the back of the house, the master bedroom in the back, two small rooms splitting the space up front. Russell pointed at the first door on the right. "That's his."

He stepped back, letting Jack make his way inside.

It was sparse with a single bed, plain wooden headboard, a matching nightstand and chest of drawers. The bed was made as if awaiting Cooper's return. Two framed pictures hung on the wall, paintings of sailboats. The air was stale and cool, like no one had been in there for ages. Jack took his time, walked the room, didn't touch anything. He knelt down, peered under the bed. Nothing but balls of dust. He turned his head and saw Russell watching him.

The two stepped out of the room, toward the stairs in back.

"That other one Eric's room?"

"Yes, that's his."

"Mind if I take a quick look?"

Russell looked surprised, maybe even annoyed at the request but then just shrugged. "Go on in."

It looked nearly identical to Cooper's. Eric's room had more personal items lying around, like a person who really belonged. But there was nothing that would help him find Youngblood. He knelt one more time, peering under the bed. This time, there was a well-worn cardboard box. He carefully slid it out.

"What did you find?"

He looked back at Russell, pointed at the box and gave a look that said, "Are you okay with me searching?"

Russell waited quietly in the hallway without a sign of protest.

Jack reached into his jacket pocket and pulled out a pair of latex gloves. He peeled back a red sweater on top, revealing several books and a banded block of envelopes, letters.

"Correspondences, notebooks." Jack said, as if to himself.

The letters were addressed to a Madelyn Cooper at an address in Newport Beach.

"They're Cooper's," Jack said.

Russell still said nothing.

Jack flipped through the envelopes and read the names listed to and from. All from Alvin Cooper, sent when he was in Europe. Jack placed the letters to the side of the box on the floor and scanned the remaining items. Four spiral notebooks, each with a different color cover. Jack flipped through the first notebook, noticing pages of handwritten paragraphs, each page dated and timed. He read the first line from each, getting a sense of what he was reading. It didn't take long to realize what he had: Cooper's journals. A worldview through a serial killer's eyes. Suddenly Jack felt excited and disturbed at the same time.

"I'm taking these." He wasn't asking.

"Go ahead."

Jack placed everything back in the box. The letters drew his interest but he had to read the journals if he wanted to understand Cooper's mind. What made him tick, and possibly what made him kill. He thanked Russell for his time and gave him a business card.

"Call me if you remember anything that may help us locate Cooper or your nephew, Eric."

They stood by the bay view window as they shook hands, Russell's eyes betraying anger and regret.

It was getting late. The afternoon sun had passed above the row of beachfront homes, casting Jack's shadow the width of the street.

Russell stood at the doorway for a minute, watching Jack get into his rental, before he turned and disappeared back into his house.

25

Jack took a bite of the turkey and avocado sandwich he grabbed at Harry's Grill, on Broadway off the Coast Highway. He hung a left toward the sand and walked down by the shore where he found an empty park bench. Cooper's box under his arm, Jack found a quiet spot to concentrate, while the low sun on the horizon reflected brightly off the expansive ocean. Jack ate his sandwich, scanning the pages of Cooper's notebooks. With everything going on, he'd forgotten how hungry he was, fueled only by coffee and a small bag of pretzels courtesy of United Express. Slipping a latex glove over his right hand, Jack flipped through the pages, his bare left handling sandwich and greasy chips duty. Slices of avocado and tomatoes spilled from the edges and onto the sandy ground under his legs. A man with a latex glove on one hand, eating a sloppy sandwich, reading a bunch of tattered notebooks on a beachfront table. If this were any place other than Southern California, Jack would have stuck out like a psych patient who had just wandered off the ward. But here no one seemed to care.

The first notebook didn't reveal much. It started with Cooper's returning from Hungary and learning his mother had passed. Jack found the passages about his mother's death flat, unemotional.

There was mention that he found a place to stay (the Russell home). More writings about his travels up the coast to Portland, down toward San Diego, even a stint in Mexico. In several of these passages, he made notes of unsuspecting families he watched, their children and how happy they seemed to be. These documentations piqued Jack's interest, although they were mostly observations.

By book four, the writing became far more revealing. Even the handwriting had changed. On page three, Jack found Cooper detailing his Seattle trip, rambling about a possible job offer, working at the fresh water locks on Lake Union. The tone was unremarkable, a young man's optimistic view of a steady job. Then there was a shift in focus. Jack's reading slowed, his eyes fixated on each word before coming to a stop on the last sentence of that day's entry.

And maybe I can start a family. I can't ruin this chance to start over.

Jack looked up from the notebook, pausing to let the words soak in.

Start over?

26

An hour had passed and a cool ocean breeze blew off the water. Jack returned the notebooks to the box and started on the banded mail, letters Cooper sent to his mother when he was traveling across Europe. He must have collected them after she had died.

Seagulls filled the sky; their screeching made for constant background noise, coupled with the rhythmic crashing of waves now retreating from the shoreline. He noticed lights coming on from local restaurants and businesses, a sign that nightfall had arrived. It was late and Jack needed to get back to Sacramento.

Only three letters remained. He pulled the first from its envelope and began to read. Previously Cooper had appeared upbeat, if slightly concerned about being short of cash. It was a time when Communist Europe was redefining itself, trying to see what life was really like in the West. With communism collapsing, Eastern Europeans began fleeing across open borders as opportunities became available, the Wall that once contained loyal comrades turning porous as cheesecloth. Cooper had taken advantage of the turmoil, sneaking into Hungary while it was still a communist state.

The next letter was dated two weeks later, and talked about meeting a traveler from Britain by the name of Alexander McMartin.

The two met at a Budapest nightclub and struck up a close friendship. Both low on money, they found a room to rent from a local Hungarian on the Buda side of the Danube, intending to earn a little money and find their way home.

The last letter was the one Jack found most disturbing. Far from upbeat, with Cooper constantly mentioning being homesick (although curiously he never asked his mother to send him money), he talked of the Wall between the East and West falling and people in the streets celebrating even though the Secret Police were still out in force. The police had come to their building one late night and dragged out a neighbor, who they never saw again. The landlord, a man named Lazlo Mink, told Cooper this was common and that he should not expect to see the neighbor again. The rent for the deserted room wasn't much. Cooper shaved off even more by helping Mink and his family with their "delivery business."

He wrote: *The rent is cheap and by helping them deliver their packages around town, the stay is almost free. What we are delivering, I have no idea, but it helps us get by. Truth is, they could be running black market goods because they always seem to have things no one else in the city has. The place is a little seedy, but it's all I can afford.*

The letter ended. Jack flipped it over and studied the envelope, drumming the cover with his fingers. The return address was in care of Mr. Lazlo Mink. Running illegal goods in the communist black market in exchange for cheap housing. Wall or no wall, it wasn't smart to write about these activities in a letter leaving a communist state. More than likely this information would've made Cooper a target, and placed the Mink family on the Hungarian Secret Police's hot sheet. Jack peered inside the box for more letters. But there were none.

The wind picked up, darkness settling. Jack tossed his garbage into a wastebasket, tucked the box under his arm and headed for the car.

He drove back to the 405 South, the traffic heavy. He jumped over to the carpool lane hoping that a cop wouldn't notice, and sped down the highway, making the airport just in time to catch the next flight to Sacramento. By the time he found his seat, fatigue had taken hold. His head fell against the headrest as he closed his eyes and let his body succumb to exhaustion. He managed to sleep through the bumpy flight, waking to the flight attendant's voice crackling over the cabin speakers asking all passengers to store their tray tables and lock their seats in their original, upright positions. Jack rubbed the stiffness in his neck and peered out the plane's window.

Ladies and Gentlemen, welcome to Sacramento International....

27

Homer Landley pushed the bridge of his glasses. They slid down his nose from the combination of grease and perspiration, something that always happened when the room warmed. And it happened often. His air conditioner forever on the fritz, and Landley didn't have the time, money—or energy—to fix the problem.

He leaned back, rocking in a kitchen table chair that doubled as his computer chair. The monitor blinked on and off, colors changing every time Landley swatted its side.

After two hours of filtering though various websites, Landley's eyes ached. Besides surfing for kiddie porn, which was his real job (if you considered that a "real" job), Agent Marquez had him looking for JPetroski, a twenty-four carat scumball. She didn't give Landley all the specifics but offered a big reward if he could find him.

He flooded his eyes with Visine, blinked out the sting and continued searching for any sign of the guy. No one in the chat room heard from JPetroski since Marquez's conversation with him the previous day. Landley leaned against the table, the computer humming at full speed, digital pages materializing one after another, none of which yielded anything fruitful. He puffed his cheeks and blew out short breaths like a steam locomotive.

Landley rubbed his chin, elbow planted firmly on the table, and launched another site, one of his old favorites. A second passed and the screen refreshed. Landley whistled softly as he typed in a series of passwords, entering with the cyber equivalent of candy and a trench coat.

wuz up, dog? a message flashed welcoming Landley home.

nothin tell me something gud

got sum new pics fuckin off the hook

grown ups or lolita? he messaged back.

they look yung . . . u tell me

Landley's computer chimed with an attachment from his friend. Landley perused the images, some color, many black and white, some even homegrown.

Landley muttered to himself as he cycled through. "Seen these before. Don't waste my time."

wat do u think, the message came back.

Landley typed, *ho hum . . . been there done that*

ya well I tride. at least u replied. unlike ur friend

wat friend?

family man . . . wat a weener!

Landley scooted his chair close to the table and tapped frantically at the keyboard. *do u mean jpetroski*

that's the 1 . . . he used a different moniker but i new it was him. fuckers a creep

when did u talk???

2day

when?

today i say

Landley shook his head, his frustration elevating. *wat TIME?*

2 hors ago, guess

wat name

There was no immediate answer. Landley's fingers drummed a nervous staccato on the top of his mouse. *hello?* he typed. *how about a response.*

After a long wait, the computer chimed a message. *faust*

Landley leaned forward, his face squishing into a contorted stare. "What the fuck is a Faust?" He typed out another message. *did he say if hes coming back?*

don't no . . . why

no reason. got 2 go

Landley jumped up and grabbed his jacket off the couch, rushing out the door. He patted his pocket, felt his cell phone and car keys, then made his way through the parking lot. He opened his car door, allowed the day's heat trapped inside to escape, before sliding behind the wheel and turning over the engine. As he left the lot, Landley hit the speed dial button to Agent Marquez, glancing at his cheap Casio watch, hoping to catch the detective before her shift ended.

She picked up on the second ring.

"What's up, Homer?"

Landley stuttered, finding it difficult to talk and drive at the same time. "I think I found him. The guy."

"Slow down. What guy?"

"Your J Petcock . . . Petski, that dude you asked me to find. Him!"

Marquez's tone smoothed and dropped a few decibels, words slowing to calm Landley. "Are you talking about J Petroski?"

"That's right, that's the one. Only now he's calling himself Faust."

"Faust, as in Dr. Johann 'sell your soul to the devil' Faustus?"

"Is that a TV show?"

"Yes, Homer. Right after Dr. Phil and before Jerry Springer." Marquez waited for him to get the joke, but he didn't. "Dr. Faustus was a 16th Century literary character. He made a deal with the devil."

"Fits his personality. Look, you want this guy, meet me at the undercover off-site. Time is money Lucy, let's go!"

"All right, nice job." Before Homer could say anything else, she added, "And Homer, don't ever call me by my first name again."

Landley's smile evaporated as he sheepishly replied, "Yes, ma'am."

Homer Landley's apartment was empty, the only sign of life the hourglass tumbling on his computer. In his haste to hook up with Agent Marquez, Landley forgot to sign out, leaving his friend dangling on the other end. The low hum of his ancient refrigerator was interrupted by the chime of an incoming message.

Yo dog, faust was looking 4 u. said it was important. he promised me he wouldn't tell but i gave him ur phone number. he's going to call u. wants to see u right away

The empty apartment fell silent again before the sound of more chimes blinked up Landley's screen.

u there dog?
hello?
hello?

28

Back on the 5, Jack called Marquez, updating her on his findings.

"That's great, Jack," she said. "But we may have stumbled on something better. I think Homer found Cooper online. He's now going by the name of Faust."

"I assume you're referring to the four-hundred-year-old dead guy?"

"Maybe he ran out of friends to kill."

"Are we going to get a chance at talking to Mr. Faust soon?"

"That would be Dr. Faust, and, yes, I have Homer coming over to the off-site to start scanning the Internet looking for him."

Jack made a fist and rapped on the top of his steering wheel. "Good. I'll get a team ready."

"Meeting us there?"

"You bet."

"One last thing," Marquez said. "Ray Sizemore from Seattle got in this afternoon. He's coming out to the site with Harrington."

Jack was glad to hear Sizemore had made it in. Maybe he'd be able to shed some light on Youngblood's travels to Washington State. Jack had begun wondering if Cooper wasn't the only one involved in the Grace Holloway kidnapping case.

Outside the radial tires buzzed. Jack couldn't say how many times he'd driven down this stretch of highway. As a kid, he remembered sitting in the back of the family station wagon, his father commuting back and forth every weekend from San Francisco. Jack's grandfather, Hank, owned a butcher shop there. A blue-collar man through and through. Jack's dad, Sean Paris, took a different route, going to college and becoming an engineer. He married Jack's mother, landed a job in Sacramento, which took him away from his parents but never for long. Every weekend, Sean Paris made the drive back to the Bay Area to help out with the butcher shop. Young Jack went with his dad because it was his time with his father. Like Hank Paris, Jack's father worked long hours and long days. But he was committed to his parents and to his family. Jack didn't really appreciate why his dad did what he did until late in life after Jack's mother died of cancer. Hard, honest work was Hank's discipline, but he knew the real reason for living.

The drive grew quiet giving Jack time to let his mind wander. He looked up and saw the exit for downtown, glanced at his watch and decided to make a quick pit stop, pulling off the freeway and heading toward Capitol Avenue. Moments later he was in front of The Waterboy, considered among the best restaurants in Sacramento, where his son, Michael worked. Jack found an open meter, squeezed his car between a Mercedes and a Volkswagen and jumped out.

The place was busy so no one really noticed him walking around back. Still he pretended to be on his cell phone so he wouldn't be bothered. He wanted to peek into the kitchen, to see his son. Jack leaned against the wall and peered through a swinging door, pushed open by a passing waiter. A group of chefs scurried, carrying large metal trays over their heads. Smells of broiling meat and spices rolled out in waves. In the middle of the crowd stood Michael, the sous chef, dressed in a white chef uniform, apron stained. Early on in life, Michael said he wanted to be a chef, not a cop, which was fine with Jack. After high school, he immediately enrolled in the Culinary Academy in San Francisco, earning his degree.

Jack stood there and watched as Michael worked. Flames leapt over beautifully carved pieces of meat, sauces drizzling from silver pouring containers. They were Michael's tools and he had mastered them. Jack saw how focused his son was, how in control of his surroundings. He realized his son had grown up. Michael had become a man. It made Jack proud.

A waiter approached Jack and asked if he needed any help.

Jack held up his cell phone. The waiter smiled and darted into the kitchen.

He took one last look, then turned away.

Marquez watched Sizemore shuffle a stack of papers, tap them straight on the table. An open folder to his right exposed a series of black and white crime scene photos from the Grace Holloway murder in Renton, Washington, over a decade earlier. Behind him, Homer Landley was scrolling through websites, searching for the kidnapper/killer they now knew as Faust.

"Faust, eh?" Sizemore's voice was filled with sarcasm. "I didn't know Cooper was so well educated."

"You can get college credit in prison," Marquez quipped.

"The reports don't seem to have much on his family prior to his arrest."

"Wasn't much there. Mom died while Cooper was traveling through Europe. He comes back to an empty house, rents a room he finds in the classifieds, gets a job, moves on...."

"Didn't Jack say he befriended the landlord's son and that they traveled together?"

"Youngblood," Marquez said. "Eric Youngblood."

"Was Youngblood in Seattle during the time our victim was found dead?"

"I can't be certain. You're going to have to wait and ask Jack."

Homer groaned loudly and shoved his computer mouse off its pad. "Nothing! Guy's all over the place, talking to anyone who'll listen, but I can't seem to find him anywhere!"

Marquez leaned back in her chair and glanced in Homer's direction. His eyes looked tired, his whole body a wet shirt on a wire hanger. She actually felt sorry for the guy. "Ease up, I have faith in you."

Homer sucked in a lungful of air and went back to clacking on the keyboard.

Sizemore turned to Marquez. "What was Youngblood doing with Cooper fifteen years ago when they were hitchhiking up and down the coastline?"

Marquez knew where Sizemore was going with his question. Placing Youngblood with Cooper at the scene of the Holloway murder meant more than identifying a murderer; it meant a possible conspirator, one who could be turned into a witness. Pit one against the other, someone to squeeze. A two-for-one deal. The question was, who was the weaker of the two?

"You get any DNA other than Cooper's?" Marquez asked.

"No. Got some unidentified latent smudges. But only Cooper's DNA."

"Then I guess we should look for Youngblood as a material witness."

"If Youngblood was present during the Grace Holloway kidnapping and murder, it's possible he knows what's going on with your current wave of killings, including the Baker abduction."

Marquez agreed. "There's too much smoke to ignore. The question is, why now? Why does Cooper risk escape and kidnap a child less than a year before his release? Why not just wait until his time's up? Draws less suspicion."

Sizemore shrugged. "You're being too logical. Men like that are not guided by rational thought."

Sizemore was right. Child abductors and murderers rarely allowed logic to dictate their actions. In most cases, it's an urge that drives them to act, no matter the circumstance.

"Still, it just doesn't feel quite right," she said. "I can't help but think Youngblood is involved in the Baker kidnapping."

"Anything's possible," Sizemore said. "You got evidence showing the two have been in contact since his incarceration?"

She shook her head, recalling a report that Jack had received from Butte County jail. It was Cooper's visitor's log and employment records. State of California special agents also reached out to Cooper's coworkers after he went missing and interviewed everyone. There was no evidence Cooper had been meeting with anyone fitting the description of Eric Youngblood.

"To the contrary," Sizemore continued, "there's a good reason why I don't think they're together."

Marquez tilted her head and glanced at him sideways. "Let's hear it."

"For starters, why do we only find one dead body every time Cooper changes his identity? Why not two? One for Cooper and one for Youngblood?" Sizemore shook his head and tossed the reports back on the table. "No, if they were together, I would think we would be finding pairs of dead bodies. At least a pair of dead bodies with common M.O.s. One new identity doesn't help anyone."

"Make sense," Marquez replied.

"We haven't spent that much time looking for him. For all we know, he's left a trail as wide as Sherman's March to Atlanta."

"Could you check to see if Eric Youngblood has ever drawn the attention of law enforcement in the state of Washington?"

Sizemore nodded and pulled his cell phone from his pocket, holding the phone to his head, waiting for the switchboard operator in Seattle to answer.

"Find me a parking ticket," he said, griping out loud. "Anything."

While he waited on the line, Marquez asked, "Was there a lot of news coverage of the Grace Holloway abduction?"

"Every damn day."

"I mean, film coverage? Did they film a command post filled with volunteers, the search and rescue teams, things like that?"

"You bet. When a kid comes up missing, the whole world volunteers, and the news is there to capture it. We had people handing out flyers, walking door-to-door, all that."

"Do you think you can get your office to pull the tapes of the coverage?"

"You think we'll find Cooper as one of the volunteers?"

"I'm hoping we'll find one of them. Or if we're lucky, both. Killers like to find themselves in the middle of the commotion, liking the thrill of it all."

Sizemore turned back to his phone and started talking. "Get me to Squad 8." He stood up and walked to a quiet corner, his words now reduced to a murmur.

Marquez looked over at Homer, who was staring at the monitor, screen flipping from one webpage to another. Although Homer was doing everything he could to find Cooper, he wasn't having much success. Marquez looked down at her hands and noticed they were gripped tightly on the edges of the table. She was feeling as anxious as Sizemore. All she could do right now was hurry up and wait. Cooper's jail cell had been tossed for clues, and Search and Rescue was out in full force. Hoskins was handling forensics, and earlier that evening the whole world had been put on notice by every television and radio station, including the Spanish, Vietnamese and Russian broadcasts. If someone hadn't heard of the Baker kidnapping by now, they were either dead or living under a rock.

A door slammed shut, and Marquez's head snapped up to see Jack enter the room carrying a cardboard box under his arm.

She smiled. "Welcome back. I hope you got something good from your trip."

"What I got are the rambling thoughts of a madman."

29

Jack let the box slide out of his hands and land squarely on the table in front of Marquez. He shrugged off his jacket and glanced at Sizemore, still standing, on his cell phone.

"Sizemore?" He motioned.

Marquez nodded, then hooked a finger on the corner of the paper-filled box and sifted the sealed plastic evidence bags. "Any of this crap any good?"

"I think so." Jack extracted several notebooks and fanned them across the table, a series arranged chronologically.

Marquez stared at them, each a different color with the dates covered in black marker. "What's this?"

"Cooper's journals when he lived with his buddy, Eric Youngblood," Jack said as he slipped on a pair of gloves and removed last notebook from its plastic sleeve. Carefully he flipped through the pages, stopping near the end of the notebook. He read a tabbed passage:

We met this family. Nice folks, lovely daughter. She cried most of the time, there at the park. Dad did nothing to make it better. What a prick! Poor thing. She needed love. She needed a father.

Jack flipped through several pages, then started to read again.

I decided to follow them. They went to a home off the main road.

Looks like a tri-level. They pulled into the garage and I couldn't see them get out before the garage door closed. I waited outside for the father to leave.

Jack lowered the notebook, the pages falling together. He tossed the book on top of the plastic sleeve and took a chair.

"Stalking," Marquez said. "Just like with Jessica Baker."

"Yeah," Jack responded. "Just like Jessica Baker."

"So, who'd he grab?"

Jack shook his head. "Doesn't say. Like a story without an ending."

"Where did you find these?"

"Cooper's old bedroom. Youngblood's uncle kept them."

"Lots of information to be spilling for your roommates to see."

"It's obvious Youngblood knew what was going on."

"You think Youngblood's involved in the Baker kidnapping with Cooper?"

Jack shrugged.

"Sizemore's got the office running a check on Youngblood. If he got cited for spitting on the sidewalk, we'll find him."

Jack looked down at his watch. Jessica Baker—now missing almost thirty hours without her meds. "Homer find anything?"

"Homer," Marquez called. "Anything?"

Homer didn't bother turning around. Just lowered his head, a sign of failure.

Marquez turned back toward Jack. "Doesn't look good."

"Anyone heard from Colfax?"

"He called in about an hour ago. Search and rescue is still out searching the surrounding fields and abandoned buildings. The hotline's receiving a crapload of calls. The PD is shagging them down as fast as they can."

"And?"

Marquez shook her head. "A waste of time."

Sizemore returned to the table, clipping his phone back on his hip. He stuck out a hand at Jack.

"Welcome to Sacramento, Ray," Jack said.

"Wish it could have been under better circumstances."

For the next thirty minutes, the three sat and reviewed the documents taken from the Russell house. Letters from Cooper's mother, others from persons unknown with addresses in Colorado, Michigan, and Florida. Innocuous letters about travels and homesickness. The journals painted a different story, however, portraying Cooper's haunting dark side. Although none of the entries actually stated Cooper committed the Holloway kidnapping, they danced close enough to indicate his involvement. Jack watched Marquez read, her face conveying depth and horror.

"It's like looking through his eyes," she said.

"Take a look at this entry." Sizemore tapped at a page in one of the notebooks. "*Eric still upset with me, can't understand why. I tried hard to make things right, let him know that I understood how he felt but couldn't let it get in the way of our friendship. Said he didn't know if that was possible. I wonder if he has lost his mind, lost his nerve. I don't know if he can even be trusted.*"

Sizemore flipped to the next page. He shook his head, then looked up at Jack and Marquez. "That's it. Nothing explaining why he was upset or the reason for not trusting Eric." He checked the date. Three months after Holloway was reported missing. "This entry looks like it happened after he returned to Orange County."

"Whatever happened, Eric started to have second thoughts," Marquez said.

Jack tented his fingers on his chin, lips gently touching fingertips. "Maybe Eric started to have remorse over the Holloway kidnapping and Cooper feared he would run to the police."

A voice blared from across the room. "Then why didn't Cooper just kill him. He didn't seem to have too much of a problem using that as a silencing technique."

"You have a point, Homer," Marquez said.

"Then there was an entry I found in one of his notebooks," Jack said. "It talks about 'starting over.' What the hell did he mean by that?"

"A new life? A family? Maybe it's fantasy?" Marquez was reaching.

Jack remained silent.

Nearing midnight, Jack's cell phone rang. He pulled it from his hip. "Yeah."

The phone conversation went on for a few minutes, everyone watching in silence, waiting for Jack to finish. He ended the call, took a deep breath.

"That was Colfax," he said.

"What'd he have to say?"

"Staked out the address for Klaus Monroe. The one he got from the phone number. A small duplex in a shithole area of Chico. Said he sat on it for a couple of hours, looking for any activity. No lights, no movement, so he finally just knocked. A young man by the name of Graham Buckley answered. Says there's no Monroe living there. Says he doesn't even know a Monroe."

"How long has Buckley lived at the duplex?"

"Not long, less than a week. He gave Colfax the name of the landlord. He's contacting him as we speak. He'll let us know what he finds out."

His phone vibrated again. Answering the call, he placed it on speaker so that everyone could hear. This time it was Hoskin.

"Got something for you." Hoskin's voice sounded over-modulated. "We were able to identify a bank account for Monroe at Washington Mutual. Unfortunately, he used a private drop box for his address. Manager said it's filled with junk mail, nothing that would help us locate him. However, we did learn that his ATM card was used yesterday."

"Where?" Jack asked.

"Local. Cash machine at a 7-11 in Auburn. I know the spot. They may have surveillance cameras."

"We'll head out there now. Maybe we'll get lucky and find latents. I'll get someone to pull the camera."

Hoskin gave Jack the address and directions to the Mini Mart, estimating it was going to take them thirty minutes to get there, barring any traffic.

"My money's on Cooper using Monroe's card."

"I ain't takin' that bet," Sizemore said.

Marquez glanced back at Homer, who stared sad-eyed at the three of them, like he was waiting for an invite to their club.

"Homer," Marquez said. "We're done here. Go home and I'll call you in the morning."

Homer looked like he might cry. "Why can't I come?"

"Not this time, it could be dangerous."

"To check out a video? Are you nuts?"

"I appreciate your enthusiasm," Marquez said. "Go home and continue scanning the Internet for Cooper. You call me if you hear anything and I promise, we'll make sure you're included on any raids."

A smile stretched across his skinny face. He grabbed his jacket, slapped Marquez a high five and headed out the door.

Sizemore leaned close to Marquez and whispered, "You take your informants to raid sites?"

"He can sit in the car far, far away. It makes him feel wanted."

Sizemore grinned.

"We've got to get moving," Jack said. "It's been almost twenty hours since Monroe used the ATM. We want to get there before they recycle the tape."

30

Homer fidgeted with his keys in his pant's pocket as he strolled toward the front door to his apartment. The pathway through the complex was partially lit by a lamppost, two of the three bulbs burnt out, the air still warm and heavy from the day's heat wave. From a distance, Homer could hear the pool pump and smell chlorine. It was late and Homer felt tired and hungry. He just wanted to get inside and lay down.

His steps clicked on the concrete walkway, echoing between the three-story buildings that boxed him in on both sides. As he passed a row of mailboxes, he thought he heard footsteps. He canted his head to the left, then right. Nothing. A second later, he picked up the sound of heels clicking a slow pace again. Because of the echo, it was difficult to determine where it was coming from.

Picking up speed, Homer made his way to the front door of his apartment, the porch light flickering from a failing bulb. He stabbed his key into the door, twisted the handle and kicked the strike plate with his boot. The door creaked open as the porch light popped, leaving Homer in total darkness. He slid his hand across the interior wall, feeling for the switch plate. That's when he felt a hard thump across the back of his head.

Homer stumbled forward, glasses flying off, unable to keep his balance. Another hard thud against his head, the pain now ringing in his ears, then a strangle hold around his neck. He couldn't move or breathe, couldn't see, the pressure becoming tighter. His fight or flight instinct kicked in. He chose flight. He grabbed at the arm knotted around his neck and pulled to get away but he wasn't strong enough. The grip around his neck tightened, restricting blood and air, his head starting to feel light, tingly. He needed a weapon. A gun or a knife, two things he had never carried or ever wanted to. He grabbed at his front pocket and felt something, a pen. He tore the ballpoint from his shirt pocket, held it like a dagger and in a swift motion, swung it hard, down and behind. The pen slammed into his attacker but didn't penetrate. He felt the steel tip stop against clothing. Homer cocked his arm and swung again, farther and harder. This time the tip pierced skin. His attacker let out a loud growl, then bent forward at the waist, a gap now between their bodies, giving Homer his opportunity.

Homer broke free and dropped to the floor, arms and legs flailing, trying to gain traction on the slick wooden entryway. He grabbed a fistful of carpet, and his left leg found the corner of a wall. He made a break for the back room, bumping in the darkness, body slamming into the kitchen table that blocked his path in the unlit room, knocking over several chairs. His hand swiped a framed picture off the wall and it shattered at his feet. He dove into the bedroom and kicked the door closed, locked it, and scrambled behind the bed. He listened for movement. Nothing but his own labored breathing. He tried to force himself steady but couldn't stop shaking.

"I've got a gun!" Homer screamed.

Silence.

"Look, you son-of-a-bitch, I got a gun and I'm not afraid to use it! You hear me?!"

Homer's head twisted left to right, listening for the sound of footsteps, crunching glass, the twist of the doorknob. He reached down and patted the floor under the bed, feeling the end of a baseball bat, an Easton Thunder Club. He choked up in his most aggressive stance. Then he remembered his cell. He groped at his jacket pocket. It wasn't there. Must've fallen out during the scuffle. But his assailant didn't know that.

"I'm calling 911!" Homer shouted.

The only other phone was the cordless he'd left in the living room, next to the computer, as usual. He made a pact with himself that if he survived this he'd stock a phone in every room.

Creeping forward with the Thunder Club held tightly in his hands, Homer pressed an ear to the door. Silence. As he started to pull away, Homer heard footsteps. His heart raced. He drew the bat back, ready to swing. Live or die, he was going to get in at least one good whack. Then he realized the sounds were becoming fainter, more distant. His attacker was leaving.

Homer bent down to his knees, peering at the space between the floor and bottom edge of the door. Moonlight blue filtered through the crack. Homer stared at the gap, waiting to spy a shadow, movement of any kind. Everything was still. He gently cracked the door, his eyes adjusting to the darkness. He could faintly make out furniture tipped over, the front door wide open. No curious neighbors were roaming, trying to find out what all the commotion was about. *So much for Neighborhood Watch.*

Making his way into the living room, he found his computer monitor on the floor, the screen cracked like a San Andreas Fault. He pushed the screen aside with his left foot and spotted the cordless, covered in shards.

"Where the hell are my glasses?" Homer mumbled as he dropped to his knees and swept his hand over the carpet. He caught the corner of something unfamiliar. A small notebook. Homer was ready to toss it aside but then hesitated. It wasn't his. He flicked on a lamp and held it close to his face. And then he realized what he'd found.

He stumbled his way to the kitchen table, paused for a second, took the notebook and slid it under the table rug. He crawled back into the living room and leaned the bat against the wall, and dropped to his knees, hunting for his glasses, feeling toward the front door, where they'd been struck from his face. There, near the entrance, Homer spotted a fuzzy black blob glittering in the moonlight. He pushed them onto his face. The world became clear. So did the figure standing in front of him.

Before he could react a hand shot forward and clamped hard around his throat. He was forced into a spin, an arm squeezing around his neck for the second time that night. This time, Homer had no pen in his pocket and no other weapon at his disposal. His Thunder Club rested against the wall just out of his reach. The pressure around his neck increased until he felt like his head would explode. His vision blurred, funneling to a pinpoint view. His attacker leaned heavily on his back, dragging him down to the apartment floor. He fell to his knees, bone striking hard onto wood. Then he felt a sharp prick in his lower back. He winced once before a rush of warmth engulfed him. His body went numb.

"Take my money," Homer slurred. "Just don't . . . hurt me." His head fell, cheek pressed against the cold floor.

"I don't want your money, Homer." The man leaned close to his ear and whispered, "I want you to stop poking your nose where it doesn't belong."

Homer's eyes widened briefly.

Then they closed and his mind faded into darkness forever.

31

The 7-11 was at the corner of Auburn-Folsom and Racetrack Street, not too far from the County Fairgrounds. The interior glowed with florescent lights, standing out in the rural area like a UFO in the middle of a forest. Jack nosed his vehicle into the parking lot. Marquez sat in the passenger seat, scrolling through her notes. Sizemore had taken his rental back to the office to catch up on what Hoskin had learned.

A single Chevy coupe was parked directly in front of the doorway, a haggard female passenger leaning her head out the side window, blowing slow smoke rings into the night sky.

Inside, the clerk was ringing up a large fountain drink, Twinkies and smokes stacked on the counter. The customer never took his eyes off the clerk, even when Jack and Marquez pushed through the front glass doors.

Marquez maneuvered around the news rack where the ATM stood, gazing back at Jack, who pointed above the beer cooler, at a surveillance camera aimed directly at her.

"Good coverage," Marquez said.

They walked to the counter. Jack threw down a pack of gum along with a five-dollar bill, and Marquez flashed her credentials at the clerk, who peered up at Jack.

Jack nodded. "Yeah, me too."

After explaining the reason for the visit, the clerk took them to a back room the size of a closet, where a beat-up VCR sat perched on top of a metal and wood shelving unit.

"It records for twenty-four hours," the clerk said as he thumbed through a catalogue of tapes.

Jack reached up and hit the stop button. The screen went black. "You change the tape in the past couple of hours?"

The clerk shook his head. "Shift's not over."

"Were you working yesterday?"

"Every day, all day."

"You remember seeing this guy come in here?" Jack flipped out a photo of Cooper.

The clerk squinted at the photo and his bushy brows furrowed.

"Can't say for sure."

Jack looked around the store, seeing no one. The Chevy out front had departed and the street looked empty.

"Doesn't look all that busy. You sure you don't remember anything?"

"You can go through the video. Maybe that will help." His tone was less than concerned.

Marquez pulled up a dirty chair from the back office, and Jack settled onto a couple of plastic crates. They rewound the video, starting around 9:55 p.m. the previous day, when Monroe's ATM card was used. The grainy video showed a handful of customers scanning magazines, purchasing smokes, blurry and unfocused. Jack could barely determine if a customer was male or female, let alone their suspect. Marquez leaned in toward the screen every time a figure entered the frame only to be disappointed. The clerk grew bored and excused himself to the front counter.

"Are we close?" Marquez tapped the screen next to the time clock.

"Inside a minute."

On screen, a figure entered. Presumably a man, he was slight, wearing a gray hooded sweatshirt, hands shoved into his pockets. The clerk at the counter straightened the beef sticks. He glanced at the customer, nodded and went back to his duties. The figure moved closer to the ATM, but because of the angle and quality, it was near impossible to see his face.

Marquez muttered, "Come on, look up."

Next to the ATM, the suspect dragged a card from his back pocket, shoving it into the machine. A few seconds passed before he glanced nervously around the store, then briefly toward the camera. Jack punched the pause button, catching most of the suspect's face. The two stood in silence as they studied the blurry image.

"What do you think, Jack?"

"Hard to say. But I know one thing." He tapped a finger on the screen. "That ain't Cooper. That's Youngblood."

32

Marquez studied the grainy blend of black, white, and gray. "What makes you say that?"

"Similarities." Jack touched the screen next to the suspect's arm. "Look at his wrist."

The snapshot showed an exposed right wrist with a steel banded watch. Jack pointed at it. "Left handed. Cooper's right."

"How do you know that?"

"We usually wear watches on the opposite wrist." Jack lifted his right, which sported a black-faced Tag Hauer Chorograph Carrera SLR.

Marquez grabbed his wrist and studied the watch. "Nice. Buy that on a Bureau salary?"

Jack shook his hand free. "It was a gift."

"Uh-huh." Marquez replied through pursed lips. "Okay, so if this is Youngblood, we've got two suspects involved in the kidnapping of the Baker girl."

"Looks that way," Jack said. "But why isn't he hiding his identity like Cooper? Maybe there's another reason why Youngblood is here in the mix. Let see what else our boy does."

Jack pressed the play button and the video advanced. The man pushed numbers, withdrawing cash from the machine. He counted the bills, holding them in his right while sifting with his left, another sign of a left-hander. He shoved the money in his pants and started toward the door.

"Look," Marquez said.

As he exited the store, Youngblood turned right and walked along the open glass, still in view of the camera. Youngblood stopped, half his body now out of sight.

"What the hell is he doing?" Marquez said.

Jack stepped out of the room and stared into the open area. He turned around, smiling. "He's using the pay phone."

Both hurried out the back door toward the telephone. A man sifting change walked toward them. Jack put up a hand, gently touching the man on his chest as they met in front of the payphone. The man peered up, startled at first, then looking insulted.

"Sorry," Jack said, pointing to the phone. "Police business."

Jack returned his attention to the payphone, inspecting the black plastic and weathered chrome phone box and receiver. He pulled a pair of latex gloves from his jacket pocket and slid them on. He lifted the handset and eyeballed it at an angle.

"You see any latents?" Marquez asked.

"Looks like there's a couple of smudge marks, maybe a print or two." He paused for a second, then added, "I think we can do better than a couple of prints."

He rushed to the trunk of his car where he retrieved a pair of wire cutters and a plastic bag. Back at the payphone, he snipped the stainless steel cord.

Marquez asked, "What do you think you're doing? That's private property."

"Arrest me, Agent Marquez."

"I know you've got a print kit in the trunk of your car."

"This is more fun."

"It's not necessary."

"It's the phone company. Of course it's necessary."

Marquez shook her head.

"Everyone spits into a phone." Jack lifted the receiver and cord, which swayed in the breeze like a dead snake, and dropped it into the plastic bag. Jack looked up at Marquez. "DNA."

"What now?"

"We'll send it to the lab to see if we can confirm Youngblood was here."

"That could take some time. Will it help us find the Baker girl?"

"At least it will let us know if Youngblood's involved. If so, it tells me he's in the area so we can hunt him down and find out what he knows. And fast."

They knew the players; they just needed to confirm who did what.

"Let's get out an A.P.B. with Youngblood's picture transmitted to every agency in the western states." Jack sealed the plastic bag with evidence tape. "Make sure Washington Mutual doesn't put a freeze on Monroe's ATM card. Maybe we'll get lucky and Youngblood will get greedy and take another shot at using it."

Marquez nodded. "I'll get Hoskin to subpoena the telephone company to find out who Youngblood called. Might get lucky and get a hit on where the Baker girl is being held." She looked at Jack's face. "You look tired."

Jack exhaled, turned and stared at the empty parking lot. "She's around here, Lucy. I can feel it."

They took the road back down Auburn-Folsom, a windy, tree-shrouded route with million dollar homes sprinkled along the trail, looming steel and brick walls secluding them from the regular folk. Jack listened to Marquez talking to dispatch at the FBI field office, giving out the description of Youngblood for the A.P.B. Marquez wasn't one to waste time on nonsensical jargon. She rattled off straight-up, need-to-know information for the bulletin. After her request to transmit to all western state law enforcement agencies, she had dispatch transfer her to Chris Hoskin's phone. She waited for the call to connect, all the while biting down on the glossy red fingernail of her right pinky.

"You keep chewing like that and you'll end up taking off a finger."

She pulled her hand away. "Nervous habit."

"It'll be all right, Lucy. We'll find her."

She nodded grudgingly, then popped up in her seat, rubbed her right eye with the palm of her hand and spoke into the phone. "Chris. We got something for you to dust for latents and possible DNA." Pause. "The receiver from a payphone." Another pause. "No, you don't need to get to the phone. It'll be coming to you. The suspect used it less than twenty-four hours ago." Pause and a grin. She turned to Jack. "Chris wants to know if you thought about taking the coins in the box?"

Jack snapped his fingers. "Should have thought of that. Prints on the coins."

Marquez smiled. "I'll call the telephone company to see if they will pull the coin box for us. No one's going to be using that phone tonight anyway."

As they headed back to the office, Jack thought about the notes he read in Cooper's journals, still troubled by the words "starting over." Starting over from what? This was before he'd killed his family.

"What are you thinking about?" Marquez stared at Jack.

"Cooper's journals and letters home. Strange things I just can't put a finger on."

"Maybe they need another set of eyes"

"I think you're right. I'll ask Sizemore or Colfax to give them a look over."

Marquez punched Jack, hard enough to cause him to jerk. "I meant me."

Jack smiled. "I know."

Marquez picked up her cell phone and placed a call. A few seconds later she blew an exasperated breath and shut the phone.

"He's not home," she said.

"Who's not home?"

"Homer."

"You need to let him know his time belongs to you."

"He's pretty good about that. Probably on the computer with the ringer off."

"Now that's dedication."

It took thirty minutes to get back to the office and hook up with Sizemore and Hoskin. Marquez carried the box of journals and Jack handed the plastic bag with the payphone receiver to Hoskin, who disappeared to the ERT room to begin processing for DNA, which would involve gassing the entire receiver with a boiling container of cyanoacrylate and ninhydrate inside a closed box for about two hours. The process was simple. The hard part would be finding a useable print to confirm Jack's suspicion.

Marquez pored through Cooper's notebooks and letters at the undercover off-site, taking notes as she read. Jack pulled a stack of papers off his desk. The Meridian PCS records had come in over the fax machine on the phone number from Officer Cambridge, which showed the phone hadn't been used shortly after Monroe was cited. The cell phone was subscribed to Klaud Morrow. With Meridian PCS, anyone can subscribe to a phone in any name without verification. In the past, Jack had pulled phone records under the name of Mickey Mouse and Adolph Hitler. Tracking and identifying criminals using Meridan's system was nearly impossible. A crook's go-to service. It was obvious that Klaud was actually Klaus Monroe. The billing address was also bogus. Jack noted the numbers called most frequently, then fired out another salvo of subpoenas to the phone companies, and either begged, threatened or guilted the late night representative into getting him the information immediately.

"Jack," Marquez called out from across the bullpen, still staring at the journal, right arm held high above her head. "Phone's for you."

He walked back and picked up the line. "Yeah, Paris speaking."

"Agent Paris, this is Cingular Wireless. I have the information you requested from your emergency subpoena request."

Jack grabbed his notepad. "Go ahead," he said.

The woman from Cingular rattled off names, addresses, and any other information provided by the subscriber. When she got to the third one, Jack recognized the name. Andre Burke. She didn't have to read the address: Jack already knew it. He cupped the receiver and shouted to Colfax. "Mark, where's our porn boy, Andre Burke?"

"Still at County Jail."

Jack wrapped up his call with Cingular, and grabbed his jacket and briefcase.

Marquez looked up from her notepad. "Where you going?"

"County lock-up. Mr. Burke may have the answer to where Klaus Monroe lives . . . or lived."

Colfax, notebook in hand, joined Jack and Marquez. "I spoke with the owner of the apartment where Monroe told Officer Cambridge he lived. Terrance O'Brien says the prior occupant was a husband/wife couple by the name of McGarrett. His records showed they moved to Huntsville, Alabama, an address to mail their security deposit."

Marquez chimed in. "I'll get a hold of the Birmingham Division and have them run out and interview the McGarretts."

"In the meantime," Jack said. "I'll take Mark with me to talk to Burke."

Marquez nodded as she copied information from Colfax's notes. "Let me know what our boy has to say."

Jack waved an acknowledgement as he and Colfax headed out the back door.

It was late, but the air still felt like heat radiating from a toaster.

"Cross your fingers, Mark. Let's hope Burke can give us an address where we can find Mr. Cooper."

Colfax opened the driver's side door. "Right now, I'll settle for Jessica Baker."

Jack agreed. "Let's get them both."

The Bureau radio lit up with traffic from the Special Operations Group as Jack cranked the engine. Several locations, called in to the command post, were staked out. Colfax swiped his hand across his face; beads of sweat had formed in the short time it took to get to the car.

"It's midnight and it's still so fucking hot out here."

Jack blasted the air conditioning as the Crown Vic sped out the front gate toward Interstate 80 West, on their way to the Sacramento County Jail.

33

Jack waited in the jail's interview room for the guards to bring Burke in for questioning. Colfax leaned against a stark white wall, tapping his knuckles to the beat playing in his head. Jack leaned back in his chair, rocking slowly.

"You think he's going to play stupid?" Colfax asked.

Jack shook him off. "Burke can't play stupid. He *is* stupid. But I think he'll do anything we ask to get out of jail. Even if that means giving up Monroe."

Moments later, a latch clicked and the door swung wide. Burke entered wearing an orange jumpsuit, his head hung low. He looked miserable, hands cuffed in front, led by a hulking deputy the size of a small Buick sedan.

Burke peered at Jack. "You said I could go home. What the fuck?"

Jack put up a hand. "Cool your jets, Burke. I had no idea you were still in lock-up."

Burke held his hands straight out in front of him, the shiny chrome cuffs secured on his wrists refracting fluorescents. "You think I want to be here?"

"No. I don't. So sit down and shut up. Maybe we can work something out."

"You mean to get me out?"

"Yeah, Burke, get you out."

"Tonight?"

"For Christ's sake. Sit down."

Burke fell into the hard plastic seat at the table in front of him.

Jack stuck a finger in Burke's face. "If you want my help getting out, listen carefully and answer my questions, okay?"

"Are you going to get me out?"

"You're not listening."

Burke sucked in a deep breath, letting it out like a pool toy with a pinhole. He nodded.

"Good." Jack planted his hands on the table and leaned toward Burke. "You know a guy by the name of Klaus Monroe? His phone records show a number of calls between you two."

"I got no idea who you're talking about."

Colfax jumped in. "You better come clean or you'll be a pin cushion for some lonely inmate."

Perspiration dotted Burke's face as he locked on Colfax. "I swear! You got to believe me."

Jack waved a hand, redirecting Burke's attention his way. He spread out the telephone records on the table and pointed at the calls between Burke and Monroe. "Take a look at these calls. Is this your number?"

Burke looked down, eyes scanning the pages. "Yeah, that's my number, but I don't know who that is."

"Check the dates and time. That help?"

The room grew quiet, only the sound of Burke's steel handcuffs could be heard scratching across the metal table.

"They were at night, Burke, late at night." Jack flipped a couple of the pages around to get a better look, running a finger before stopping halfway down page two. "I just counted twelve calls with your number listed. Eleven of those calls are Monroe calling you. Pretty close in time, like he was desperate in getting in touch with you."

Burke reached over with his cuffed hands and twisted the pages back in his direction. He studied the pages for a moment before something clicked.

"Holy shit, that's Carlos."

"Could you mean Klaus?" Colfax said, less threateningly.

"Yes. Klaus, Klaus Monroe. That's the guy who I met a couple of months back." Burke's pitch dropped an octave and his body slackened low in his chair. "That asshole called me over and over."

"Okay, I get the picture," Jack said. "Now tell me how you know this guy."

Burke sat up straight in his chair and pitched forward. "See, I meet this guy on the Internet, says he likes to trade pictures." He paused and gave both Colfax and Jack a hard stare. "Am I going to get into more trouble over this?"

"No. Continue."

"So this guy wants pictures, which I send him. We start talking some more. He wants to meet, have a couple of beers."

"And?"

"I don't usually go out because I got other things to do, so I say 'thanks but no thanks.'"

"How'd he get your phone number?"

"When we spoke over the Internet, we kept on getting interrupted by others joining in on the chat. He dogs me to give him my number so we can talk more in private, so I give it. After a while, he kept calling me, leaving me voicemails, so I call him back and meet him for a couple of drinks. That's it. I met him that one time."

"Where'd you meet him at?"

Burke rubbed his chin and thought for a moment. "A bar in a town called Paradise. Real close to Chico. I think the name of the bar was O'Reilly's or O'Rourke's. Off Clark Street."

Colfax spoke. "I know the place. O'Rourke's. Clark Road, just north of Elliott."

"Thanks, Burke." Jack stood as he gathered up the papers. Colfax hammered at the interview room door with two sharp cracks from his fist. The door opened and Colfax made his way out. Jack reached down and shoved the papers into his briefcase, right on his heels.

"Hey," Burke yelled. "What about me? When can I go?"

Jack stopped and turned back. "I'll talk to the desk sergeant and see if we can get you cut by morning."

Burke dropped his head onto the table between his folded arms, rocking side to side, his response low and muffled.

"Fuck."

34

Colfax walked into the bar first while Jack checked out the parking lot looking for the pickup truck he saw Cooper speeding off in two days ago. Already way past midnight, the lot was still half full. Most of the cars were compacts, American made, couple of Toyotas, a new Lexus with paper plates. Jack entered and made his way to the counter where Colfax stood alone, looking toward the bartender, who was waiting on a customer. The bar area was compact, dark wood edged in a black vinyl cushion dotted with brass studs, which stretched down the right side of the room, curving back toward a darkened alcove. The wall behind the bar was lit from underneath, low wattage casting elongating shadows upward, giving each bottle a glistening appearance. The rest of the place was covered in a blanket of darkness, each shadowy figure shrouded in anonymity and privacy. From what Jack could tell, there were about half a dozen patrons seated at various tables. Only one customer sat alone, however, a long neck bottle balanced between the tips of his fingers. Jack gave each a good look. None of them matched his subjects.

"You talk to the bartender yet?" Jack asked.

Colfax dipped his head and glanced to the right. "Not yet."

179

They stared over at the bartender until he sensed their presence and glanced their way. He pitched his chin sharply, indicating he'd be over. The bartender finished a tall pilsner from the draught spout and slid it toward the customer, before dragging a towel across the counter. He took in a short breath, walked down and gave them both an exasperated look. "What can I get you?"

Colfax flashed his badge and leaned forward, resting his left hand on the bar as he spoke in a low tone. "I'm looking for one of your customers." Colfax reached into his jacket pocket and pulled out a picture of Monroe. He slid it low on the counter, tapping the top edge twice. "You seen him?"

The bartender tipped his head down slightly, studied the photo briefly before looking back at Colfax. "Yeah. But not for some time now."

"When was the last time he was in?"

"A week, maybe two, three. Why you looking for him?

"He's been killing bartenders," Colfax said.

"We're trying to find a sixteen-year-old who's been kidnapped," Jack said.

The bartender pointed toward the lone patron cradling the beer bottle. "You see that guy over there?"

Neither Jack nor Colfax turned to look. "Yeah," Jack said, "I see him."

"I'm pretty sure he's friends with your guy."

"What makes you say that?"

"They sit together at that same table. Otherwise, that dude sits alone."

"You know his name?"

"Paul something. Not all that talkative."

Jack turned and gave the customer, Paul LNU, as in Last Name Unknown, a passing glance. "How much longer are you open?"

The bartender checked his watch. "Another half an hour unless you tell me differently."

"A half hour is fine."

"Anything else?"

Jack shook his head and stuck out a hand. "Thanks for the help." The bartender took it, and then walked back toward the other end of the bar.

Colfax turned to Jack. "What do you think?"

"I think we don't have a whole lot of time. I say we go talk to Paul LNU."

The two turned and made for Paul, who was in his own world, before turning his gaze as they approached.

Jack presented his credentials. Then he and Colfax took up the empty chairs, sandwiching Paul LNU between them.

Paul scooted back, head swiveling between the two.

"I already spoke to you guys."

"About what?"

"That missing girl."

Jack looked over at Colfax. The only people talking about the Baker kidnapping were the officers following up on tips.

"They came to my house already," Paul said, tapping the beer bottle on the wooden table. "Said they were checking all registrants in the area."

Colfax pointed a finger at Paul. "You a Two-ninety?"

Paul's face tightened. "Not voluntarily."

Two-ninety is public code for the registration of all convicted sex offenders. In California, anyone convicted of a sexual crime must register with the local police department. Failure to do so could land them back in jail.

Jack placed a hand on the beer bottle, stopping Paul's nervous tapping habit. "What's your full name?"

"Paul Ulysses Blunt."

"Mr. Blunt, what did you tell the officers when they spoke to you?"

"I said I don't know nothing about any missing girl. I don't kidnap kids and I am not a sexual deviant."

Colfax pulled out the photo of Monroe. "You know this guy."

Blunt barely glanced. "Don't know him."

"Look again," he said.

"I said I don't know him. Now leave me alone."

Colfax rubbed his chin with his left hand, his other still on the photo. "Blunt . . . Blunt.... I remember you. Aren't you still on probation?"

Blunt squirmed in his chair then dropped his head like a turtle trying to retreat inside his shell. "My last year."

"Last I checked, you still have to cooperate with law enforcement, one year or one day."

Blunt remained silent, staring down at the table but not at Monroe's photo.

"I don't think your probation allows you to be in a bar either. Am I right?"

Blunt blew out a noisy breath laced with profanity as he slapped a palm on the photo. "Okay, maybe I know this guy. He comes in for drinks every once in a while. He knows I'm a registrant so he sits with me because we have something in common."

"You know his name and where he lives?" Jack asked.

"Klaus. I've been to his house, but only once." Blunt made his point, knowing that as a sex registrant, he was not allowed to associate with other sex registrants. "I drove him home one night because he was wasted and I was afraid he was going to end up killing somebody in that truck of his."

"You know he has a truck?"

"Yeah, white, a beater with a camper shell."

"You have any way of calling Klaus?"

"No. Just know where he lives."

Jack and Colfax stood from the table as Blunt's eyes followed them. "Why don't you take us there?" Jack said, pointing toward the door.

Blunt didn't budge, lower jaw hung open. "Now?"

Colfax answered, "That wasn't a request."

Blunt pulled out a wadded bill from his pocket and tossed it on the table. He pushed back his chair and marched toward the door. "You're not going to give me up, are you?"

Colfax said, "You gonna leave a better tip?"

Jack jumped in. "No, Paul. Help us out and we'll forget you're associating with a known sex offender at a prohibitive establishment to trade porn."

"I never said I was trading porn."

"Should I search your residence?"

Blunt turned away and shook his head.

"Then show me where Monroe lives."

35

After twenty minutes of driving down wrong turns and dead-end streets, Colfax was starting to get irritated with Blunt. From the backseat, Blunt kept saying the next one would be the right one.

"Come on, Paul. Think." Jack maintained his composure but he, too, was growing impatient.

"Cut me some slack, will you? It's been a while." Then Blunt leaned over the headrest, pointing to his right.

"Take that next turn."

Jack headed east on Deer Creek Highway, the street lined with big trees and older homes.

"Anything look familiar?"

Blunt fanned his right hand. "Yeah, hold on, I think I got it now. There, turn right."

Jack turned south onto Forest Avenue, a more rural section, with large, white warehouses on both sides. "I don't see houses, Paul."

Blunt jabbed a finger over Colfax's shoulder. "Make another right."

They pulled down a dirt road shrouded by canopy trees. Kicked-up dust from the tires drifted through the headlights, as they crawled to a fork twenty yards ahead. Jack slowed down.

"Okay, Paul. Which way?"

Blunt hesitated. "I'm not sure."

"Great," Colfax said.

"The house is down one of these roads, I'm sure."

Colfax looked over at Jack. "Take your pick."

Jack turned to the left and followed the road for another fifty yards before killing his lights and gliding to the side. "Get out, Paul, we're walking."

The three exited and trudged down the darkened road. If Cooper was there, Jack didn't want to alert him to their presence. They cleared a row of trees into a large, open patch of dirt and grass. To their right was an L-shaped one-story with a detached garage. All the lights were off. There was a pickup truck parked in front but it didn't look like the one Jack saw the other night.

Jack tapped Blunt on the shoulder. "Is this the place?"

Blunt squinted hard at the house and shook his head. "I think so. I can't say for sure."

"That isn't good enough, Paul."

Jack gave it a few seconds before turning back. If Blunt wasn't sure he wanted to look down the other side of the forked road first. The three jogged to the car and walked down the other side along a stretch of magnolia bushes, where another house sat thirty yards away. Jack peered around a large oak tree. The porch light was on, a good sign.

"Okay, Blunt, get a good look."

Blunt's head bobbed up and down. "Yeah, I think this could be the one."

"What do you mean you *think*?" Jack asked.

"Look, it's one of these. I can't remember. They all look alike."

Colfax groaned. "For Christ's sake."

Jack raised his right hand, trying to quell Colfax's anger. They could set up on both houses. Jack would take one, Colfax and Blunt the other.

Jack told Colfax to park the car at the top of the street, out of sight.

Blunt threw up both hands. "Why can't I just go on home?"

"You're the only one here that has actually seen the guy," Jack said. "I need you to point him out."

"He looks just like the photo."

"Good," Jack replied. "Then you won't have a problem picking him out for us." He tossed the keys to Colfax, who turned and pushed Blunt up toward the main road.

Jack jogged down the path back to the first house, stepping behind a row of trees where he kneeled low and tried to get comfortable knowing this could be a long night.

An hour passed without seeing any movement, Colfax and Jack updating each other on the Nextel direct-connect. Jack wondered if it was worth staying much longer. Colfax suggested they call in his narcotics team to take over the surveillance, more bodies with fresh eyes. Not a bad idea. Jack could at least catch an hour of sleep before covering other leads.

"You think you can get the team for this morning?"

"I'll call the sergeant," Colfax replied.

Jack leaned against a tree, careful not to become too lax. Few minutes later, Colfax phoned back.

"They can be out at six."

Jack looked at his watch. 4:05 a.m. "I'll take it."

Another hour passed with no activity, Jack's legs beginning to cramp from squatting too long. He stood behind a tree and stretched his back, stiff knees popping like bubble wrap.

He gazed down the roadway, hoping to hear the narc team coming to relieve them. A spear of light crossed the path before disappearing behind the thick foliage as rolling tires approached.

Jack tapped the direct-connect on his Nextel. "I see headlights. I think your team has arrived."

Jack watched the road but no vehicles approached. Twenty seconds later, Jack's phone chirped. Colfax, his voice a whisper.

"It's not my team, Jack."

36

Jack held his breath.

"I got a pickup driving up to the garage," Colfax whispered. "Driver's stopped and is exiting the truck."

Jack's heart started racing. If this was Cooper, the Baker girl could be inside. Approaching now would be a gamble. If Jessica Baker were being held elsewhere, they would lose the option of following him to the stash house, essentially jeopardizing a rescue. She'd become another Grace Holloway. The best thing to do was to give it a few more minutes of surveillance and assess the situation.

Jack called Colfax on the Nextel, his voice anxious. "Is it Cooper?"

"Can't tell. Too dark."

As much as Jack wanted to head in their direction, he couldn't risk it. He told Colfax and Blunt to get in closer to record the license plate, then call his sergeant and get an ETA. With the recent development, they could use back up.

Jack had moved to the other side of the road, getting closer to the second residence, when a voice yelled out, commanding someone to stop. Jack bolted toward the fork in the road; Colfax's voice came over the Nextel, screaming frantically. "He's running! I lost him."

"I'm coming down the road!" Jack sprinted along the edge of the bushes, peering in between openings, hoping to see Cooper cutting in his direction. This time, he would not let him escape. Between the fork and the two houses, a dense V-shaped patch of bramble led into the woods. If Cooper made a break for it, he would have to weave himself through it. The noise of snapping branches and crushing ground cover would give him away. Jack pushed himself into a thicket of shrub brush. He stopped, hearing movement directly in front of him. He crouched low behind a dense hedge, squinting into the darkness. Colfax's voice sounded over the Nextel.

"I don't have him, Jack."

He gave Colfax his location and told him to enter from the side road so they wouldn't get caught in a cross fire in the event of shooting. The bushes rustled louder and Jack caught sight of something leaping through a wall of green foliage to his left. It was definitely a person, but it was too dark, the suspect moving too fast to get an ID.

"I got him heading toward the first house," Jack whispered into his Nextel, not waiting for Colfax to respond. He sprinted through the thick overgrowth, chasing the dark figure, hoping whoever it was didn't make a hard turn in the opposite direction. Snapped branches told him he was heading in the right direction. The unlit path brought Jack back on the other side of the road, by the first house.

"Shit!" Jack's head swiveled up and down the road searching for movement. He ran north, speculating his suspect would make a break for town. He hadn't taken two steps before something exploded from the darkness made by the hedges, tackling Jack to the ground. Jack's head hit hard on the dirt path as the two men tumbled across the road and into a dry ditch. Twisted into a knot with his attacker, Jack drove the heel of his palm up into the perpetrator's chin, making solid contact. The man's head snapped back, opening a space between the two of them. The full force of a boot struck Jack squarely in the chest, lifting him off the ground and tossing him back against the other side of the culvert, the wind knocked out of him. Struggling to catch his breath, Jack scrambled to his feet, watching his attacker try to gain traction and flee. Jack dove at his legs, grabbing, pulling hard. The man fell onto his stomach, body slamming with a heavy thud. The man groaned, scraping at the ground but with too little energy left to get away.

"I got him!" Jack screamed, sliding, his right leg first, into the ditch, landing on top of the attacker, knee falling squarely on the suspect's back, pinning him to the ground as Colfax ran up, pair of handcuffs pulled from the back of his jeans.

"Are you okay?" Colfax asked, fighting to get the cuffs secured.

Jack rolled over and dragged a sleeve across his chin, wiping away the sweat and dirt and blood from the fight. He nodded, glad it was over.

Jack got to his feet, checking for injuries. His chest felt like it was hit with a hammer. Colfax lifted the suspect, who offered little assistance, his body limp on wobbly legs.

"Let's get a look at you," Colfax said as he straightened up the man, holding him steady by the shoulders. Jack made his way around to the other side so he could face his attacker, the moonlight bright enough to illuminate his features in blue and gray hues.

Blunt appeared, standing just above them on the dirt road. He pulled his right hand from his jacket pocket and pointed at the man. "That's him. That's Monroe."

The attacker squinted at Blunt and tilted his head. Blood dripped from his chin as he heaved in deep breaths. "What the fuck are you talking about?"

Colfax straightened out his arms, pushing the attacker back a few inches to get a better look. Jack walked up and studied the man's face. He knew it couldn't be Monroe because Monroe was most likely dead.

"This isn't Monroe." Jack turned toward Colfax, frustrated. It was obvious Blunt would ID his own mother at this point. The guy wasn't Monroe but it also wasn't Cooper.

"Who are you?" Jack asked.

The man lifted his head. "Why are you chasing me?"

"Why were you running?" Colfax jumped in.

"I saw your car up on the road and you two sneaking around my house." He pointed his bloody and scraped chin at Colfax and then at Blunt. "Thought you were looking to rob me."

"No one's going to rob you," Jack said as he pulled out his Maglight and shined it on the man's face. He studied it for a second. "I know who you are." Before the man could respond, Jack answered for him. "You're Eric Youngblood, Alvin Cooper's friend."

"Yeah," he said. "That's me."

Jack closed his distance to Youngblood and tapped him on the chest with an accusatory finger.

"Well, Mr. Youngblood. You've got some explaining to do."

37

Colfax parked the Crown Vic just past the fork in the road, while Jack waited with the prisoner, who sat cross-legged in the dirt, his hands cuffed. Jack had confronted Youngblood, who denied any involvement in the Baker abduction. When Colfax returned, they stuffed him in the back, head first, before getting in themselves, Jack in the driver's seat, making Blunt ride beside the suspect.

"Can I go home now?" Blunt whined.

"In a minute," Jack said. "We're a bit busy." He threw his right arm over his seat and addressed Youngblood. "Is anyone in the house?"

Youngblood shook his head. "Like I just told you, I had nothing to do with that girl being kidnapped."

"We're going inside to find out."

Jack steered the car carefully to the front, scanning the area for any movement.

Colfax gestured at Youngblood and Blunt. "What do we do with these two?"

"We take Youngblood with us." Jack pointed at Blunt. "Get out and stand by the back of the trunk. If you hear gunfire, run."

Blunt rolled his eyes, muttering, "Oh, fuck me."

Jack got out of the vehicle, and led Youngblood out by the elbow. Colfax snuck up from around back. The front door was still ajar from when Youngblood bolted into the woods. Jack pushed him in front, like a shield.

"If anyone in there has a gun, you're taking the first round."

Youngblood tilted his head and sighed deeply. "I swear there's no one in there."

Jack drew his pistol, keeping it close to his side. With his left hand, Jack grabbed a handful of Youngblood's shirt. Colfax followed, covering Jack's flank.

They entered a modest nook that led to a small kitchen, living room to the right, boxes scattered over a hardwood floor the color of pale beer. There was an overstuffed couch, a Barco-lounger, and two wooden dining chairs. Everything looked recycled from a second-hand store.

"Police!" Colfax called out.

"I told you I'm the only one. Cooper's not here."

Jack pushed Youngblood down the hallway and through two bedrooms and a bathroom.

The house was clear. Nothing. No sign Jessica Baker had ever been there.

During their search, Jack found a rental agreement in the kitchen under the name of Charles Petersen. Jack figured an alias for Monroe. Dools ran Monroe's name through DMV and came up with only the Southern California address. Two hundred and fifty hits on Charles Petersen, but none listed to this place.

They returned to the living room and sat Youngblood on the couch. Jack grabbed one of the wooden dining chairs and placed it in front of him; Colfax fell into the Barco-lounger.

"Okay," Jack said as he removed his ballistic vest and stood it by Youngblood's feet. "Where's the girl?"

Youngblood shook his bowed head. "I don't know. Cooper's the only one that knows."

"Then tell me where I can find Cooper."

"I've been waiting for Alvie to show up for two days now." Youngblood sank into the couch. There was a bit of hesitation in his voice, like he was struggling to find the right words. "This is his place, sort of. He told me that it belonged to a friend. Guy named Monroe."

"You ever meet Monroe?"

Youngblood shook his head. "No. I spoke to Alvie two days ago, at night. He asked me to meet him back here at the house. He told me Monroe was dead."

"Is that why you're using his bank card?" Jack asked.

Youngblood closed his eyes and exhaled. "Cooper left it for me. Said I could use it if I needed money."

Colfax leaned in. "I'm lost. You're a friend of Cooper, you're crashing in a dead man's house, you use his bankcard, and yet you're saying you had nothing to do with Monroe's death or the kidnapping of Jessica Baker?" Colfax spat on the floor. "Bullshit."

"Look, let me explain." Youngblood shifted his weight, pushing himself up to sit taller. "It's been over a week since I received an e-mail from Cooper. Out of the blue, there it was."

Jack asked, "Prior to that, when was the last time you two spoke?"

"It's been over five years. Before he murdered his family. After that incident, I wanted nothing to do with him."

"So why'd he reach out to you after all this time."

Youngblood shrugged. "I can't say. We were best friends for a long time. Traveled together, shared a room. Alvie came to our house right after he returned from his trip to Europe. Found his mother had died and needed a place to live. So he moved in, gets a job and we became friends. We traveled, did things together. Then, sometime during one of our trips, I found out something about him. He started acting really weird, scary. I don't know, he just freaked me out."

Colfax spoke. "You travel with him to Seattle back in '89?"

Youngblood wouldn't look at Colfax.

"I asked you a question, Eric. Were you there with Cooper?"

"You want to know if I had anything to do with that dead girl? The one you found in the church?"

"Bingo."

"Nothing!" Youngblood shot back without a moment's pause. "I had nothing to do with that girl's death. It was Alvie. Alvie kidnapped her and killed her. That's why I didn't want to have anything to do with him. That's why I asked him to leave. Leave my uncle's house and get as far away from us as he possibly could."

"I don't buy it." Colfax hovered over Youngblood, shoving a finger in his face. "Don't lie to me. You either tell me the truth now or you won't have to worry about being extradited back to Washington because I'll kick the shit out of you myself."

"I swear I had nothing to do with that girl's death."

Jack reached up and gently placed a hand on Colfax's arm, then slid his chair, up close and personal with Youngblood. "Eric," he said calmly, "you got five—strike that—you got two minutes to tell us what you know or you'll be looking at murder charges in Seattle and possible kidnapping charges here."

"The girl, the one in Seattle, I didn't kill her." Youngblood's lips tightened into a straight line. "I was there when Alvie met her at Pike Place. We were looking for a bar that would let us in. She was in front of a restaurant with another friend. We talked for a bit and, the next thing I know, she's following us around."

Colfax lowered his voice. "Her name is Grace Holloway."

"What about the friend?" Jack asked.

Youngblood shook his head. "Left after an hour or so. I don't remember. All I know was her friend was gone and that Grace girl was tagging alongside of us."

"So far you're with him and her," Colfax said. "Sounds like conspiracy to me."

"It's not like that. We spent the rest of the night bouncing between bars, getting kicked out of some, left alone in others. At first, we didn't know she was sixteen. She looked older. By the time the sun started to rise, we were driving south toward Renton. Grace wanted to take us to this abandoned building, said she liked hanging there because it gave her time away from her mom and dad, you know, maybe smoke some weed. A place to think. Alvie started acting like he's real interested in her well being but I guessed he was only trying to get in her pants."

"What about you? You want to get into her pants too?"

Youngblood's face wrinkled like taking in a bad smell. "Fuck no. I wasn't going to screw a minor and get my ass thrown in jail. I'm not that stupid."

"But Alvie is?"

"I don't know and I don't care. I'm not his mother. Besides, things were already going south between us. I really didn't care *what* he wanted to do. I just wanted to get away."

"So what happened next?"

"We made our way back to Tacoma, where we found a cheap motel. I told Alvie to leave me there and those two took off on their own. They disappeared for the day. I couldn't go anywhere because I had no wheels. I was bouncing off the walls until Alvie came back early evening, this time by himself. I asked him, 'Where's the girl' and he told me she wasn't worth his time."

"What did he mean by that?"

Youngblood closed his eyes. "I pushed him for an explanation and he kept laughing like it was some kind of joke. Said he got aggravated and left her to die."

"In those words?" Jack asked. 'Left her to die?'"

"Yeah. It wasn't long after that I saw the TV stations broadcasting the story of the missing girl and her photo. Then they found her body."

"Why didn't you do something?" Colfax demanded.

Youngblood shook his head emphatically. "I didn't know where she was. I kept yelling, trying to get Alvie to tell me if it was that abandoned building, but he laughed at me, said that would be the first place everyone would look, so he took her somewhere else. A place no one knew about, including me. I pressed him for the location but he wouldn't tell me. He said she was a pain and needed to die."

"Why didn't you go to the police?"

Youngblood rolled his eyes. "Look what you guys are suspecting me of right now. Alvie told me that because we were all together, we were both responsible for her death. Said if he fell on the murder, so would I." Youngblood bit down hard on his lower lip. "I got scared. I didn't know what else to do but to go along with it and get the hell out of Seattle."

"So if you two had a falling out," Jack asked, "why did he reach out to you now?"

"Said he wanted to talk. Said he was getting out and needed help. I told him no. After a few e-mails and a couple of phone calls, he started threatening me by bringing up the Grace Holloway murder. I had to meet with him."

"You got a phone number or an e-mail that he's using right now?"

"I got a number, his cell."

"Give it to me," Jack said.

Youngblood recited the number, looking over at Jack's notebook to make sure he got it right.

"I left him a message on it today so I know it's still good. Do you want me to call him now?"

Jack thought about it, then shook his head. "Let's wait until we get the phone tapped."

Colfax stood up and thumbed toward the door. "I'll call Hoskin with the number and get started on tracing it. You finish up here."

"He told me he took another girl," Youngblood continued. "I couldn't believe it."

"Why is he doing this?"

"He's looking for a family," Youngblood said. "And he's starting with a daughter."

"He killed his last daughter."

"I can't tell you why that happened. I can just tell you that he's looking for a replacement. It isn't sexual. He told me. He wants a family again and to settle down." Youngblood laughed. "Like he could settle down after everything he's done."

"You knew he kidnapped a girl and never came to law enforcement with that information?"

"He was threatening me with Grace Holloway!"

Jack made a tight fist and jammed it in front of Youngblood's face. Youngblood pulled back as far as he could. "You better hope she's still alive, for your sake."

"That's why I came here. To find her and put an end to this mess."

"And how were you going to do that?"

"I came here to get him to tell me where the girl was."

"Then what?"

Youngblood paused. "I was going to get her back. Alive."

"What makes you think Cooper would let that happen?"

"I wasn't going to give him any options." Youngblood spoke in a voice filled with no doubts. "I was going to make him tell me. Then, I was going to kill him."

38

Marquez sat at her office desk, scribbled in her notebook after reading the last pages in one of Cooper's journals. She had jotted down a few items of interest, hoping they would help her learn more about him. She turned her neck to stretch out the stiffness, glancing toward where Sizemore was sitting. He too was mulling over Cooper's paperwork, concentrating on the letters.

"You find anything?" she asked him, yawning.

Sizemore frowned and shook his head. "Nothing Jack hadn't already mentioned, but I'm not even close to finishing." He flicked the stack of letters with a gloved hand, the papers sliding down into a pile.

Marquez pitched open the next journal and began to read.

Five pages in, Marquez's eyes began to burn. Between the small print and ranting diatribes, she needed a break. Or at least some coffee. At the pot, she poured herself a cup and pulled her cell to check messages. Nothing. Marquez was surprised not to hear from Homer. He called more than her mother. She rang him again but got only his voicemail.

"Lets go for a ride," she called to Sizemore.

"Where to?"

"Check up on my informant."

Marquez pulled up to the Bureau security gate in the Chevy Tahoe and waited for the slider to roll open and let her out.

"Do you give all your informants this much attention?" Sizemore asked.

Marquez shook her head. "Homer's different. He wants to be a cop. He's very loyal. Given a task, he'll go after it like a dog gnawing a bone."

The Tahoe lurched forward, squeezing between the steel fence and the moving gate, onto the main road. Marquez placed a call to Jack. Voicemail. She left a message she was heading over to Homer's and to call, then closed the phone, took in a deep breath and tried to calm her nerves.

Ten minutes later, Marquez was pointing out the driver's side window toward a large apartment complex in a nearly abandoned section just off the freeway.

Sizemore nodded. "Looks pretty quiet.

"Out here, no one calls the police unless there's a dead body."

Marquez pulled out her cell, speed-dialed Homer and got his voicemail again. "Hey, I'm here. See you in a second."

She found a spot near Homer's building. Moving toward his apartment, Marquez sensed something wasn't right. She hoped she was wrong.

39

O'Rourke's lot was empty except for Blunt's 1996 Chrysler LeBaron. Colfax walked him to his car, all the while talking and poking a finger. Blunt never looked up as he jammed a key into the door. Colfax reached into his jacket, pulled out his business card and passed it along, Blunt taking it like he didn't know what to do with it.

Jack intended to keep Youngblood close by. As soon as they got a pen register and a trap and trace on Cooper's phone, the plan was to put in a call to Cooper, lure him out. Jack needed his boss's help so he rang Frank Porter, who got the cell phone trackers online, tech agents with boxes of computers and antennas that allowed them to chase cell phone signals to within fifty feet of their location, out and running. Jack hoped Cooper would be in custody before long.

Youngblood slouched in the rear of the car, head tilted all the way back, rumbling an arrhythmic snore. Before they left Monroe's house, Jack tried to convince Youngblood that killing Cooper wouldn't help clear his name of the Grace Holloway murder; in fact, it would make matters worse. Youngblood reluctantly admitted he wasn't sure he had it in him to kill Cooper anyway; he was frustrated and at his wit's end. But that didn't change his opinion that Cooper needed to die.

Waiting for Colfax, Jack listened to his voicemail and caught Marquez's message. He called her back but she didn't pick up. "Tag. You're it." He hung up just when Colfax made it back to the car.

"Just got a call from Marquez," Jack said to him, then peered over at Youngblood to make sure he was still asleep. He dropped his voice. "She's over at her informant's."

"Everything all right?"

Jack felt uneasy. "I hope so."

"What do you want to do?"

"We better get out to Homer's," Jack said.

Jack hit Interstate 5 South, calling Marquez again to let her know they'd be there soon. When she didn't pick up, he immediately dialed Hoskin.

"How're we doing on the trap and trace?"

"The company phone is Meridian Cellular. We're having a problem getting a hold of the night duty rep. I'm hoping we can get the phone up in an hour."

Jack ground his teeth. "We've got a missing girl, Chris. An hour is too long."

Hoskin's voice was apologetic. "We'll do the best we can."

"Call me as soon as the pen register is live." Jack hung up.

He looked down at his watch: 6:03 a.m. The sun was rising, temperature already starting to climb. According to Jack's calculations, Jessica Baker had been missing for almost forty-eight hours, long past when a non-ransom kidnapping victim usually survives. Usually. The word punctuated his thoughts, as if statistics, numbers, and opinions made a difference. The only thing that mattered was getting Cooper to bite on a pretext phone call. One call. One chance. Jack worried he may not get a second if Cooper suspected Youngblood of cooperating. If that happened, Cooper would disappear and the chances of finding Jessica Baker would fade with him.

The freeway reader board read: Truxel 4 1/2 Mile. Jack swung the car three lanes over, setting himself up for a quick exit. The vehicle decelerated from 90 mph, before entering the steep off-ramp, bending north, Youngblood waking from his slumber. He rubbed the stubble on his face, then glanced out both sides of the car.

"Where are we?" Youngblood asked, groggily.

"We're heading to a friend's house. When we get there, you stay in the car."

Youngblood didn't respond.

They were still fifteen minutes away from Homer Landley's apartment complex. The car went quiet, everyone waiting for something to happen. The silence broke when Jack's cell phone buzzed. Hoskin.

"You're pen is up and running. We should have triangulation on the cell as soon as you put in your call."

"Who's the subscriber on the cell phone?"

"A bogus address and name. Monthly prepaid. The phone's off right now. I'll let you know if Cooper turns it on or if he places any calls."

After he hung up, Jack turned to Colfax and relayed the news.

Colfax reached down and pulled up his black nylon tactical bag. "If what you are telling me about Cooper is true, he's one dangerous asshole." He rummaged inside for a moment and removed two .45 caliber magazines. He slid the two side-by-side and tapped the top edges against his palm, making sure the rounds were properly seated.

"If he doesn't cooperate," Colfax said, "Cooper isn't leaving unless it's in a body bag."

40

Marquez stepped into a shallow puddle of water. The sprinklers were running early in the morning to keep the heat from sucking it all up before the ground could soak it in. She pointed down the walkway toward Homer's unit.

Sizemore reached behind his lower back, making sure he had his handcuffs, then checked his double magazine pouch and knocked on his undercover ballistic vest.

Marquez crept along the pathway, Sizemore following five feet back, watching for suspicious activity through the tall hedges. Approaching the fork, Marquez peered in the opposite direction, away from Homer's unit. Moths and insects fluttered and buzzed in chaotic patterns, illuminated by lamppost light, and patches of leafy green melted into a black backdrop that daylight was unable to penetrate. Marquez concentrated on these areas, searching for movement. Seeing nothing, she headed toward Homer's. Fifteen yards from his apartment door, she stopped. His lights were off, curtains hung askew, blinds bent and hanging at an unnatural 45-degree angle. Sizemore came up from behind.

"Where's your boy?"

She didn't have an answer. Marquez pulled her phone from her hip and dialed Homer once again. Still nothing.

Sizemore pointed at the front porch light. "Let's go check it out." He stepped in front of Marquez but she held him back.

Her brow wrinkled and her mouth fell opened. "Something's wrong."

"What?"

"I don't know. I just got a weird feeling."

"He's probably cowering in the corner with a steak knife after what he just went through."

Marquez paused a moment. "Maybe you're right." She stood straight and moved closer.

The door was ajar, giving her a partial view of the interior. She angled up and pushed it open, exposing the kitchen and a wooden dining table, where Homer sat, hands stacked atop one another. Homer faced Marquez but his eyes were rolled skyward, transfixed and dull.

"Are you all right?" Marquez asked as she crossed the entryway.

Homer didn't respond. Marquez slowed.

His body remained still for another second before it fell forward, his head slamming hard on the table; blood leaked from the back of his neck. A thin rod capped by a wooden handle protruded from the base of his skull, the shape of a screwdriver or an ice pick. Marquez jumped back, bumping hard into Sizemore, who had already drawn his weapon. She tried to adjust her eyes to the dark room but it was too late. She was shoved off balance. A gunshot rang out and Sizemore grunted in pain. She turned but could only capture blurry movements, a struggle behind her, heavy bodies slamming against the front door, then onto the floor. Two more shots rang out, the air lighting up white.

Marquez screamed, "Ray!"

Sizemore howled filled with agony.

"Ray!"

Marquez could make out the tussling of bodies, uncertain who was who. She had no choice but to turn and dive into the fray and find out. Dropping to her knees, she slid out her ASP baton, slinging it to full length. She squinted and strained to see, then leapt and threw the baton over the assailant's neck and yanked hard, raking the bar across his Adam's apple, then eased up on her stranglehold just a hair—if this was Cooper, she needed him alive to find Jessica Baker. She applied just enough pressure to peel him away from Sizemore. But the man was strong, and she felt his weight shift to her left, driving her almost directly underneath him. This was bad. Marquez kicked out her legs, tried to gain leverage, then hooked her arm under the handle and squeezed the steel bar like a vice against his throat. The man grunted, resisting. A surge of energy from her attacker and he had broken free. He struck the side of her head, neck snapping to the left, head rung. Another strike and Marquez lost the baton. She reached for her weapon, pushing it forward and squeezing the trigger. A loud pop and another grunt. She cried again, this time in a weaker voice. "Ray."

She heard moans, more struggling.

Her vision started to fade. She was losing consciousness.

Then there was a final bright flash as another gunshot rang out.

41

Jack closed his cell phone as he pulled into Homer's apartment complex. He had left three messages for Marquez and gotten no response. Youngblood was reaching for the handle of the car when Jack turned.

"You're not going anywhere," Jack said, then turned to Colfax. "Cuff him."

Colfax took out a pair of cuffs and secured it to Youngblood's right wrist, the other side to a steel bar bolted to the back seat that's used for prisoner transport.

"Am I under arrest?"

Jack shot Youngblood a quick glance. "I'll let you know when I get back."

With Youngblood restrained, the pair exited the car and moved forward together, side by side, scanning for any signs of Marquez or Sizemore. In front of Homer's apartment, a man stood by the front door. Dangling from his right hand was a gun.

Both Jack and Colfax crouched down and drew their weapons.

"Freeze!" Jack yelled. Colfax sidestepped to his right, trying to get another angle in case it turned into a firefight. Jack continued to advance slowly. He didn't want the man diving into the apartment and gaining the advantage of cover. The man's eyes bulged out, glaring at Jack and Colfax.

"FBI! Drop your weapon now!"

The man's hands started to rise. Jack slid his finger into the trigger housing and leveled his sights squarely on the man's chest.

The man's hand started up but the gun, a shiny chrome revolver, fell to the ground. It bounced before settling into the shrubs by entryway path. He raised his hands high over his head. "Don't shoot. Please don't shoot."

Jack shuffled forward, covered by Colfax. He spun the man around, grabbed him by the back of his T-shirt and pushed him against the wall. He holstered his weapon and pulled out his handcuffs, securing the man from behind.

"I got him," Jack said to Colfax, as he dragged his prisoner backward and away from the front door, forcing the man to his haunches before he drew his weapon again, pointing toward the entrance. Colfax dropped low, skidding up to the frame. He clicked on his flashlight and shined it into the apartment.

"I got movement inside." Colfax's voice was low and authoritative. Jack dragged his prisoner backward to a metal bench situated near the path, and with another set of cuffs latched him to the sturdy steel frame.

"Stay here," Jack commanded.

Colfax aimed his weapon into the dark. "Show me your hands."

A moment of silence, then rustling.

"Hold your fire. It's me, Marquez. I'm coming out."

Jack lowered the muzzle of his gun and Colfax did the same.

Marquez stumbled to the doorway, bleeding from the left side of her head, her hair tossed and the sleeve of her blouse torn loose. Jack holstered his weapon and ran to her side. She fell against the door jamb, her whole body shaking. Jack tapped Colfax on the back as he ran past to let him know he was clearing his right side, and Colfax followed to provide cover.

"What the hell happened? Are you all right?" Jack tried to be calm but his voice was tense. He slid Marquez's right arm around his neck and guided her out toward the bench where the suspect was handcuffed. Marquez sat beside him and sighed.

"Shit! He almost killed us, Jack." She rubbed the sides of her temples with both hands, keeping her stare toward the pavement.

"Can you cut me loose now?"

Marquez looked over at the man on the ground. "Oh God, cut him loose."

Jack looked at Marquez, then down at his prisoner.

Marquez waved a hand. "He's the neighbor."

"I'm Carl," the man said. "I heard screaming so I ran over to see what was going on. It was over by the time I got here."

Jack bent down and peered into Marquez's eyes. "Are you okay?"

Marquez grabbed his arm and she squeezed her eyes shut. She didn't say anything.

"Where's Ray?" Jack asked.

Marquez pointed at the apartment. "I think he's hurt."

Jack uncuffed Carl and dusted him off with a quick apology, then ran back to the apartment. By this time, Colfax had turned the lights on and cleared the living room. The place had been ransacked. Furniture busted, pieces scattered throughout the room. Crimson ran up and down the hallway wall in bold streaks, blood from someone being jacked up and violently tossed around. Colfax stood over Sizemore, who was lying on his back in the living room, his right arm over his chest, covering a hole oozing bright red, his white shirt soaked in blood. Sizemore had taken a round through his shoulder, and was trying to stay focused through the pain.

"I called for an ambulance and back up," Colfax said. "He's lost a lot of blood but I think he'll be all right." Then he pointed up toward the table. "I can't say the same for your informant."

Homer lay face down on the table, blood dripping from the edge of the chair, a large circle pooled around his feet.

Colfax studied the blade protruding from the back of Homer's neck, and shook his head. "Looks like a leather punch stuck right through."

"This guy likes to make his killings up close and personal," Jack said.

Colfax knelt down, studied Homer's body, his placement. He peered under the table. "I got something."

Jack slipped on a pair of latex gloves and knelt next to Colfax. Wedged under the table was a small booklet. A notebook. Jack reached for it, careful to avoid the blood still dripping from Homer's neck.

Jack flipped through the pages, then looked up at Colfax. "It's one of Cooper's journals."

42

It took seven minutes for the ambulance to arrive but another five before the medics approached the apartment. The fire department's protocol was to wait until the area was cleared of any danger. Colfax told them that the attacker had left but the shift captain insisted on waiting until a patrol unit met with Jack and gave the all clear. The medics started Sizemore on a large bore IV but he refused any meds for the pain. Marquez suffered several lacerations and a hard blow to the head. The medics suggested the ER for a PET scan. She refused. Homer didn't have an option. He was placed in a body bag and transported to the county morgue. Hoskin and nine ERT agents arrived to conduct a crime scene examination, briefed by Marquez while the medics examined her.

Although physically sound, it was visible to Jack that Marquez was mentally shaken. She kept on repeating she should have listened to her gut instincts, knowing something wasn't right. Periodically, Marquez would slam her fist against the bench, exploding in anger before shifting into a well of grief and tears. Her anxiousness to track down Cooper almost got her and Sizemore killed.

A medic knelt beside her, stethoscope hanging loosely around his neck. He rubbed her arm softly. "You're going to be all right and so is your partner," he said. But she refused to look up, tears falling to her lap.

Squeaky wheels and rattling metal drew Jack's attention back to the apartment, where EMTs maneuvered a gurney down the narrow pathway, Sizemore lying on top, his upper torso covered in a white blanket. Jack tried to catch Marquez's eyes. They were closed, her head resting in her palms.

"I'm going to go check on Ray," Jack told her.

She nodded.

Jack made a b-line to Sizemore, who was strapped down on the gurney, his eyes closed. Cables from a portable three lead ECG were taped in place and a liter bag of saline was held high by an attending medic. A nasal cannula crowded under his nose, the clear fluoropolymer tubing hissing from an O2 tank cranked high up. Jack trailed as the medics wheeled him to a waiting ambulance.

Jack tapped the gurney railing, and his wedding ring clanged against the chrome bar. "Doc says you'll be okay."

Sizemore opened an eye, rolled his head toward Jack. "I know he's hurt."

"You think you hit him?"

Sizemore nodded. "Got off several rounds. I think so, but I can't be sure."

"Any idea what happened?"

"We got here before he had a chance to leave."

Cooper was probably waylaid looking for his lost notebook. Somehow Homer must have gotten it from him and wedged it under the table to hide it. Good plan. Bad timing.

If Sizemore was right, Cooper would be bleeding heavily and in need of medical attention. Cooper would never go to an emergency room; all gunshot wounds were reported to the police. He thought for a moment before placing a call to Frank Porter, asking him to have the surrounding drug and liquor stores canvassed for anyone matching Cooper's description. If they got lucky, Cooper would need a lot of alcohol to numb the pain and supplies to bandage his wounds. Patrol officers were instructed to keep a close eye out for any abandoned vehicles, as well.

Back at Jack's car, Youngblood was leaning out the rear passenger window, his right wrist still secured to the metal bar. He blew out a cloud of cigarette smoke before flicking the butt to the ground. Youngblood gave a nod as Jack approached.

Jack glanced at the parking lot filled with lights glowing bright red on their windshields. The morning sun had risen above the horizon and the heat was already pushing the mercury far above comfortable. He was starting to wonder if the summer heat would ever break.

A handful of agents shuffled through the maze of bodies and vehicles, sweating in their all-white Tyvek coveralls. Another group in dark blue windbreakers, FBI – Evidence Response Team in bold yellow lettering, stood talking and pointing in every direction. The scene bordered on chaos.

"He knows you're on to him," Youngblood said. "You know what he's going to do?" He squinted into the bright morning sun and spat out the rear window.

"He's going to change his identity again, isn't he?"

"Agent Paris, I'm not telling you how to do your job, but no one knows Alvie better than me."

"What's your point?"

"You got one option to stop this guy."

Jack remained silent.

Youngblood pulled tobacco from his teeth, gave it a look of disappointment and then spat again. "You're going to need me to deliver him to you."

43

Marquez sat in Jack's car, looking out the window, remaining quiet. Colfax took Youngblood in tow, following Jack back to the off-site in Marquez's Tahoe. Jack reached out and gave her a gentle touch, just to remind her he was there. She looked up with an appreciative nod before turning away to lean her head against the side window. The glass fogged each time she exhaled.

Jack turned around with his right arm over the front seat as he maneuvered in reverse. He considered taking Marquez to the office and leaving her with another agent, not wanting to add any undue stress.

"Why don't I take you—" he started to say,

Marquez's hand shot in front of his face.

He took the hint and kicked the air conditioner on high, accelerating back to the off-site.

Fifteen minutes put them around the corner, Jack's Crown Vic in the lead, Colfax in the Tahoe directly behind him. Jack slowed, pulled out his cell phone and called Colfax.

"What's up?"

Jack rolled down his window and pointed out to his left. "Take a spin around the back side. I'll go the opposite direction and meet you there."

"What am I looking for?" Colfax asked.

"Someone who may want to kill us."

It was clear Cooper didn't have any problem hunting down Homer or going after FBI agents and cops. He'd drawn a line in the sand the minute he tried to kill Marquez and Sizemore. Now it was time for Jack to cross it.

The two vehicles cruised the block but spotted nothing out of the ordinary. Porter had sent three agents to secure the perimeter in case Cooper was planning on coming later. Other cars were starting to fill the parking lot, employees from businesses within the complex. Jack eyed each suspiciously, and entered the office, the air conditioner whirring loudly.

Colfax held a hand up to the vent on the wall that divided the front reception area from the back, wiggling his fingers, feeling the cool air filter through them. "Man, it's hot here," he said.

Jack pinned the thermostat as far to the left as it would go, then walked over to his desk and dropped a full evidence bag on the table. Marquez, across the way, sat staring at the package.

"Is that the notebook?" she asked.

"Found it under the table next to Homer's lap."

"Why didn't Cooper take the book?"

"I'm guessing he dropped it when he first attacked Homer, realized it was missing and tried to beat it out of him."

"Only Homer didn't give it up."

"He must've hid it under the table. You and Sizemore got there before Cooper could find it."

"If Homer just gave him back the book, maybe he would be alive to tell us what happened."

Jack shook his head. "Cooper wouldn't have been that generous."

Jack slid on a pair of gloves and took the notebook from the plastic bag, filtering through the pages. Colfax stood next to him. The room stayed quiet, the only sound coming from the grind of the air conditioner and the turning of each page. Near the end of the notebook, Jack encountered a single message that appeared different from the rest. It read "Rabbit Hole," with an arrow pointing to a crude drawing of an envelope. The words were worn, as though written first. Jack stared at the entry, tapping a pencil on a separate notebook.

"Rabbit hole," he repeated. "Like a hiding place."

Colfax glanced at Youngblood, who was leaning against a dividing wall, not paying attention. He appeared startled when Colfax called his name.

"You know anything about any . . . rabbit hole?"

Youngblood's jaw dropped.

Colfax curved an eyebrow.

Youngblood hesitated. "Yeah, I know about a rabbit hole."

He walked over to where Jack sat, bent at the waist and gazed down at the notebook. Without touching it, his finger glided above the page. "I haven't used it since before the time Alvie went to jail."

Jack cocked his head toward Youngblood. "What is it?"

"It's an old e-mail account," Youngblood replied. "Not the one he recently contacted me from. I thought he stopped using this one after he went to prison." Youngblood rolled back an empty office chair and sat down. "Before Alvie got arrested for the murder of his wife and kid, he started communicating with me by writing messages in his e-mail account."

Jack responded, "You mean from his e-mail account."

"No. The thing was, Alvie was scared the police were monitoring his e-mail. Like a wiretap. He was so paranoid, he told me never to write or call him. Just use the rabbit hole."

"You just said he didn't want you to communicate with him. Wouldn't that include e-mailing?"

"That would include *sending* an e-mail. Alvie said if there was something important that I needed to talk to him about, I should access his e-mail account, write an e-mail and save it in his draft folder. He created the Rabbit Hole just for our contacts. They were never sent."

Colfax tapped a finger on his forehead. "I don't get it."

Marquez chimed in. "There is a difference. By not sending the e-mail, the message never makes its way over Internet where it may be intercepted. By writing a message and saving it in the draft folder, the message never leaves the Internet provider's server. Kind of like being parked. Youngblood simply draws up the message left in the draft file, reads it, then writes his own message back, leaving that one in the draft file for Alvin Cooper to read. No e-mails floating in cyberspace, no lost messages hanging in other people's e-mails to be read. And deleting them would prevent the message from ever being retrieved."

Youngblood nodded. "It was his way of keeping contact with his close friends hidden and private."

"Hence the reference 'The Rabbit Hole,'" Jack interjected.

"Do you think you can still access his account?" Colfax asked.

Jack was thinking the same thing. Bait. Better than a phone call.

"That was over five years ago," Youngblood said. "I have no idea if he still has the same account."

Marquez rolled her chair to another table, where an undercover computer rested in sleep mode. She shook the mouse and it sputtered to life. Marquez hooked a finger at Youngblood. "Let's find out."

44

For the past hour, Jessica Baker's eyelids fluttered open and shut. She remembered a dark and empty room void of sound or movement. Then she saw a window with shafts of gold and yellow light filtering through a dirty curtain. Then she was back in the dark. Different times, different places. She was being moved, but where? There was no way to know how much time had passed during those brief moments of consciousness. But for each of them she was conscious. She was still alive.

Jessica shifted, arms and legs bound from behind, trying to find a position to stop the pain radiating up her back. A short rope ran along her spine and connected her wrists to her ankles, keeping her from standing, contact points rubbing the skin raw and numb. She managed to cope with her cramped legs, but her head was in a bleary haze from a combination of stress and fear, and the lack of insulin was making her panic. She tried repeatedly to convince herself that this was all just a bad dream. But she couldn't.

As she rolled to her left side, perspiration dripping down her forehead, the air in the room hot and heavy with the smell of dust, her body pressed deep into a pile of clothes, rags on top of some kind of dirty cushion left flat on the floor. It reeked of age. Whatever she was lying on, it hugged close to her skin, damn near suffocating her; it didn't allow her body heat to dissipate, causing her to swelter

217

in a slick pool of sweat. She was so tired and dazed, she didn't much care.

Jessica noticed a thin strip radiating beyond her ankles, and she tried to focus her blurry vision. The glow became clearer. A gap between the bottom edge of a door and the hardwood floor. She tilted her head upward, eyes following the dark seam of the doorframe. Halfway up she spotted a pinpoint glimmer of reflective light bouncing off a curved surface. A brass doorknob. Suddenly Jessica felt a spark of hope. If she could get to the handle, maybe she could find her way out. She paused and listened for her captor but only heard the sound of her own heartbeat and labored breath. Straining to hear over the noise, searching for any signs of life on the other side of the door, she sucked a lungful of air, then forced her legs as straight as possible, pushing against the door. It bowed, allowing a sliver of white to filter around the edges. She tried it again, but it would not give. She realized she didn't have the power to kick it open. The energy needed was more than she had and she was growing weaker by the minute.

If she could gain more leverage, more extension, perhaps she could pop the latch. Jessica spotted a tarp slung over a pile of junk three feet high. Unable to use her hands, she lurched forward with her jaw, biting down on the edge of it, and yanked her head back. She rocked, trying to gain enough momentum to roll off the stacks of clothing. The tarp pulled partially away, revealing a small collection of framed paintings and photos, which tilted, then tumbled onto Jessica's face. The weight of the frames and glass pinned the tarp over her nose and mouth, causing her to cry out. Jessica struggled, flailing, fighting to shake the tarp from her face so that she could breathe. She twisted and broke free of the heavy objects. The glass in the frames cracked in thick fissures across the artwork, and her body fell still, exhausted and limp.

Jessica squeezed her eyes closed, her jaw tight. Tears steamed from her face, rolling off her left cheek and onto the dusty hardwood floor.

She lay still for a few minutes, waiting for something to happen. To be rescued. For her captor to come get her. To just die. Her eyes, now adjusted to the darkness, fell upon one of the framed photos, broken, leaning sideways against the wall. It was a black and white of a small town gas station, probably taken in the early '40s judging by the bulbous round cars and men wearing fedoras standing around antique gas pumps. Then she noticed her reflection, her face fractured into sections, divided by the cracks. Broken glass with sharp, jagged edges. Good enough to cut through rope.

With a single kick, she smashed the glass. Most of it shattered into small pieces, too small to use for cutting, but one piece, in the shape of a dagger, lay flat on the floor, large enough for Jessica to get her hands around. She rolled over, slid her body over the shards, feeling for the larger piece. Glass dug into her skin with every push of her feet, searing, stabbing pain, but she didn't care. Her fingers fished blindly. Finally, she felt the long, sharp edge. Her dagger.

Her heart raced, and she found it difficult to breathe. She started to cry, unsure if it was from joy or fear. Carefully, she pressed the bindings between her wrists across the glass, and started to move it up and down. The glass slid easily over the rope, but ten frantic minutes later, the rope still held. Jessica wanted to continue but she had nothing left. Completely drained of energy, she let her hands fall limply to the floor, both of them void of any feeling, body sagged and softened like a setting fog. Her mind wandered, spinning off, away from her ugly reality. She fantasized about warm summer days, playing basketball, doing homework, lying lazily by the pool. In the darkened room, Jessica closed her eyes and drew a broad smile, mind floating in a daydream. As the seconds ticked away, Jessica started to feel the warmth of the room engulf her, more embrace than strangulation. Her breathing slow, she felt a flush, like a chilled body dipped into a warm bath. She could taste her breath. It was sweet. She'd felt like this before. It was the feeling of her body shutting down, falling into ketoacidotic shock, a diabetic coma. Jessica Baker knew she was dying, and she felt relieved.

45

The three investigators hovered over Youngblood, who had been briefed on what to say—but it would still be up to him how to say it. Bait Cooper out into the open and hopefully lead the team to where Jessica Baker was being held. That was the goal. It had been two days since her abduction, and with each passing minute without her meds, Jack lost a little more hope of finding her alive.

Youngblood typed in the web address, then punched in Cooper's username and password. The inbox was empty and there was nothing in the trash. But it was valid. Youngblood sat back and threw his hands in the air.

"I fucking can't believe it. It's still active."

Jack thinned his lips into a tight smile. "We're one for one. Let's see if he's still looking at his messages."

Youngblood took a moment and thought about what to say, fingers resting on the keyboard without making a move. Then he started typing his message, pausing, backtracking, trying to get it just right. The last thing he wanted to do was make Cooper suspicious.

Alvie, Youngblood started. *Your phone's off and I've been waiting at the house all day without hearing from you. I can only think you're in trouble. I ran out of ideas on how to contact you. This was the last. If you*

are in trouble, reply and I'll come get you. I'm on the move in case they
know about me.

Youngblood removed his fingers from the keys and looked back at Jack, waiting for approval.

Jack studied the message, then nodded. "I guess it's as good as any."

"What do we do next?" Youngblood asked.

"Wait."

The command post buzzed and the Chico PD, in conjunction with the FBI, had teams of officers and agents scouring every inch of the area. But the waiting was killing Jack.

"Eric, why do you really think Cooper killed his family?" Marquez asked.

Youngblood shook his head and grimaced. "I wish I knew. Something he was hiding, that his wife may have found out about?"

"Something worth killing your wife and child over?" Marquez's tone was filled with disgust.

"He killed that Holloway girl. That's pretty bad. Maybe she discovered that, and that's what drove him to kill again."

"How would she have learned about Grace Holloway?" Jack asked.

Again, Youngblood shook his head. "Who knows? I told you, I had very little contact with him until he reached out to me after he murdered his family. Between those times, I can only imagine he had made other friends that shared his interests."

"Like killing young girls?" The question was rhetorical.

Youngblood shrugged. "Look, Alvie came to us after his mother died. Before that, I didn't know him from Adam."

Jack glanced at his watch. "How long it usually take for Cooper to respond?"

"Minutes, no more than an hour. But that was years ago."

It had been over an hour. Youngblood folded his arms on the desk and settled his head on top of them with his eyes closed.

Marquez was on the phone with Jim Harrington, getting updates on tracking Cooper's cell phone and e-mail. Nothing. Jack returned to Cooper's journals, nudging Youngblood every so often to ask about a phrase or a place mentioned. Youngblood was able to give some speculation here or there, but nothing of much substance. Jack tapped Marquez on the back.

"Check the Rabbit Hole."

Marquez rolled to the undercover computer. As she launched into the website, Youngblood lifted his head and craned his neck in her direction.

Marquez leaned forward, then tapped it with a finger. "I think we got something."

46

The response to Youngblood's message was short and simple: *Where are you?*

"You think he knows we're on to him?" Marquez's voice was cautious.

Jack shook his head. "I doubt it or he wouldn't have responded." He looked back at Youngblood. "Tell him you were contacted by the police at Monroe's house and that they're accusing you of the Grace Holloway murder."

Youngblood said, "If he thinks I'm hot . . . that'll drive him away."

Jack nodded. "It could. But helping Cooper escape will ensure law enforcement can't pin the Holloway murder on you, guilty or not."

"I told you, I had nothing to do with her death."

Jack put a hand on his shoulder. "I heard you the first time. I just want to give Cooper a reason to hook up."

Colfax glanced at Youngblood and pointed a finger. "You know when we get him, he's going to implicate you in the Holloway murder, or just say you killed her."

"He can say anything he wants." There was a quiet moment, a feeling of uneasiness electrifying the room. Then Youngblood asked, "Are you saying you'd believe him?"

223

Colfax shrugged without saying a word.

Jack rapped the table gently to break the tension, and told Youngblood to craft a reply to Cooper to see if they could meet. Youngblood never shifted his focus away from Colfax, the brittleness still apparent between them.

Marquez slid her chair to help draft the response, as Jack rang Harrington to fill him in.

"I'll put a call into the server, see if they got a location where Cooper launched his e-mail."

"Push them hard, Jimmy."

In the background, Youngblood and Marquez formulated the message. It had to be short and to the point. Words were important. Too many wasted ones would certainly draw suspicion, thus killing any hopes of getting Cooper to show himself. Jack was already concerned that Cooper was aware law enforcement was on to him. He'd proven his desperation by murdering their informant and trying to off cops. It wasn't only Jack tracking Cooper now, and their killer was lashing back, eliminating anyone who got in his way. Maybe Cooper had already decided it wasn't worth the trouble keeping Jessica Baker alive. Start over with a new victim, a new target of opportunity.

"We're ready," Marquez said.

Jack nodded once. "Pull the trigger."

The message was placed in the draft box and Youngblood signed out of the e-mail account. They'd cast their imaginary fishing pole. Now they'd wait for a bite.

"He knows your hunting him," Youngblood said, breaking the silence.

"He probably does," Colfax replied, "but I'm betting he's not going to pass on your help. The heat's on and you're his only friend. At least the only one he hasn't killed yet."

Youngblood folded his arms across his chest. "You don't like me, do you?"

"I don't like people involved in killing young girls—"

"I told you—"

"*Or* those who know about the crime but choose to keep the information to themselves because they're scared."

Youngblood's gaze fell toward his lap. "I'm sorry," he said to no one in particular. Or maybe to everyone, including Grace Holloway and Jessica Baker. Colfax clenched his teeth and walked away.

Jack's cell phone vibrated. It was Harrington, his voice sounding anxious.

"Tell me something good, Jimmy."

"Jack," Harrington said. "We got a location."

47

The room at the FBI field office was filling fast with brass from every nearby agency. Harrington unfolded a large map on the conference room table and ran his hand across the heavy paper, smoothing out the folds as people crowded around, jockeying for space to get a good view. Jack stood to Harrington's right, tossing his notebook on top of the map. Against the back wall, a satellite view showcased where Cooper accessed the Internet on a wall-size, pull-down screen. Rumbling in the room grew to a moderate roar.

Jack looked around, trying to get a head count on how many people were present. "Let's get started," he said, and the room instantly grew quiet.

"For those who have not been updated," Jack continued, "we have several initiatives in the works to help locate and rescue sixteen-year-old Jessica Baker and apprehend our subject, Alvin Franklin Cooper."

The screen changed to display two photos, side-by-side, one of Baker and the other of Cooper.

"The first is a trap and trace and pen register on what we know to be Cooper's telephone." Jack gestured for Harrington's input.

"Although we're confident that the cell number belongs to Cooper," Harrington said, "the phone has been off since we went up. At this moment, we don't have a bead on him."

"We do have the server of his e-mail account monitored," Jack continued. "Not more than two hours ago, Cooper launched his e-mail on a Wi-Fi network at a Starbuck's in downtown Sacramento. Three patrol units and an FBI surveillance team were dispatched to the area. They're searching every building, park, and alleyway for Cooper. We're also looking for the last vehicle he was known to be driving." Jack held up a photo of a white Chevy pickup with a camper shell. Notepads flipped open as the attendees started hastily scrawling.

Someone in the audience raised a hand. "Has there been a demand for money?

"No demand."

A low grumble confirmed what everyone in the room knew: no ransom meant no bargaining. Which left only two possible outcomes. Either he was going to keep her. Or he was going to kill her.

"We were able to get an associate of Cooper to post a message via e-mail with the intent of drawing him out into the open. It didn't take long for Cooper to take the bait and ask for a meeting."

The screen changed, projecting an overview of Sacramento's midtown section. Rows of tightly fitted Victorians with tall evergreen and oak trees lined shaded streets just east of the town's center, gentrification making its mark with many houses expensively refurbished or converted into law offices.

"Cooper has instructed his friend to meet him tonight at Harlow's, a nightclub near 27th and J Street." Jack used a laser pointer to shine a bright red dot on the south side of J, just before the Capitol Freeway. "As most of you know, that's a busy commercial area, lined with businesses, bars, and restaurants. It's going to be busy tonight and I think that's why Cooper chose this place at this time."

Jack ran the red laser in a broad circle around the area. "We got S.O.G. staking out the outer perimeter with SWAT on stand-by just down the street in case we get him contained in a stand-off location."

A lieutenant with Sacramento PD raised a hand. "I got every detective waiting to be deployed into the area as soon as you're ready."

Jack gestured at Hoskin, who stood deep in the crowd. "Chris will meet with your team and get them updated with our best photo of Cooper and the associate he's supposed to meet."

Hoskin wedged through the crowd over to the lieutenant, where they conveyed plans before exiting the conference room together.

Jack scanned the crowd. All eyes fixed forward, waiting for direction. He leaned with both hands square on the table and checked his watch. Four p.m. Two days and approximately eight hours had passed since Jessica's abduction. With Cooper's awareness that law enforcement was in pursuit, a haunting portrait of Jessica Baker's future emerged. He thought about her condition, about the possibility of a diabetic coma. When would Cooper decide it wasn't worth keeping her alive any longer?

Between Jack and Colfax, the audience was briefed and assignments handed out. A perimeter was secured around Harlow's with a covert surveillance team. Tech agents with the cellphone tracking equipment were also deployed, circling the area in case Cooper's phone came to life. Youngblood was provided a car, a red Chevrolet Malibu. The vehicle, part of the Sacramento FBI's covert fleet, was wired for sight, sound, and GPS tracking. Youngblood himself was wired as well. If Youngblood had to pick up Cooper, Jack and the security team would be able to monitor the conversation and follow at a safe distance without getting burned during the surveillance. Hopefully, Youngblood would be able to convince Cooper to take him to where Jessica Baker was being held. At that point, Youngblood was instructed to step into view of the surveillance team, place both hands on top of his head and say, "It's a green light." Between the microphones, video feed, and surveillance, someone was going to get the cue.

The crowd started to thin as the team leaders began talking on their cell phones, informing their respective teams of their assignments. Several of the commanders stopped in front of the map, running their fingers along the street lines surrounding the meet location. The roar of the crowd returned and Jack knew this meant game on.

Colfax rapped a fist on the map. "This isn't going to be easy. Cooper's not stupid and he's certainly not going to make the same mistakes he's made in the past. His head's going to be on a swivel, and if he spots surveillance, that girl's history."

Jack nodded in agreement.

"If he meets Youngblood on foot," Colfax said, "he could take him down those alleyways to clear himself of any tail. The body transmitter is only good for a short range. He gets any distance on us, and Youngblood's on his own."

"We'll have a bird up."

Colfax shook his head. "A plane's a great asset, but it'll be night in a few hours. There's no guarantee they'll be able to keep an eye on two small figures darting in and out of the dark."

Jack knew there weren't answers to every contingency. All he could do was lay the foundation of a rescue like he had done in the past: perimeter surveillance, outer mobile surveillance, tracking system, air coverage. Tactical, negotiation and rescue teams trailing the pack. A command center was set up at the Sacramento County Sheriff's Office because it was closest to the meet location. There wasn't much else Jack could do but wait.

Jack nervously scratched the two-day-old stubble on his chin. "Where's Youngblood?"

"Harrington's got him," Colfax replied. "He's being fitted for his transmitter."

"Let's go see him. I got one more piece of insurance I want to stick on him before we cut him loose."

48

Youngblood tightened the leather belt around his waist, adjusting the buckle to face perfectly straight.

"How's that?" Youngblood pulled his hands away from his body, palms up, and aimed the shiny belt buckle directly in Harrington's line of sight.

Harrington studied Youngblood's waist. "That'll do. Just remember the mic is in the buckle. Don't cover it up or everything'll be muffled."

Youngblood's head canted down, eyes fixated on the buckle.

"Act natural. You concentrate on that transmitter too much and Cooper's going to know something's up."

Youngblood blew out a nervous breath. "Just knowing there's a microphone down there makes me feel like I have a brick stuck to my belly."

"Everyone feels that way, believe me. Just forget it's there and he's not going to find it."

Youngblood forced a smile. "He won't have to. If he suspects anything, he'll just kill me."

Harrington patted him on the shoulder. "We'll make sure that doesn't happen."

"Everything okay?" Jack asked as he walked into Harrington's office with a black duffle bag slung over his left shoulder, Colfax right behind him. Jack placed the bag on the workbench, pulled open the zipper and removed a cell phone, placing it in Youngblood's hand.

"Keep this on your hip."

Youngblood studied the phone, turning it over. "I got one already."

"This one's better."

Harrington took the phone from Youngblood, checked the battery.

"This one has a longer battery life and allows for autodial in case you're in trouble." Harrington clipped it on Youngblood's side and gave it a pat. "Just hit any key and it will call us direct. No need to dial. We'll come get you."

Jack pulled out another phone exactly like the one he gave Youngblood. "I'll be able to listen in with this one."

"I'm all choked up that you care so much for my safety," Youngblood said looking at Colfax.

"Just get him to tell you where Jessica Baker is," Colfax said. "We'll do the rest."

Jack pulled up a work stool and sat next to Youngblood.

"Eric, tonight is critical to the rescue of our victim."

"Just tell me what you want me to do."

"You're going to drive one of our undercover vehicles over to Harlow's and park around the back, just like you told Cooper. We'll have surveillance already set up to keep an eye on you."

Youngblood nodded that he understood.

"When Cooper arrives, see if you can get him inside your car to talk. It will give you both privacy, and we will be able to monitor the conversation better without the outside noises interfering."

"What if he comes in a car and asks me to get in?"

This was always a tough call. When Jack worked undercover, the rule was never to get into a target's car. It didn't allow for the security team to provide cover if the suspect decided to take a drive. And that could get an undercover killed.

"Tell him your car is safer, that you just bought the car in a false name, paid cash so the police wouldn't be able to find you."

"And if he says no?"

"Look, Eric, I can't tell you to go with him because it's too dangerous." Jack paused. "But you know him better than any of us. If you feel you can get him to take you to Jessica Backer, I'll let you make the decision."

Youngblood nodded glumly.

"I know it can be a tough but only you can make that call. You just need to convey your intent over the wire so we can respond. If you don't go, I'll still have the ability to follow him. Hopefully he'll lead us to Jessica Baker, but I can't let him get away."

Youngblood stared into Jack's eyes, before glancing quickly at Colfax, who was still shadowed in the corner. "Okay, I'll try to get him in my car. Otherwise, count on me going with him."

49

Thursday – 4:59 p.m.

The radio chatter was constant but controlled. The mobile surveillance units pointed out vehicles and suspicious individuals around Harlow's, running license plates to see if any of the cars were recently sold or reported stolen. Low light, closed-circuit cameras hidden on rooftops and inside stationary box vans observed pedestrians, people roaming the streets, hopping bar to bar.

The sun would be setting shortly but the heat was still going strong. Surveillance agents complained about the temperature inside their vans. They couldn't run the air conditioner without drawing suspicion, forced to swelter inside a metal box. Stripped down to shorts and T-shirts, they wrapped bags of ice around their necks to keep from passing out.

Jack was driving around the area in a Toyota Camry trying to stay clear of the surveillance team. Marquez kept watch out the window while nervously finger-tapping the glass. It sounded like falling rain.

"An hour or so and it will be dark," she said.

"I don't expect Cooper until it is." Jack had already instructed Youngblood to park around back of Harlow's in case Cooper showed up early. Cooper hadn't specified a time. Before the evening crowd arrived, Jack wanted Youngblood to get a good parking space, which would provide the best view for the team. An agent called over the radio that Youngblood was in the lot and out of his car, leaning against the hood having a smoke.

Marquez pushed the seek button on the radio, skipping through anything that sounded like a nuclear explosion or a cat in heat, settling on a saxophone riff, bluesy and soulful. She pitched the volume down to where it hovered just above the background noise. The melody brought a brief moment of calm, and Marquez started humming. Marquez loved music, all kinds, but found jazz most comforting.

Her eyes were closed and her humming sounded soothing but Jack saw tension around her temples and forehead. These past three days had been more than she could deal with. At least, more than music could cure. Her jaw flexed every so often, a clear sign that the stress was getting to her.

Jack's phone vibrated. He pulled it off his belt and checked the ID. His son, Michael.

"Hey, Mike. What's up?"

Jack could hear the clatter of pots and pans. "I heard you came by the other night. Why didn't you say hello?"

Jack felt a twinge of guilt. "You were in the middle of a cooking storm. Didn't want to disturb you."

"Never. Next time, come on in and I'll fix you something to eat. OK?"

Jack had to smile. In his mind, his son still couldn't even tie his shoes. Now, it was Michael who was going to take care of his father. "I'd like that, Mike."

They talked for a moment longer, Jack apologizing for having to cut it short because of work. Jack didn't go into details. Michael understood. He'd been there before. At the end of their conversation, they promised to talk again soon and Jack told Michael he loved him and to make sure he checked in on his sister and mother. "Always do," he replied. That was exactly what Jack needed to hear.

The Bureau radio crackled. An agent announced a cross street that he was going to stake out. More radio traffic, a couple of chirps, license plates checked.

"I don't think the music's working." Marquez rocked side-to-side like shaking off a restless night's sleep. The side of her head sported a bandage that covered the gash she received from her fight with Cooper earlier that morning. The drape of her hair concealed most of the wound, but the surrounding area was starting to darken into a bruise.

"How's the head?"

"Nothing that a couple of Advil and vodka couldn't cure."

She must have been feeling better.

"The Advil I can get. You're gonna have to wait on the booze until after Cooper's in custody and our girl is safely in our hands."

Marquez rolled her eyes.

Jack drove south on 25th Street until coming to a stop at J, then hooked left toward Harlow's, driving by the front to get a good look at the nightclub, the MoMo Lounge, a cocktail bar above Harlow's. Nightclub patrons could slip up the side stairs for a little more leisure. A number of Sacramento celebrities were known to frequent the MoMo. Not too long ago, an overly aggressive superstar athlete and his entourage decided to tune up a couple of the patrons. A fight turned into a brawl, which turned into gunfire. The MoMo was a concern. Another set of stairs led out the back to the parking lot where Youngblood was waiting. Cooper could easily slide undetected into the lounge and look for surveillance before ducking into any number of the unlit alleyways connected to the lot. Jack ordered additional surveillance south of Harlow's to watch for any movement through the back passages.

Jack cruised slowly past the entryway. The outdoor seating was filled with customers, martini glasses crowding the metal tables. Marquez gave each person an appraising look. The front door pushed open and an African-American male wearing black slacks, a black button down shirt and vest stepped out. A beefy guy—six-two, two fifty—with the look of a Whirlpool frost-free side-by side.

"That's Clayton Browning," Jack said. "Sacramento PD. We put him in there with a couple of detectives in case Cooper tries to make a break for it."

He swung the Camry right on 28th to check around back where Youngblood stood waiting.

"He looks a little nervous," Marquez said.

"That's what happens when you're asked to wait for a serial killer to pick you up."

Jack sped on by, drove down to the next block, and turned right onto K Street, where he pulled to the side and parked, several blocks away from Harlow's, far enough away in case Cooper was cruising the streets but still close enough to move in if they had to. Jack killed the engine and rolled down the windows. The temperature outside the car was even hotter than the air inside but the fresh air felt good.

The sun sat squarely on the horizon directly in front of their view, causing them both to squint. Marquez shaded her eyes with a hand as she dug into her bag for her sunglasses, finding and sliding them on. For Jack, there was a moment of stillness, like that episode of *The Twilight Zone* when the guy found a pocket watch that could stop time. Time had stopped, and in a kidnapping, time will kill. It made Jack irritable, anxious to get this thing moving. To spot Cooper. To rescue Jessica Baker.

Jack checked the time. "Okay, Marquez. Let's go hunting."

50

The cigarette in Youngblood's hand had been smoked down to the menthol filter. He squeezed the stub between his thumb and middle finger and flicked it into the center of the parking lot, where it bounced off the rear bumper of a white, late-1950's Plymouth Fury. He recognized the model. Power-Flite, push-button automatic transmission and rear tailfins that would give any person a lifetime membership in the Caped Crusader's Club. Youngblood's mother had one just like it. She was proud of that car. It helped her compensate for not having a husband; for Eric not having a real father. Youngblood remembered when he was small, he would look over, see his mother lost in her own world as she cruised along the Pacific Coast Highway, bright weekend morning, her lips glossy wet with red lipstick that filled an expansive smile, like that car was the only thing that gave her pleasure. It reminded her she was still alive.

He stared at the Fury, studying the heap of metal that was probably once a nice ride. Now the tires were bald and the fenders spotted in rust. It showed more than age. This car may have been built in the same factory, but that's where the similarities ended. Like Youngblood and Cooper, two men on very different paths.

He stared at the Perko's parking lot across the street. It was packed. Youngblood couldn't tell which cars belonged to customers

237

and which ones belonged to cops. It made him feel both safe and nervous at the same time.

A few people appeared, spilling into the lot and making their way up the back steps to the MoMo Lounge. Two parking attendants in black slacks and white shirts greeted vehicles as they pulled up to the valet stand. Everything sped like a movie on fast forward, especially compared to Youngblood, who felt stuck on pause. There was a wreck of a transient who had been slouched across the bus stop bench for as long as Youngblood had been there, greeting every pedestrian that crossed his path. So far, everyone seemed to ignore him. He'd stand, wave his arms like he was leading an orchestra, before taking a bow with the grace of a busted ladder.

Youngblood turned his attention back to the parking lot and the feeder alleyways that opened to the south and west, cars pouring out and filled with young couples. A band started playing upstairs at the MoMo, a male voice belting Van Morrison's "Moondance," the bass beat heavy. The air was still thick, the atmosphere electric with evening life. No one knew there were more cops and guns in the area than patrons. Youngblood lit another cigarette and took a deep drag, blowing the smoke through both nostrils. He started to feel antsy, wondering if Cooper was really going to show. Maybe he was already out there, watching him, wondering if this was a set-up. Which, of course, it was. He knew if Cooper suspected him of cooperating with the police, he'd kill him without hesitation.

Feeling shaky, he pushed himself away from the Malibu and erected board stiff. He didn't have a clue what he was doing or why; he just needed to do something. He launched his cigarette into the street, the embers bouncing and rolling like a Chinese sparkler, and then turned to the left and headed down the sidewalk toward the front of the building, checking the streets, studying the crowd coming and going. He squinted at the evening sky, the horizon fading from dark orange and darker purple. Youngblood continued to study the crowd, now starting to fold into a sea of bodies. He turned around and started back to the car.

A bus pulled away from the corner, the motor rumbling and spewing exhaust stink. The transient was still standing by the bench, bent over, arms apart, taking another bow. Youngblood picked up the pace, hoping to make his way past the bum before he had a chance to beg for money. No such luck. The man reached out and placed one hand on Youngblood's jacket, his other pressing against Youngblood's stomach.

Youngblood stopped abruptly, trying to retreat from the smell of foot rot.

"Spare some change?" the man whispered through a face full of matted whiskers.

"Sorry, got no change." Youngblood upturned two empty palms and tried to push away, but the man held tight.

The transient forced out a phlegm-filled laugh. "That's okay, my friend. I got paid already."

Youngblood felt the bum's hand, still on his stomach, pat twice. He looked down and saw a piece of paper sandwiched there. The transient put a finger to his own lips, then he pulled the paper away far enough for Youngblood to see a message written on it.

Don't talk, don't alert the police. Go upstairs to the bathroom at the MoMo.

The man placed both hands on Youngblood's chest and gave him a pat. "Have a nice day," the man said as he stepped back with a bow.

Youngblood took the note, crumpled it in a tight ball and tossed it in a nearby trash can. It hit the rim and bounced to the sidewalk. He looked around, still unable to tell the cops from the pedestrians, and made his way back to the Malibu, where he pulled out another cigarette. He paused a second to think. Then dipped his head toward his belt buckle.

"If you can hear me," he said in a low voice. "I got to take a piss. Be back in a sec."

51

Marquez kept her eyes locked on Youngblood as the Camry sped past the corner next to the bus stop.

"Looks like your boy is being shaken down by a drunk."

Jack shifted his head in time to catch a bundle of dirty clothes crowding Youngblood's body.

"Marquez, you get a good look at the transient?"

"It's not Cooper. Guy's too tall."

Jack grabbed his radio microphone. "Does anyone have an eye on that transient accosting our source?"

A voice came back, one of the surveillance team members. "I've got 'em. He's been here the whole time and he doesn't seem to be making any move away from the area. We got a call to the Metro Transit Authority to have an officer come out and shake him down for disturbing riders. Should be able to clear him."

Jack turned down the Bureau radio and turned up the volume on the one transmitting Youngblood's body wire. A lot of road noise, muffled conversations, the sound of shuffling feet. Then a voice came through clearly: "Have a nice day."

By now, Jack and Marquez were two blocks down, waiting at an intersection for the stoplight to turn green. They strained to hear

Youngblood's voice, the transmission nothing but footsteps and the scratchy sound of fabric rubbing against the mic.

Jack swung the vehicle to the right and accelerated, hoping to catch the next corner before the light turned red. Before too long, Jack would be out of the transmitter's range. Then he heard Youngblood talk, and the two leaned closer to the speaker.

"Did he say piss?" Marquez asked.

Jack nodded. "Yep. Nature called."

"Some undercover man."

The Bureau radio crackled and a surveillance agent informed them that Youngblood was walking up the back stairs into the building.

Jack circled the area, trying to keep some distance so that Cooper wouldn't spot them. The Metro Authority arrived and gave the transient the heave-ho down the street. More pedestrians crowded the sidewalks, Harlow's customers starting to spill out onto the terrace.

A surveillance agent came back on the radio, his tone elevated, voice shaky against background noise. Jack could hear the agent breathing heavily as though running.

"This is Shadow 5. Your source tossed something on the ground after contacting the transient. It's a note."

Jack started to get that sinking feeling. He strained to hear the rest.

"Your target is up there. Repeat. Your target is inside the building."

52

Youngblood stood by the bathroom door, staring at the little man stenciled on tarnished brass plate. Hand on door, he paused, wondering what he was waiting for him on the other side, and hoping it wasn't a knife to his throat. He kept quiet, not only for Cooper's sake, but he didn't want the surveillance crew finding out. Youngblood wasn't worried about Cooper's freedom; he just knew that if Cooper suspected the police were closing in, he wouldn't survive another second. It was best to find Cooper on his own, then decide what to do next.

Youngblood reached down and unbuckled his belt, sliding it out, rolling it neatly, and shoving it into a nearby trash can. He took a deep breath, then gave the door a push.

The bathroom was small. The light on the ceiling bathed the room in a golden tint, making the black and white checkerboard tile appear stained. A hand grabbed him and spun him around. Youngblood stared into a familiar face. Although a bit older, worn down, it was still Cooper.

Youngblood began to speak but Cooper cupped his mouth and held a single left finger to his lips.

Cooper reached behind him and locked the door, grinning as he held up a note card in front of Youngblood's face.

Are you wearing a wire? The words were written in dark felt pen.

Youngblood tried to feign offense, shaking his head. Cooper stepped back and waved an open hand, directing Youngblood to turn around slowly. Youngblood spun around while Cooper patted him down, looking for a transmitter or a recorder.

"Where are the cops?" Cooper's voice was quiet, controlled.

Youngblood shook his head again. "No cops, I told you."

Cooper leaned against the bathroom door, arms crossed. He remained silent.

Besides being ten pounds heavier, a few wrinkles sprouting around the eyes, Cooper looked exactly like he did fifteen years ago. It was his personality, an aura emanating fury.

Youngblood swallowed and nervously scratched the back of his neck. "I was surprised you still were using the Rabbit Hole."

"I keep all options open." Cooper paused. "How did you remember to use it?"

"I don't forget much, Alvie."

"Alvie," Cooper said, smiling. "I haven't been called that in years."

"That's because only your friends call you that."

"Yeah, don't have many of those left, now do I?"

Youngblood didn't answer right away, then said, "What do we do now?"

Cooper pushed himself away from the door and reached into one of the bathroom stalls. He pulled out two black, shiny, nylon baseball windbreakers. Large, white lettering embroidered across the back read "Van the Man Band." Cooper handed one to Youngblood.

"Where did you get the jackets?"

Cooper chuckled and, impersonating Elvis, said, "We're part of the band, man." He pointed with his chin at the door as the music kicked into high gear. Van Morrison's "Domino" started to rock and the crowd roared.

Youngblood slid on the jacket. It was a little big and smelled like weed.

"Let's go."

Cooper reached around Youngblood and cracked the door. He stuck his head into the hall, giving the area a quick look before nudging Youngblood out.

As Cooper was leading Youngblood down the small cove between the restrooms, a man appeared from around the corner. Black, about six-two, two fifty. Youngblood instantly recognized him as the bouncer from Harlow's. Before Youngblood could say anything, he was shoved from behind, tumbling forward, falling into the bouncer's arms. He tried to stand but a hand pushed hard against his back, not letting him regain his balance. The bouncer had an earpiece, a curly wire trailing down behind his back, the same type all the police officers wear. The bouncer tried to shove Youngblood off, but it was too late. Cooper lunged, a knife in his right hand. He drove the steel blade deep into the bouncer's chest. A heavy thud followed by a gurgling groan. Cooper pulled back and stabbed the bouncer again, and again, until the body collapsed in a heap, like a sack of wheat.

"Quick," Cooper said, "help me get this guy into the bathroom."

Youngblood remained still, his eyes fixated on the large man pumping blood across the wooden floor. "What the hell did you do?"

Cooper looked up. "He's a cop. I can tell."

"He's a bouncer, Alvie."

"He's also a cop and I'm not taking any chances." Cooper hooked both of his hands under the dead man's armpits and struggled to drag him forward. "Come on, Eric. Give me a hand before someone else shows up."

Together, they dragged the bouncer into the bathroom, leaned him up against the back of the door and slipped out. They heard his body slide against the wall, blocking the doorway from being pushed open, like a drunk had passed out on the bathroom floor. It wouldn't take long to discover the mess but by that time, Cooper and Youngblood would be safely away.

"Where are we going?" Youngblood asked, wiping blood from his hands.

"We're getting the hell out of here. Far, far away." Cooper paused. "But first, I got something to show you."

"Something or some*one*?"

Cooper laughed and wagged a finger in Youngblood's face. "You were always the smart one, weren't you?"

53

Jack watched the back stairwell to the MoMo, nervously tapping his cheek with a fountain pen. He positioned the Camry across the street in the Perko's parking lot for a better view. The front was covered by agents sitting in unmarked cars, patrolling on foot, swarming like bees. Instead of rushing in, the plan was to sit and wait for Cooper or Youngblood to show. If Cooper was already upstairs, capturing him would be easy but that didn't help find Jessica Baker. Jack knew Cooper would rather let her die first than give her up. Jack's best chance was something on the wire. A town. A street. Anything.

But the wire was quiet, muffled noises, nothing they could make out. Marquez finished her conversation on the cell and slid it into her jacket pocket.

"That was Sac PD. They sent Clayton Browning, our bouncer, upstairs to check it out."

"Anything?"

Marquez shook her head. "Hasn't reported back yet. They're going to give it a couple more minutes."

Jack had a bad feeling. "Why aren't we hearing anything? Water running, a flushing toilet, anything."

Marquez caught his eye. "Something's not right."

Jack shoved the pen into his shirt pocket and pulled on the car door handle. "Let's go take a look."

They made their way through the parking lot, neither attendant giving a second look. Jack grabbed the railing of the stairs and vaulted two at a time, pushing past a kid dressed in black leather sporting a glossy black Mohawk. A blonde, Christina Aguilera look-alike stumbled her way down the stairs in stilettos.

"Make a hole!" Marquez commanded.

The girl's eyes grew wide and she raised her hands like she had to protect her perfect make-up from being smudged, heels clattering on the wooden stairs, a confused egret trying to balance on a rocking platform.

The entryway door was open, the inside dark. Streaks of light flashed from table lamps with colorful shades next to modern leather sofas. The Van Morrison band at the far end of the room was cranking it up, leading into "Blue Money," women holding onto martini glasses, men with beer bottles. Jack filtered around the corner, taking the hallway toward the bathroom. It had been about ten minutes since Youngblood left the parking lot, too long for a quick piss. Jack felt his chest starting to thump. A crowd gathered around the bathroom. Jack rushed to the door and pushed. The door budged a crack, butting to a stop. Jack leaned down to get a look at what was blocking the door. Then he knew what had happened. His capture plan was unraveling.

"Fucker's passed out drunk," a customer yelled into Jack's ear.

Jack turned toward the man and gently pushed him back. "Not this time."

The man quick-stepped back down the hallway.

Jack leaned his body on the door and shoved hard. The door gave a few more inches, wide enough to wedge open and for him to squeeze through. Marquez was already on the radio, alerting the surveillance crew and requesting medical assistance. Multiple stab wounds in Clayton's chest and neck, blood pooled beneath him.

There was nothing Jack could do. The blood wasn't spurting out, meaning his heart wasn't pumping. He placed a hand on Clayton's chest, felt no movement of breathing. Two fingers on his carotid artery, no pulse. Jack was a certified EMT, but even a blind man could tell Clayton Browning was dead.

"You think Eric did this?" Marquez asked.

"I don't know. Could be Cooper and now he's taken Eric hostage."

"Or they both were in on it."

Jack had already torn open Clayton's shirt when the medics pushed through the door and took over the scene, going to work, intubating their patient and starting compressions. They drew an IV line on his right arm, hung a bag of saline. They pushed on the heart to pump fluids, even though there wasn't much hope.

Jack stood back and allowed the medics to do their job. He punched the knob on a water faucet and stuck his hands under the stream. The sink filled with red. He grabbed a handful of paper towels that had been neatly stacked in a decorative woven basket, and wiped his hands dry.

Jack pulled out his hand radio.

"We have an officer down and the source is out of pocket. He may be alone or with Cooper. If you spot them, they are to be taken." The words gave Jack the sense of failure. It was too late to surveill Cooper to locate Jessica Baker. Their suspect had killed a cop and they couldn't risk his escape. Things had escalated too fast. And now they'd gone too far.

54

Thursday – 5:35 p.m.

"Where're you guys going?"

A skinny teenager with long, stringy hair under a black ball cap with the word "Crew" stenciled in front stood holding a clipboard, sheets of wrinkled papers rustling at the end of a pencil-thin arm. Youngblood looked back at the kid, furrowed his brow, and turned away as if he never heard the question. Cooper was already pushing through the front door of Harlow's, following closely behind two other roadies. He was carrying an empty box and wearing a pair of aviation sunglasses to conceal his face. Youngblood grabbed a box marked "Cables" and sandwiched himself into the crowd, hunching low.

They jogged across the street, following the flow of workers to a white Econoline van, whose doors were swung wide exposing stage equipment. Youngblood glanced around for any signs of surveillance, then back at Cooper, who jerked his head for Youngblood to follow. Past a row of metered vehicles, Cooper led them to a burgundy Lincoln Continental that looked like it had been seized from a Detroit drug dealer during the disco era.

Cooper pointed with his chin. "Get in."

Youngblood tossed the box next to the Continental and slid into the front passenger's seat.

Cooper pulled away slowly from the curb, taking his time, using his blinker, not wanting to risk getting pulled over for something as stupid as a traffic violation.

He headed straight for the freeway. Once there, his whole body seemed to relax.

"Where'd you get the wheels?" Youngblood asked.

Cooper peered into his rearview mirror, then adjusted it to the right. "Borrowed it from a friend."

Youngblood leaned his head back and closed his eyes. "We had this conversation, remember? You don't have any friends, Alvie. Besides me."

Cooper shrugged but didn't comment.

"Okay, so what the hell did you do to bring the heat directly onto you?"

"The girl." Cooper shook his head but held his stare forward. "It was the girl."

"We got to get rid of her."

Cooper remained quiet.

"Did you hear me?"

"I hear you."

"Where is she?"

Cooper smiled slightly and reached for the radio but Youngblood placed his hand on Cooper's arm, stopping him.

"Where, Alvie?"

Again he glanced in his rearview. "She's fine, Eric. She's protected." Cooper pointed skyward with a single finger and gave Youngblood a wink.

"Protected? What does that mean?"

"By God."

"God don't help guys like us." Youngblood fell back in his seat. "Look, God or no God, you better decide on what you plan on doing with her and quick."

Cooper nodded but kept silent.

"Well? Are we going to get her?"

Cooper opened his mouth but nothing came out. When he did speak, his words were smooth, calm. "Yeah, we'll get her. First, I need to get my things."

"You got . . . things? Don't you think you should have taken care of that before now? Forget the *things*. Let's get the girl and get the hell out of here!"

Cooper cruised with the flow of traffic in the middle lane, blending between cars in case there were any cop cars trying to get an ID. He signaled to his right, slid over and jumped off at 12th Avenue. He slowed way down. The cars behind him started honking. He crawled the Continental to the main feeder road, turned left and got back on to the freeway.

"What the fuck are you doing?"

Cooper glanced at Youngblood, then back at the rearview. "Making sure you're clean."

Youngblood shoved a finger toward his own chest. "I'm clean?"

"Okay . . . we're clean."

Youngblood pulled his arms tightly across his chest. "So tell me, Alvie, what do we do after we get the girl?"

Cooper's eyes narrowed. "What do you mean?"

"Just what I said. What do you plan on doing with her?"

Cooper face tightened as he bit down on his lower lip. "I can't go back to prison."

Youngblood understood what that meant. No body meant no case. But through his talks with Agent Paris, Youngblood also knew there was a string of murders already linked to Cooper. Whatever happened with the Baker girl, Cooper still had other issues to deal with if arrested. "You really raised a shitstorm since taking her."

Cooper shrugged. "One thing at a time, Eric." He checked his rearview mirror, then exited at 16th Street.

Youngblood checked his watch. Time was running out. Soon Agent Paris and his team of sharpshooters would find them. By then, Youngblood hoped to have Jessica Baker in his grasp. As for Cooper, Youngblood would do what he originally planned on doing. Everyone wins. He reached over and tapped Cooper on the arm. Cooper looked over, waiting for Youngblood to say something.

"Hey, you got a...." Youngblood made a gesture with his hand, mimicking a gun, which he pointed at Cooper's face.

Cooper gave a quick nod, indicating to look in the back seat.

A red gym bag bounced in the center, unzipped. Youngblood reached inside, felt the smoothness of cold metal. He pulled out a Smith and Wesson Model 27, .357 Magnum. He cradled it in his hand, gauging the heft of the large frame weapon. "Kind of a big gun, don't you think?"

"I get what I get. Besides, I don't like guns." He paused for a beat. "I knew you'd want one so I borrowed it."

"Yeah, don't tell me. The same friend you *borrowed* this car from?"

Cooper said nothing.

Youngblood shoved the gun in his waistband and pulled the nylon jacket shut. "Okay, Alvie. Get me the girl. I'll take care of her. You get everything else arranged for us to get out of Dodge."

"A shame, isn't it? I still think she'd come with us."

Youngblood thought Cooper was becoming delusional. "And when she says, 'fuck off,' what then?"

Cooper frowned. "Then we do what needs to be done."

Youngblood nodded. He ran his hand over the cell phone Agent Paris gave him. He slid it from his waist and switched it off.

Cooper glanced his way. "What are you doing?"

Youngblood casually let the phone fall to the back seat floor. "Getting rid of my past."

55

There were more flashing red and blue lights in the area than at a Macy's Day Parade. Road blocks were set up, stopping every car coming and going within a four-mile radius, and K-9 units were brought in. News crews swarmed the perimeter. The dogs sniffed the Malibu, the bathroom, and everyplace Eric Youngblood may have been, anything he might have touched. One of the K-9s took off in a sprint, the handler chasing close behind. The atmosphere during a kidnapping is already tense, add in the brutal killing of a police officer, and the whole scene stiffens tighter than cooling steel.

Jack sat in the passenger seat of the Camry, on the phone with Harrington as Marquez drove, cruising every block. The odds of spotting Youngblood or Cooper were slim, but they weren't willing to give up.

Jack wasn't in the mood for pleasantries. "Talk to me, Jimmy."

"Okay, first, your boy Youngblood turned off the phone. But, as you know, it doesn't matter."

Jack told Youngblood the phone was for safety, but what he failed to mention was that the phone also contained a GPS tracker, which worked whether the phone was on or off. An insurance policy.

"Where is he, Jimmy?"

"We got him moving down 16ᵗʰ Street, northbound."

Jack cupped the mouthpiece and looked at Marquez. "Get over to 16ᵗʰ."

The Camry took a sharp dive to the right, engine whining a higher pitch as Marquez stepped hard on the accelerator.

"Give me a cross street."

"Okay," Harrison growled, "the system shows him at 16ᵗʰ and R. No, Q. Wait, P. P Street. There's gonna be some lag time so I suggest you get there as fast as you can."

"How much lag?"

Harrington grew more frustrated, his words now a stutter. "Lag. Long. Go."

That's all he had to say. Jack shook two fingers toward the windshield and Marquez jammed her foot to the floor. The small Camry engine struggled to meet Marquez's demand for more power.

Jack scoured the area, searching for anyone who resembled Youngblood as they punched through two red lights and a stop sign, drawing blaring horns and middle fingers. They slowed near John C. Fremont Park, the vicinity where Harrington directed them to look hardest.

"He's got to be somewhere close," Jack said.

The Camry was almost at a standstill with a long line of cars forming behind.

"Pull over." There was a parking space to the right, the only space within a long row of vehicles. They got out and the gazed across to the park, studying the pedestrians. Jack spoke into his phone, "Where are they?"

"The signal is there. Must be stationary."

"I don't see him, Jimmy."

"What about the cars?" Harrington suggested. "Check for vans."

Jack hesitated. "You mean something that could conceal a body?"

Harrington paused for a beat. "It's not out of the question."

"Okay. If you see any change in the signal, call me." He hung up and turned to Marquez. "You go that way," Jack said, pointing south. "I'll go there."

Marquez nodded and took off in a jog, checking the parked cars along the row. Jack did the same in the opposite direction, peering into each but trying not to look too obvious. He passed a Pontiac Grand Prix, a Chevy Camaro, a few foreign cars, all void of any people. He was approaching P Street when he came across the last car in the row. The meter was signaling time had expired. He looked in. Empty. He picked up the phone one more time and called Harrington.

"Anything?" he asked even though he knew the answer.

"No, Jack. It's there."

"I don't see it."

"I've notified CTT. They're coming out to help you."

CTT stood for Cellular Tracking Team. Agents with boxfuls of gadgets attached to an antenna resembling a small version of an AWAC recon plane. The technicians can track a signal to within feet of their transmission.

Jack stared back into the empty car and something caught his attention. He looked harder. There, on the passenger seat, a black jacket with words embroidered on the back. Van the Man Band. Jack got Harrington back on the line. "Hold on, Jimmy, I think I've found our signal."

56

Cooper pushed the key into the lock and twisted the knob. With a nudge from his foot, the door creaked open. The house, one of the old Victorians remodeled back in the '70s, looked like it had recently been vacated by a business. No furniture, boxes of correspondences abandoned in hallways and corners.

Cooper started up a dark flight of stairs to the right of the entry, Youngblood right behind him. The old wood creaked under the strain of their combined weight.

"Is she here?" Youngblood's voice was filled with annoyance.

"No." Cooper continued trudging up the stairs to the second floor without turning around. "Don't worry, we'll get her."

"Let's hurry up so we can get out of here."

The two entered a small room at the top of the well. Two large suitcases sat beside a neatly made bed with a single pillow in a white pillowcase. Youngblood pointed at the suitcases with his chin.

"Those your things?"

Cooper nodded, then knelt down and shoved his hands under the bed.

"If you want, I'll pull the car around and we can get that shit in the trunk."

Cooper started tugging, pulling out a box filled with notebooks just like the ones he had when he lived with Youngblood.

"Where'd you get those?"

Cooper smiled as he sat cross-legged on the hardwood floor, holding a handful of notebooks. "They're mine. I kept them safe since my incarceration."

Cooper stacked the books, straightening them into a neat square. He glanced back at Youngblood, eyes hooded. "I kept them so that I wouldn't forget."

Youngblood hesitated. "Forget what?"

"Them. Mona, Dorothy . . . Grace."

Youngblood tried to hold steady but he could feel his hands start to shake. "Yeah, well, you didn't have to kill them."

Cooper tilted his head, like he didn't get Youngblood's response. "What do you mean? I didn't have a choice."

Youngblood said nothing.

"The letter. I got the letter, Eric." Cooper smiled, grabbed up a thick stack of papers and headed toward the stairs. "Help me carry these down, Eric."

Youngblood grunted and then snapped up a box and followed Cooper out of the room.

It took less than five minutes for unmarked cop cars to flood the area, uniforms patrolling the perimeter. Jack didn't want Cooper or Youngblood escaping but he still wanted to take one last shot at finding Jessica Baker. Let the plain clothes make a run at it first, then let the chips fall.

His phone rang. Colfax.

"Where you at, Mark?" Jack asked.

"Not too far away. Couple of blocks north. I'm with one of my Chico detectives. We'll scope out around here."

"Okay. I got a vehicle here with a Van the Man Band jacket inside. I'm guessing it's how they got in and out of Harlow's."

Colfax told Jack he would be making his way south. After the call, Jack glanced over at Marquez.

"What's wrong?" she asked.

Jack opened his mouth but it took a moment to find the right words. "Things have turned to shit and I got a bad feeling they're about to get worse."

Colfax hung up the phone as he stepped from his car. His partner, Detective Bernard "Bean" Conrad, exited the passenger side and moved toward a row of thin two-story structures. He hooked two fingers in Colfax's direction.

"I heard you mention that Van Morrison cover band." Bean pointed toward a row of buildings. "I saw two guys heading up the stairs of this old Victorian. One of them was wearing that band's windbreaker."

"I'll go around back," Colfax said. "You check out the front. And radio the address to dispatch. Have them find out what they can on the place."

Bean nodded and broke toward the front of the building. Colfax peeled off down a perpendicular street, heading for an alleyway, searching for a back way into the house without being spotted. He turned left and lost sight of Bean. Colfax made the sign of the cross, a nervous habit. He wasn't particularly religious, barely went to church except for the occasional wedding, maybe a Christmas service, something his wife made him do. Whatever the reason, Colfax wanted to make sure that if there was a higher power, it would be on his side today.

Creeping along a side street lined with garbage cans and skinny trees, Colfax looked up at the Victorian and saw an open window, no blinds. He stood still for a moment, watching, listening for any noise. A second later, a man walked past. Youngblood. He was sure of it.

Colfax pulled out his phone and called Bean. The phone rang three times before going to voicemail.

He hung up the phone and clenched his teeth. The right thing was to call for back-up, but part of him just wanted to kick in the goddamn door.

Then he heard the gunshot.

57

Bean stood at the bottom of the stairs leading to the porch landing of the Victorian. He peaked in the window next to the front door. A good cop, Bean had just left a DEA task force. Drug cases are heavy in informant development and surveillances. Sneaking a peek at an old home for movement was routine. Bean pulled a pack of cigarettes, shook out a smoke, and placed it to his lips. He struck a match and cupped his hands. Bean had just turned to take another peek when he saw something move on the second floor. He looked left, then right, tossing the smoke to the ground and pulling his firearm. He leaned a hand on the door, giving it a slight nudge. It pushed open easily. Bean held steady, checking the interior stairs. He could hear voices. Bean carefully made his way into the living room, which was bare, shelves empty, dust balls crowding the corners. It was clear no one lived here.

At the bottom of the stairs, he listened, trying to make out the voices above, what they were saying. Footsteps, something being dragged across the floor. He glanced at his watch. Time was precious. Bean checked to make sure he had an extra mag. He tiptoed up the steps. A single squeak could give him away.

Bean kept his focus on the open entryway to his left where the voices emanated. He could see the bay window through the door but still couldn't see the people talking. By the time he reached the top of the stairs, the conversation stopped. The quiet made Bean uneasy. He stood still. Then someone spoke. A whisper but he understood what was said. His eyes bulged. The words.

Get the girl, now.

"Freeze! Get your hands up where I can see them!"

Cooper was caught off guard, his hands filled with notebooks and binders. Stopped dead in his tracks, he looked like he was weighing his options.

"I said get your hands up!"

Cooper flung the notebooks at his face, and Bean swung an arm to knock them away, trying to keep his gun level at his target. An immense force slammed into his body from the side, and Bean fell backwards, stumbling against the wall, his right foot giving way. He slipped off the landing and onto the stairs, tumbling with the weight of his body, the hardwood of each step assailing his ribs and head until he crashed in a heap at the bottom. His eyes opened to see the front door, and then he turned his head to see Cooper flying down the stairs. Bean squeezed his right hand, searching for his gun. It was empty. He struggled to push himself up but he couldn't feel his legs, his head swimming, body feeling like it was filled with electricity. Then Cooper was standing over him.

A voice came from behind Cooper. "Who the hell is he?"

The man came into view. Their missing source, Youngblood. He had a surprised look on his face. Cooper bent down and picked up Bean's service weapon. He checked the gun to see if there was a bullet seated in the chamber. Then he pointed it at Bean's heart.

"You don't want to shoot me. There's a lot of us just outside." Bean turned his head toward the door.

Cooper glanced at the open door, then back to Bean.

"No, I don't believe you."

"What are you going to do?" Youngblood asked.

"Like you said, Eric, I'm going to fix the past."

Cooper pulled the trigger. A loud bang followed by the sound of spent brass casing clanging against the railing and then dancing across the floor.

Misty red drizzled down the wall.

Then there was silence.

Colfax pulled his gun from its holster and sprinted back to the front of the house, grabbing his hand radio.

"Dispatch, this is Nora 31. Shots fired. In need of assistance immediately."

The dispatcher responded, shutting down all radio traffic and sending every unit available.

Colfax made it to the bottom of the outside stairs. In a single fluid motion he bolted to the half open door and kicked it in, his weapon drawn forward, front sights guiding his direction. Bean was lying at the bottom of the steps, upside down as if he had fallen from the top. Eyes open, neck contorted. His shirt soaked in blood.

Colfax bent down on one knee and checked for breathing sounds. Nothing. He felt his carotid. No pulse. Colfax tore open Beans' shirt and saw the gaping hole through his chest.

Pointing his weapon up the stairwell, Colfax jumped up and took two stairs at a time. Before the top landing, he heard a noise below, around the back. Footsteps, running, the sound of a door being kicked open. Colfax rushed down. A fence gate was pushed wide. Over the radio, Colfax heard Jack's voice.

"Mark, we're a block out."

Colfax grabbed his mic. "They killed Bean. They ran into an alleyway. Fifteen seconds ago. I'm going after them."

Sirens wailed in the background.

"Be careful, Mark," Jack's voice crackled over the radio. "We're coming up behind you."

*

Youngblood had an awkward time trying to keep pace with Cooper, trying to run while wiping the sprayed blood from his eyes. Every time he looked up, Cooper, who had gathered up his precious notebooks before fleeing the house, had taken a turn down another alleyway. Why these journals were so important mystified Youngblood. The FBI already knew he had kidnapped Jessica Baker, and they had the evidence to charge him with the kidnapping and death of Grace Holloway. He was an escaped convict. What secrets mattered now?

Cars streaked past in both directions on paved city streets. Cooper skidded to a stop, glanced each way, then dashed across the road. He waved an arm, beckoning Youngblood to join him in an alleyway sandwiched between two tall brick buildings. Youngblood breathed deeply and gave chase. A car slammed on its breaks, the driver laying a heavy hand on the horn. Youngblood didn't bother to slow, just stuck out an arm like a halfback juking a tackle and kept running.

The alleyway dark, sun descending beyond city skyline. Youngblood saw Cooper tugging on a large padlock across a metal latch. He yanked hard and tore the lock open.

"Come on!" Cooper waved Youngblood into the lower level of the brick building. They entered a dark room, the air stale from the summer heat. Cooper tugged Youngblood forward as the door slammed shut.

Youngblood waited for Cooper to flip on the lights but instead he walked down a black hallway. Youngblood could barely see, eyes had not yet adjusted to the darkness. Cooper appeared to move in a blur. They turned into a room on their left. This time, Cooper hit a switch and a light flickered overhead.

"What are we doing?" Youngblood asked.

"We hole up here until the heat cools."

Youngblood tried to hold steady but his whole body was trembling. "No good, Alvie. I say we take care of the girl and get out of here."

"You fire off a gun in here and the whole world's gonna come running."

Youngblood paused for a moment, digesting what Cooper had just said. "She's . . . here?"

Cooper stared at Youngblood, and their eyes locked, a few seconds of silence that felt like an eternity. Cooper just smiled.

Youngblood had enough. He reached behind his back and drew the Smith and Wesson Magnum. He pointed it at Cooper's head.

"All right," Youngblood said. "I waited long enough. Where is she?"

58

The Camry slowed but didn't stop. Marquez pulled alongside Colfax, who was running full speed. He turned his head as Jack leaned out the window, screaming at him to jump in. Colfax piled into the back seat and Marquez gunned the engine.

"Turn here." Colfax pointed left at a long gravel road that paralleled the next major city street. "I think they went this way."

At this point, it was all a guessing game. Cooper and Youngblood had a head start and whichever direction they took, the two suspects would still be blocks ahead of them.

"I saw him. Youngblood." Colfax was angry, accusatory. "He wasn't restrained. He's working with Cooper."

Jack shook his head, his jaw tense. Had Youngblood been working with Cooper all along? Had Jack Paris been this badly played? The radio chatter grew heavy. A medic unit, in tow with SWAT, entered the building where Bean lay dead, patrol units cordoning off the area, as K-9s with tactical teams were dispatched. By this time, the media had fully descended on the operation after news of Bean's death. The PIO—Police Information Officer—took advantage of the coverage by linking a description of Cooper and Youngblood as people of interest.

Jack's cell phone vibrated. An agent at the command post.

"Just got a report of a guy running with a gun," the agent said. "Matches the description of one of yours."

The agent gave Jack the location, an alleyway not more than three blocks away. Jack directed Marquez up a side street, where the Camry coasted to a stop. Colfax reached for car door, ready to bail.

"Whoa," Jack said, reaching for Colfax. "Where do you think you're going?"

"I think we should split up." He punched a finger south. "I'll take that route. You guys head down the one in front. We'll cover more ground."

"You going alone is not a good idea."

"We don't have time to argue." He pushed the door open. "I'll be careful." Colfax took off across the street, down the back alleyway. Jack and Marquez didn't have time to stop him. They had to get moving before Cooper had another chance to escape.

Jack exited the car, Marquez following his lead. He pulled his weapon and pushed the barrel low and forward, quick-stepping ahead, as Marquez peeled off to track the other side of the alley, a few feet back. Jack came to a door on his right. He stopped and listened, before gently pushing the door open a few inches. Jack peered inside. Even with his face pressed close to the doorframe, it was too dark to see much. He spun around and saw Marquez coming his way. Jack nodded toward the entrance.

Marquez drew her pistol. "Let's go," she said.

"Why is it so important we kill the girl?" Cooper didn't seem to care that Youngblood was pointing a gun at his head. He took a couple of steps and tossed the notebooks on an old dining table, then pulled a chair and sat down.

Youngblood remained silent, gun fixed on Cooper.

Cooper's stare sharpened. "You're afraid the cops are going to pin it on you, aren't you?"

"No, I'm not worried about that. You stalked her, you grabbed her, you jabbed that needle into her with the ketamine. If someone's going to jail over it, it'll be you, Alvie."

Cooper shook his head, crooked smile forming. "My, my Eric. You're going to dime me out, aren't you?"

Youngblood didn't feel like arguing. He'd spent the past couple of days trying to find answers to this predicament. He wanted to free himself from this mess and from Alvin Franklin Cooper. For good.

"Just tell me where she is, Alvie."

"Okay. I'll tell you. I'll give you Jessica. But even if you kill her, who's to say the cops are going to believe you over me?" Cooper rocked back in the chair, front legs lifting off the ground. "Or when I tell them you are responsible for the kidnapping and murder of the lovely Grace in Seattle?"

Youngblood smiled. "They won't believe you."

"How can you be so sure?"

"Just tell me where she is?"

Cooper laughed.

Youngblood's stomach started to twist, head spinning, his blood ready to boil. His hands were shaking and Cooper could see it. "You got two seconds to tell me where that girl is."

"She's safe, Eric. And she'll stay safe."

Youngblood thumbed the hammer back. "Where?"

Cooper kept on smiling. "Under the cross of God, Eric."

"You and your fucking games."

"Do you know what's in these notebooks?" Cooper gestured toward the stack on the table. "They're my memories. Yours too. Everything we did." Cooper let the front legs of the chair fall flat. "Everything *you* did."

Youngblood glanced down at the notebooks.

"I figured the day might come when you'd betray me. This is my insurance."

"You mean was your insurance."

Cooper shook his head. "No, I mean is. There are others. They're with Jessica Baker."

Youngblood kept quiet.

"The ones with Jessica talk about Grace Holloway, in detail. Jessica Baker. The others."

The others. That's what Youngblood feared the most. The others. It was too much for him. He couldn't think straight, couldn't think logically. All he wanted to do was to end this. To kill Cooper. Killing Cooper was supposed to bury the past, leave no one to speak about those memories. Now, the equation had changed. He trained his sights on Cooper. It was the only option.

"I'll find her on my own. But I can't let you live. Goodbye, Alvie." He'd started to curl his finger around the trigger, when another voice called out.

"Drop the weapon or I'll shoot!"

Youngblood turned his head and found himself staring down the barrel of a gun.

Colfax made his way down the alley, twisting every doorknob he saw. He pulled on three before coming to one that didn't have a knob. It had a latch, which was flipped to one side the door closed. Colfax put his ear to it and listened closely, then gave it a push. It opened.

The hallway was dark but there was a light at the end. Colfax heard some rumbling, then harsh words. An argument. Then came the names he knew. Grace Holloway. Jessica Baker. Cooper and Youngblood arguing over those two girls and other . . . murders. Weapon drawn, he crept forward. "Where is she?" one of them demanded to know. Cooper blamed Youngblood for the kidnappings. Then something about Jessica Baker being protected under the cross of God.

Closer and closer he approached, voices growing louder, bolder, clearer. He heard someone say "goodbye" and knew it had nothing to do with leaving—at least not alive.

Colfax swung around the corner. He saw Youngblood and he was armed. That made him the most dangerous.

"Drop the weapon or I'll shoot!"

Youngblood and Cooper stared at Colfax, whose eyes bounced between the two but his gun remained trained on Youngblood.

Then Youngblood pointed at Cooper. "Shoot him, Colfax."

Cooper spoke, his voice calm and controlled. "That's not a good idea."

Again Youngblood cried, "Shoot him!"

Colfax looked over at Cooper. He saw Cooper was shaking his head slowly, his eyes shifting down toward his lap.

"He wants you to shoot me so his secret about Grace Holloway dies with me."

"Don't listen to him, he's lying."

"Really?" Cooper said, voice rising. "I got it all here in my journals. The places we went, the people we met. It's all here."

"Shut up!" Youngblood screamed. "Who's going to believe a guy who killed his own family?"

"I killed them because of the letter."

Youngblood froze.

Cooper looked at Colfax. "I still have it."

Colfax didn't understand what was happening but he needed to get control of the situation. He held his gun on Youngblood with his right hand and directed Cooper with his left. "Put down the gun, Eric. We're all going in."

Youngblood lowered the Magnum to his side and walked toward Colfax. Colfax flipped two fingers at Cooper ordering him to stand up. Then, from the corner of his eyes, Colfax saw a glitter. A reflection of light off blue steel. There was a flash and Colfax felt the blow, powerful, crippling, like being struck in the chest with a baseball bat. Instinctively, Colfax's hand swung toward the light. He squeezed the trigger and the muzzle exploded. The gun dropped from his hand, eyes falling to his chest and the gaping hole where crimson spread fast like brush fire. As he fell back, Colfax was blinded by another flash. People were running but it was too confusing to make anything out. Colfax had taken a bullet and lost control. He had no back up and no one knew where he was. His peripheral vision began to shrink. Even the pain started to fade. The last thing Colfax saw was Cooper leaping over his fallen body. He could not move, couldn't feel anything. Everything slowed to a crawl. Then Colfax felt the inevitable, his heart stop.

It took Cooper only a second to react when Youngblood shot the cop. Pulling his second gun to kill his friend, Cooper was thinking, "Two for one, just like before." But when the officer stumbled, his gun went off before Cooper could pull the trigger. The cop's bullet struck Youngblood, who instinctively returned fire. Cooper felt something strike his side, spinning him around. The gun flew out of his hand, ricocheting off the wall, and landing next to the officer, who now slumped on the floor. Cooper dove for the gun, two more rounds exploding past his ears. Weapon in hand, Cooper aimed in the direction of Youngblood, squeezing twice, one round striking a lamp and causing it to explode, the other finding Youngblood. Not waiting to find out how badly his friend was injured, Cooper leapt to his feet and sprinted out of the room, down the hallway, lowering his shoulder into the back door with the force of his entire body. He wasn't worried about whether cops waited outside. If they did, he would be dead. And if not? He would be free.

It was the chance he had to take.

59

Jack heard gunshots and bolted out of the vacant building. He stood in the still air trying to capture their echoes.

"This way!" Marquez shouted, pointing down the alley, her gun drawn. Jack reacted without thought. He jumped ahead, passing Marquez and running toward the place they last saw Colfax.

Jack hugged the corner and peeked around, Marquez flanking his left side. A door halfway down was wide open. Gun covering, Jack raced toward it. Dusk had settled, rendering the inside of the entryway completely black. With his flashlight guiding him, Jack quickly reached the room to his left, where he discovered Colfax sprawled on his back, eyes wide open, shirt soaked red, lying on a bed of blood. Jack panned his flashlight, the beam falling on Youngblood, who sat against the wall, legs spread wide, hands by his side. His head hung low, chest straining to take in air. Marquez shone her flashlight, filling the room with more light as she knelt beside Colfax and Jack steadied his weapon on Youngblood.

A Smith and Wesson lay next to his hand but Youngblood made no effort to reach for it. Jack kicked it away as he straddled over Youngblood and dropped to a knee to assess the wounds. Youngblood had taken a round to his upper chest, more than likely piercing his right lung, which was why he labored to breathe. Soon the lung would collapse, the plural cavity filling with blood. If it hadn't already. There wasn't much time.

"It doesn't look good, Eric."

"Just my luck."

"Where is she, Eric? Save her."

Youngblood lifted his head and stared at Jack, his eyes becoming distant under half moons. His mouth fell open but no words came out.

"Come on, Eric. Where?!"

Youngblood rocked his head to the side. "I don't know . . . I don't know where she is. He . . . wouldn't tell me."

Jack turned to Marquez, who had been listening to their conversation. She got on her phone and notified the surveillance crews.

"Does he have a car?" Jack asked.

Youngblood's head continued to swivel. He was fading.

Youngblood coughed up blood. A minute later, FBI SWAT medics arrived with the back-up team. They wouldn't be able to save him. He had lost too much blood. Jack put Youngblood's chin in his hand and forced his head up. "Tell me, Eric. Where can she be?"

Youngblood closed his eyes, his breathing shallow. He caught Jack's eye one last time.

"Cross of God," he said. "Under the cross of God."

Then Youngblood's body fell limp.

60

The hallway walls reflected the flashing blues and reds from the vehicles outside, as the tactical team stormed the unit. By then, Colfax was already dead, and Youngblood had whispered his last words, leaving Jack without the answers he came looking for. He had ordered teams of agents and officers to trail behind the tactical team. Once a room was cleared, they were to strip the walls down to their studs looking for Jessica Baker, in case she'd met the same fate as Grace Holloway, stuffed in a hole in the wall. Slamming crowbars reverberated down the long hall, followed by the creak of nails wretched from wood as the team worked in a fevered pitch.

"Under the cross of God," Jack said. "A church, maybe."

Marquez shook her head. "I thought of that. There are dozens, maybe more, in the area."

"Cooper was here. My guess is he's got our victim close. If she's not in this space, she's in a church somewhere nearby." Jack walked over to a patrol car where an officer sat in the front seat taking notes. The cops looked up, gaze locked on Jack's bloodstained clothes.

"Are you familiar with the area?" Jack asked.

The officer nodded. "I patrol this sector."

"Any churches, even abandoned ones, close to here?"

The officer didn't hesitate. "Got 'em all around. Probably a handful just within a five-block radius."

273

Jack instructed the officer to get units out to those locations, and to be careful: Alvin Cooper may be there as well. The officer radioed in to the command post.

"There is a big church a couple of blocks from here," the officer said to Jack. "St. Paul's Episcopal down on 14th."

"Is it abandoned?"

The officer shook his head. "No. This place has been around since the early 1900s. Made of all white granite from the same quarry used to build Folsom Prison."

Just then, Chris Hoskin approached with Marquez. He was covered in dust and sweat, wearing a pair of leather work gloves, a heavy crowbar clutched in his right hand.

"Looks like the building space has been vacant for several years." Hoskin gestured toward the door. "The dust is pretty thick in the rooms except for one down the hall."

Jack's stomach twisted into a tight knot.

"Found rope and tape, restraining devices. I think we found where Cooper held your victim," Hoskin said. "Sorry, Jack. We're a little late."

"Tighten the perimeter," Jack said.

Hoskin nodded and returned to his team. The patrol officer called the command post for a full search of the surrounding buildings. If Jessica Baker was close by, they were going to find her. Her chance of surviving another day, in this heat, was impossible.

Jack glanced down the alleyway. "The church, is it down that way?"

The officer nodded. "I can take you there."

Jack climbed in the back of the cruiser, and Marquez slid next to him.

"Let's take a ride," he said.

61

St. Paul's Episcopal Church was located on the corner of 15th and J Street. An impressive structure that stood out from the surrounding modern buildings, the granite walls and slate roof resembled a 16th Century English castle.

Everyone bailed from the cruiser. Jack and Marquez made their way up the front steps, as the officer walked around back toward the parking lot. Jack pulled on the handle. Locked. He knocked. The latch twisted and the door pulled open, revealing a wisp of a woman, barely five feet tall, in her seventies. She smiled at Jack and Marquez.

"We were just closing up for the evening."

Jack offered his credentials and identified himself. The woman held her smile, apparently unfazed by the unexpected guests.

Jack explained why they were there, and asked for permission to search the area.

"You can certainly look around," the old woman said, pulling the door wide, "but I doubt you'll find anyone. I know every inch of this church and there would be no way of hiding a young girl here."

Jack reached in his notebook and extracted a picture of Cooper and another of Youngblood. He held them up for the woman to see. "Have you seen either of these men before?"

275

The woman stared at the photos before shaking her head. "No, they don't look familiar."

"See *anything* unusual around the church lately? Maybe an old white pickup truck with a camper shell parked nearby?"

"No, nothing like that."

Jack didn't want to push any further. It was best to wrap up and start searching other places, other churches. He was ready to thank the woman for her time when their eyes met.

"Yes?" Jack said.

Her hung mouth opened, the fingers of her hand strumming her lower lip. "It's not a truck...."

"What's not a truck?"

"The car in our lot. It's not a truck but there's been someone using our parking lot since yesterday. We called to have it towed."

"Where is the car now?"

The woman glanced behind Jack. "May still be around back. I called about an hour ago. I would think they already towed it."

"Can you show me?"

The woman led them through the church, out the back to the parking lot. The officer who drove them waited there, shaking his head.

Jack ignored the officer, his attention focused instead on the tow truck hitching up the old car, the front end already lifted into the air as the driver secured the safety chains.

Jack called out, pointing toward the ground. "Put her down!"

The driver paused, confused at first, before realizing he was surrounded by guns and badges. He swiveled to the back of his truck and released one of a dozen levers sprouting from a metal box. Hydraulic pistons hissed as the front end of the car bounced back to earth. It was a silver Chevy Caprice Classic, four door, late-'70s model. Weathered and dusty but otherwise clean.

Jack slid on a pair of gloves and tried the driver's side but it was locked. He used his flashlight to check inside. Fast food bags, cups, and wrappers, not much else. He called to the tow truck driver. "Can you pop the lock?"

The driver nodded. "You care if I break the tumblers?"

"I don't care if you take the door off its hinges. Just get it open."

The driver retrieved a toolbox from the back of his truck.

Marquez walked around the car with the officer, her flashlight painting the back and underside with light. Jack aimed his flashlight as well, fishing around the interior from a different angle. It was difficult to see inside, windows blanketed in a layer of dust. Something caught his attention on the hood of the trunk, though. Someone had run a finger through the grime. At first, Jack thought it was an X but then realized it wasn't. More like a . . . cross.

Jack turned to the tow truck driver. "Get me a crow bar!"

The driver brought him a heavy steel bar, about two feet long. Jack snatched it and shoved one of the ends under the trunk and pried. The metal strained and stretched but wouldn't break. He pulled out the bar and rammed the sharp blade straight into the lock. The latch broke and the trunk popped up. Jack dropped the bar and stared into the dark interior, trunk filled with burlap sacks, blankets, and trash. Marquez and the officer took out their flashlights and lit up the trunk. Jack tore deep, rifling through the garbage. His hand hit something different, something warm.

Then a muffled cough.

Everyone froze. The old church woman walked up behind Jack, both hands over her mouth. She spoke in a whisper but everyone heard her.

"Oh, dear God," she said. Then she crossed herself.

62

At first, Jack could only see her hair. When he pulled away the blankets stuffed around her head her face, he was as pale as a sheet of paper, eyes closed, a rag tied around her mouth and hogtied. Based on her placement and what she was buried in, tomorrow's summer heat would have certainly killed her. It was obvious Jessica Baker was not meant to survive.

Jack flung everything off of her, giving her body a chance to cool down. Using a knife, he cut the rope and silver duct tape that bound her hands and legs. She reflexively straightened but her body was limp and didn't respond to Jack's touch. He removed the rag from her mouth, her lips dry and chapped. It had been several days since she had her insulin and, according to her doctors, they would be surprised if she hadn't fallen into a catatonic shock.

Carefully lifting her out of the trunk, Jack carried Jessica into the church, setting her on the office couch. Jack checked her vitals. Unconscious, breathing shallow, but at least it was regular, stable. Marquez had immediately gotten on the phone, and the medics would be there soon. Jack knelt next to the young girl, his stare locked on her. He knew it was crazy to think, but he was afraid that if he were to look away, she would disappear. For the past three days, Jessica Baker had been all that mattered, all he could think about. It came down to this: rescue her or live with failure. And for Jack, failure wasn't an option. But his victory came at a heavy cost. His hunt for Cooper had to wait.

Marquez walked in. She stood next to Jack, staring at Jessica.

"She going to be okay?"

"I hope so."

Marquez held out a plastic bag containing several spiral notebooks. "Got these out of the trunk. I gave them a quick look. They're Cooper's."

"Anything?" Jack asked.

"Yeah. From what I saw, it looks like he's laying out what happened with her." Marquez pointed at Jessica. "There was also stuff about Grace Holloway."

"What about?"

"About how it was Youngblood's idea to kidnap her. That it was Eric Youngblood who let Grace Holloway die."

Every law enforcement officer, agent, and detective in the area was scouring for Cooper, tightening the circle around the city. But Jack didn't hold out much hope. This guy was good at stealing identities; he was a survivor. It wouldn't be that difficult for him to morph into someone else and make his way out of this trap.

Jack slipped on a pair of gloves and pulled one of the notebooks from the plastic bag, flipping it open, and started to read. He'd barely cracked the book when the medics arrived. They started Jessica on oxygen and threaded an IV line into her arm. Jack explained her diabetic condition and that hadn't been on her insulin for several days. Her vitals recorded, they placed her on a gurney and loaded her into the ambulance. Marquez went with her to the ER. Jack wanted to join her, but he stayed to preside over the hunt for Cooper.

At a large wooden table in the church room, Jack leafed through the notebooks. He found the right timeline and read. Thirty minutes and three journals later, Jack knew everything he needed to know.

He closed the cover of the third book and settled back in the chair, taking a moment to absorb what he had just read. Now that knew what had happened, Agent Jack Paris knew what he had to do.

By the following morning, ERT had finished processing the crime scenes: The old Victorian where Detective Bernard Conrad was killed, the warehouse where Detective Mark Colfax was slain, and the MoMo Lounge where Detective Clayton Browning was murdered. Three detectives dead. They also processed the vehicle where they had found and rescued Jessica Baker. Jack stood outside the church doors, sipping a hot cup of coffee. One of the officers brought over trays of tall coffees from Peet's, the parking lot turned into a secondary command post to coordinate all the evidence collected from the crime scene. As people scurried about, Jack just watched. The radio chatter sounded like air tower transmissions at O'Hare International.

A car pulled into the lot. A familiar face got out. He pulled off his Ray Bans and nodded at Jack.

"I spoke to Agent Marquez," Agent Tom Cannon said, strutting over. "She's at U.C. Medical Center. Jessica is going to be okay."

Jack smiled through his fatigue. "That's good to hear."

"Any leads on your suspect, Cooper?"

Jack shook his head. "Doesn't sound promising."

"Look, Jack, if you need any leads shaken out, I'd be happy to help."

"You married?"

Cannon shook his head. "Maybe someday."

Jack bit down on his tongue. "Be careful, Agent Cannon. This kind of work can mess with your personal life and will get your hands dirty."

Cannon smiled. "I don't mind getting dirty. Let me know."

Jack returned a reassuring nod.

*

The ride out to U.C. Med Center was quiet, radio on but the volume low. Diana Krall was playing "Cry Me a River," her fingers smoothly dancing across the keys. It lulled him into a daydream state, made his world feel safe. He parked and went inside where he met up with Marquez, who was curled in a chair outside Jessica Baker's room. Jessica's father was inside now, and she wanted to give them this time together. Marquez stretched out her arms and legs and drew a huge yawn that would make most cats cry.

"Is she awake?" Jack asked.

"On and off," Marquez said. "Right now, she's so doped up, I'm guessing she's off."

"I read the notebooks."

Marquez held quiet, waiting for Jack to continue.

"I'm heading down to Orange County this morning."

"You learn something we should all know about?"

Jack nodded. "I'll fill you in by the afternoon. I should have my answers by then."

"See you when you get back."

He showered and changed clothes at the office. There was a short briefing with his supervisor, Frank Porter, before he phoned Omega World Travel to book a round-trip ticket back to Orange County. Before leaving, he sat at his desk and pounded out an e-mail. Twenty five minutes later, he was on a United Express jet to John Wayne International. As he sat in the aisle seat, he opened his bag and pulled out a plastic sleeve that contained an envelope taken from the back of the Caprice Classic. Inside was a letter that Jack read more than once. It explained a lot. It was addressed to Alvin Cooper. It was from Bernard Russell.

63

Jack knocked twice. Two days ago, he'd stood in this same spot in Seal Beach about to meet Bernard Russell, Eric Youngblood's uncle, for the first time. So much had changed since then. Footsteps shuffled past and Russell appeared at the cracked-open door, staring out at Jack. He remained motionless a moment, before letting his head fall.

"We need to talk," Jack said.

Russell nodded and stepped aside, and the two walked down the hallway and into the kitchen, resuming the same spots at the table as last time. But Russell didn't offer Jack any coffee this morning.

Jack pulled out the letter and dropped it under Russell's nose. "We were able to rescue the girl."

Russell solemnly nodded. Not the normal response from someone given good news.

"During our investigation, new evidence came to light, filling in the blanks about who was responsible and why." Jack knew Russell wasn't going to offer anything, so he put it all on the table. "You knew the truth all along."

Russell bit down hard, fighting the tears filling his eyes.

"You warned him, didn't you?"

"Yes, I did." Tears began rolling down Russell's face. "He's my nephew."

"That's why he went looking to kill Alvin Cooper and Jessica Baker. Because he knew that if we caught him and rescued the girl, Cooper would tell us about Eric's involvement in the Grace Holloway murder."

Russell wiped his arm across his eyes. All it did was smear his tears. "It was Cooper that kidnapped that girl in Seattle. He let her die."

Jack slid the letter closer to Russell, who let his eyes wander but he wouldn't pick it up.

"You wrote that letter to Cooper right before he burned his family alive in their home. Do you remember that?"

Russell nodded.

"You should. You caused it." Jack tapped a finger on the letter, making sure he had Russell's full attention. "In here you talk about the Grace Holloway kidnapping. You threatened to tell his wife he was responsible, even though you knew Eric had done it."

Russell shifted in his chair, wanting to run away but having no choice but to listen. "It was all Cooper," he said, weakly.

"That's a lie. Cooper wrote it all down, how Eric had a craving for young girls, an addiction you were well aware of. When Grace Holloway was kidnapped and the news hit the airwaves, you put two and two together. You knew Eric was up in Seattle, knew his history, and so you confronted your nephew on the telephone. But he denied his involvement, didn't he? Put it all on Cooper. First, you believed him, or at least wanted to. When they returned, you kicked Cooper out of your house, said to stay away. That's what Cooper wrote. But then you learned the truth. That it was Eric who grabbed Grace Holloway and stuffed her in that abandon building. Cooper only watched over her. Eric made the decision to abandon her. He let her die. And you knew it."

Russell said nothing.

"Eight years go by without a word from Cooper. Then all of a sudden, Cooper's back in Eric's life. You catch Eric talking to Cooper on the Internet."

Russell started rapping the table with a fist, uncomfortable to the point of shaking.

"When you found out they were talking, you became enraged. You confronted Eric and learned where Cooper was living, that he was married with a child. That's when you sent the letter." Jack got up out of his chair and stood next to Russell. "You threatened to tell Cooper's wife about the kidnapping and were going to blame him for the murder of Grace Holloway unless he stayed away from Eric. What you didn't know at the time was that Eric had reached out to Cooper, not the other way around. It was Eric that wanted to do it again. Kidnap another girl."

Russell buried his face in his hands, sobbing. "When Eric found out I wrote the letter, he became angry. He said if Cooper's wife knew what they did in Seattle, she would go to the police. I just wanted Cooper to go away and leave us alone."

"But instead of fading away, Cooper showed you he wouldn't be threatened. Cooper fixed the problem so that no one could ever turn him in. He killed his wife and his eight-year-old daughter to save himself. And your letter pushed him into that decision."

"That wasn't my fault!" Russell said. "How could I know he would go to that extreme?"

Jack's voice went cold. "You forced his hand."

Jack turned and walked over to the window. The thought of what Cooper did made his skin crawl. It was indefensible. So too Russell's role. "Cooper should have just told the police about Eric's involvement. Might have gotten a lesser sentence."

Russell shook his head. "No, it would have been worse. The police would have found out about the other killings. Then they both would be in jail, facing the death penalty."

Jack had read about the other victims in the notebooks. The details were vague, but it was obvious who'd been the instigator.

Russell spoke through a series of sobs. "When the police pieced the crime scene together and realized Cooper was responsible for the murder of his wife and child, Eric talked to him. He convinced Cooper to plead insanity. If Cooper went to jail on this one, when he got out, Eric would make things right. He told Cooper that the Grace Holloway murder would never come up again. That the past would be buried forever."

"But Eric didn't keep his promise, did he?" Jack said. "Before Cooper was scheduled for release, Eric contacted Cooper by e-mail. Eric had the urge again and wanted Cooper's help. He threatened Cooper once more. Only this time, Cooper was ready." Jack turned and placed both his hands flat on the kitchen table, forcing Russell to look him in the eyes. "In the notebooks, Cooper wrote about how Eric planned and executed the kidnapping of Jessica Baker."

"But it was Alvie that found Jessica Baker," Russell argued. "He wanted her."

"No. His journals said he was *sent* to get Jessica Baker. He saw her picture on the bank manager's desk, that was true. She was the one. But it was your nephew who first saw the picture of Jessica Baker when he was up in Chico, secretly meeting with Cooper before his release. It was Eric who had fallen for her originally. Eric told Cooper to go into the bank and pretend to file for a loan so he could get a look at the girl's picture, then he convinced Cooper to kidnap Jessica Baker. *Eric's* idea. Just like with Grace Holloway. Cooper was the one who always took care of the victims but this time, Cooper got smart. He decided to hide Jessica Baker from Eric. His insurance. Cooper got the girl he always wanted and Eric would have to keep quiet or Cooper would let her go to implicate both of them. She would have been the one living witness."

"When you came looking for Eric," Russell said, "I knew he was in trouble. I had to warn him."

"And you did," Jack said. "And then you came up with the plan to kill Cooper and Jessica Baker, convincing Eric it was the right thing to do. No victims, no witnesses, no more past."

Jack made a fist and slammed it on the table. Russell nearly jumped out of his chair. He jabbed a finger in Russell's face. "Because of you, three officers are dead and two others badly wounded."

"I swear to you, I didn't think it would go this far."

"It went further than you know."

Russell's stare went hollow.

"Eric's dead." Jack said it with little emotion. After what had happened, he didn't much feel the need to explain how or why. Russell had to know it was inevitable. He folded his arms on the table and buried his head in them, shuddering as he wept uncontrollably.

Jack picked up the phone and called the FBI office in Santa Ana. In thirty minutes, two agents came to the house and placed Russell under arrest. Today, it was only for obstruction, but it was a matter of time before Russell would be charged with aiding and abetting.

As officers led Bernard Russell out in handcuffs, his neighbors gawked on their front porches, wondering what was going on. By tomorrow, they'd learn all the details on the morning news.

64

The office was empty. A few stragglers remained but most had gone home. Four days straight without a break, Hoskin was sorting through the evidence his team collected, getting his paperwork in order, Harrington still pulling data from Cooper's computers, searching for anything that would help Jack locate the fugitive. Harrington tried to catch quick nap in the supervisor's office but just couldn't. He lived for computer work.

Jack turned the corner and saw Marquez sitting in his chair, doodling on a yellow legal pad. She'd heard Jack approach and swung the chair around to face him.

"Hey, Marquez. How's the head?"

She balled a fist and rapped lightly on the left side. "Hard as rock."

Jack could see Marquez had been going over the notebooks. There seemed to be more.

"We found these next to Detective Colfax's body." She pointed at two additional notebooks in another plastic envelope. "During the firefight, Cooper must've left them behind."

"Anything interesting in them?"

"Other murders. I've made some phone calls. Everyone's checking their files now. May be clearing some unsolveds. You got anything in the works for finding Cooper?"

"I may."

"You going to let me know?"

Jack thought about sitting down and telling Marquez what he suspected. Seeing the fatigue in her eyes, he reconsidered. "Yeah, when I find out myself."

Jack planted himself in front of his computer, banging out his reports, trying to get a head start before Monday morning. It was a slow process, trying to document every detail. After several hours, he was done. Feeling tired, he snuck into Frank Porter's office for a quick nap. The downtime was needed but it was restless. Too much bouncing around in his head. Then he was out, hard. When he woke it was dark. He got up, walked out into the office and found it abandoned. He glanced down at his watch. Almost midnight. He grabbed his bag.

The temperature outside retained the day's heat, air still humid. The office air conditioner thrummed like a freight train behind him. Jack took his time, making his way to his vehicle. He hadn't thought about anything over the past four days besides Jessica Baker. Now the world was quiet, and quiet was a curse. Dark images entered Jack's mind uninvited. Jessica Baker. The grainy photo posted on the Internet, the family portraits that hung in her house. Then her listless body in the back of the trunk, illuminated by the harsh glare of a high-powered flashlight. One after another. It was painful, almost debilitating. For Jack, it was that pain that drove him to do what he did. Feeding it, like an addiction. Jack and those like him became the witnesses. And although it was harsh and incapacitating at times, in the end it made them stronger.

He opened the door to his car and slid behind the wheel. For just a moment, Jack sat still thinking about what Russell had said, about the journals Cooper left behind. With everything going on, Jack hadn't had the time to put it all together. Like the fragmented pictures in Cooper's computer. Through combining everything in his summary reports, it had started to become clear. Those books, the notes, the interviews, those words—Jack had it all figured out.

"I know where Cooper is," he said softly to no one.

65

Three Days Later

Szentendre was a peaceful little town situated at the bend of the Danube River just north of Budapest, Hungary. Half a world away—literally—it was made up of small homes right out of a Hansel and Gretel storybook, complete with winding cobblestone streets. If you were to guess its age, you'd start with a thousand years and a day. From Budapest, the largest city in Hungary, it's a twenty minutes ride by car, or forty minutes by public transportation, which is actually clean and reliable.

Jack arrived at the Ferihegy Airport in Budapest. The Assistant Legal Attaché, or ALAT, in Budapest, Paul Cameron, met Jack when his plane landed. It was twenty-one hours from wheels up to touchdown, including a two-hour layover in Frankfurt. It was late morning and Jack was a bit tired and stiff but he told ALAT Cameron, who spoke Hungarian, that he wanted to get out to Szentendre immediately. They decided on skipping lunch, opting for a Hungarian version of a Power Bar that Cameron had in his briefcase. It tasted like chalk, only drier.

Cameron sat in the front passenger's seat staring at a map. He'd brought a driver, Peter Goshi, a native Hungarian and an employee of the US Embassy, to guide them. Jack sat in the back of the Land Rover, staring out at the dark green hillsides and farmland, imagining what the place looked like under communist rule. There were remnants of the old Soviet government, but like all relics, they looked tired and dilapidated, left to disintegrate into the earth while the original Hungarian culture stirred back to life, vibrantly, through the faces and homes of its inhabitants.

They crossed into Szentendre around one in the afternoon, immediately running into a wall of tourists milling around in the streets, gawking at rows of perfectly lined trinkets displayed at kiosk stands.

Cameron peered over the top of the map. "Turn here," he directed, pointing at a narrow road that led up a hillside.

The driver, Goshi, turned, barely clearing a gray Trabant, an old East German car that resembled an even worse version of an AMC Gremlin, maneuvering through a series of skinny streets that left Jack completely lost.

"That's the place," Goshi called out, motioning beyond a long, crooked picket fence, at a two-story brick and mortar structure that looked like it was built just after the turn of the century. The driver pulled over to the side and parked. All three exited, passing through the gate.

"Let me talk first," Cameron said.

As anxious as Jack was for answers, he knew Cameron had the only shot to get them.

Cameron rapped on the wooden door, and a short, old man who looked well into his seventies answered. Barrel chested under a button down shirt that, at one time, used to be white, he sported cotton trousers, worn and dark gray. His hair was thin on top but wiry and thick on his arms, his skin red and leathery all over.

Cameron greeted the man in Hungarian, then introduced Jack. The man said his name was Jozeph Mink, and that he and his wife, Heine, had been living here for the past fifty years. Cameron explained the reason for their visit and asked if he'd look at photograph. Mink called his wife in from the kitchen.

Jack retrieved a photograph that Harrington had printed from Cooper's computer. The picture showed Cooper and his friend Janos Mink, taken when they both lived here.

Jack placed the photo in Jozeph's hand. "Do you know a Lazlo Mink? I understood him to be the landlord of this residence."

Cameron translated. Jozeph listened intently, nodding the entire time. Then he spoke. Cameron waited until he was done before turning to Jack.

"He said Lazlo Mink was his brother. Lazlo and his family lived here with Jozeph and his wife."

"Are they still here?"

Cameron shook his head. "No. Just before the Wall fell, the Hungarian Secret Police was cracking down hard on dissidents and black marketeers, especially those that didn't give the police a share of the profits. The Minks were taken away late one night. Jozeph never saw them again. They were most likely killed."

"What about Cooper? Does Jozeph remember him?"

Cameron again translated in Hungarian.

"Yes, he said. He remembers the American boy that came to live with them. He befriended his brother and wife, became close to their son, Janos."

"Where is Janos now?"

Cameron paused for a moment, bowed his head and then cleared his throat. "Dead. He died in a fire."

"Tell me what happened," Jack said.

"After Jozeph's brother and sister-in-law were taken away, Janos and the American took off, hoping they could bribe the police into letting them go. Later that evening, the police returned to the house and told him that his nephew was involved in a car accident. The car caught fire and burned Janos to death."

"And what happened to Cooper, the American?"

"He doesn't know. He never came back."

That was all Jack needed to know. He pointed at the photograph that was still in Jozeph's hand.

"Is that Janos in the picture?"

Cameron asked and Jozeph nodded. Egan, egan.

Jack understood that much. Yes, yes. Jack drew closer to Jozeph and again, pointed at the picture. "Which one? Which one is Janos?"

Jozeph slid a finger over the photo, stopping on one of the faces. Cooper.

"Janos? This is Janos?"

He nodded and repeated the familiar words, "Egan, egan."

Jack stared at the photo. What Jozeph told him corroborated his suspicions. The person he knew as Alvin Franklin Cooper was, in fact, Janos Mink, the young teenager who supposedly died in that auto accident. That badly burnt body? Jack could only guess that it was the real Cooper. During that time, Hungary was in turmoil and Janos Mink wanted out. With his family arrested for black market trafficking, it would only be a matter of time before Janos would find himself in an interrogation cell. Whether his act was intentional or simply seizing an opportunity, Janos traded identities with his American friend. Jack knew this from the notebooks. He remembered noticing the handwriting from the books taken from the Russell residence, how it was different than the writing found with Jessica Baker. His penmanship had changed between the time Cooper was in Hungary and when he came to America. That's because it wasn't Cooper who came back.

Jack thanked Jozeph for his time, then turned around and walked back to the car. He stood next to the trunk and stared up toward the hillside, where a little church perched with a stone cross at the peak of the roof. There appeared to be a graveyard in the back. Yes, Jack knew where Cooper was. He was buried in a grave in the town of Szentendre, Hungary, under the name Janos Mink.

66

It had been a week since Jack had returned from Hungary. He and ALAT Cameron met with the Hungarian National Police and explained what they had uncovered, so to speak, and that the American government requested the body of Alvin Franklin Cooper be exhumed for positive identification. Jack figured if they were going to track a fugitive, they might as well get his name right.

With the days now starting to cool, Jack decided to take a couple of days off to decompress. He thought about driving to the coast and staying at a little place close to the beach, one that didn't have cell phone coverage. He pulled down a suitcase and packed. He even tossed in his golf shoes, just in case. Jack picked up the phone and called Marquez, told her he would be gone for a couple of days. She told Jack to round it up to a week. He explained his plan to keep his phone off. She laughed and said it would be like a person with OCD trying to walk past a glass table with fingerprints. He told Marquez that when he found out where he was going, he would call her with the number. She told Jack not to worry. The world still turned without him.

He was packed and ready to leave when his cell phone vibrated. He looked down and saw it was his wife, Emily, calling. He pressed the talk button and drew the phone to his ear.

"Hey."

"Hey back. Haven't heard from you in a couple of weeks. Thought I'd check in with you to see how you're holding up."

Jack pulled his feet up onto the couch so that he was in full recline. "That's very nice of you. I'm sorry I haven't called; we had our hands full with the kidnapping."

"I was following on the news." Emily paused. "How's the girl?"

"Considering everything that has happened, she's doing pretty well."

"You did good, Jack."

Jack fell silent. When they weren't arguing, to Jack, there was nothing sweeter than Emily's voice. Like a warm blanket on a winter's night.

"Thanks." It was all he could think to say.

Jack could hear Emily fumbling for the right words. She cleared her throat to speak, then stopped. "When I heard Baker's father pleading on TV for his daughter's safe return, I knew you would be the one who would bring her home."

Emily always knew the right thing to say. It made him feel uncomfortable and proud at the same time. He melted. "So what are your plans for the weekend?"

Emily let out a deep breath. "Actually, nothing exciting. The usual stuff. House cleaning, grocery shopping...."

"I'm going to see the sun set," Jack said.

Emily hesitated, "I figured you'd have a stack of paperwork to do."

"Nothing that can't wait. Would you care to join me?"

"That depends."

"On?"

"What you plan to do with your cell phone."

Jack didn't miss a beat. "Funny you should ask. Think I lost it."

Emily laughed. "Okay."

They talked for a few more minutes but Jack needed to get off the phone. A slight change of plans in his itinerary. He thought he'd better repack. He tried to keep things in perspective. Didn't want to lose sight of reality. It was important that he didn't forget about the fights, the screams, the crying and the compromises. Having Emily join him at beach didn't suddenly make everything right again. But it was a start. One step at a time, he thought.

He pulled his cell phone one last time and glanced at his new messages. He played one left by Border Collins, who said he understood why Jack hadn't called him back—the kidnapping—but reiterated the board was still interested in hiring him. Jack just couldn't make that call. Not today. Of all the criticism, self doubt and second-guessing that came with the job, there was nothing more rewarding than prevailing, beating those who took advantage of others. He hit 9, saving the message for another thirty days.

Minutes later, soft bag over his shoulder and keys in his hands, he stood at the open front door, hot air from outside invading the cool apartment. He reached to his waist and unclipped his cell phone. He stared at it for a second. It was only for the weekend. What could possibly go wrong? Carefully, he set it on the entryway table next to the front door, giving it one last look, the kind you give your child when he leaves for his first day of college. Then he walked out the door and locked it.

Janos Mink held the throwaway cell phone to his ear, waiting for Jack to pick up. It rang several times before going to voicemail. He patiently waited to leave his message.

"Agent Paris, this is…." he paused. "It's me. I got your message in the Rabbit Hole." He wagged a finger at the phone. "Just so that you know, I do remember you. From our first encounter many years ago. Since that interview at the Chico Police Department, I always thought of you as a smart man, Mr. Paris. Truly, a smart man. I just want you to know that with the passing of my dear friend Eric Youngblood, you should not have to worry about children being kidnapped for pleasure. At least by Mr. Youngblood. As for me, I can't say what I plan on doing, or, as you know, as whom. I enjoyed being Alvin Cooper but I know that is no longer possible.

"A name is nothing more than something to be called, you know. What identifies a person is his character. Goodbye, Mr. Paris. I can only hope our paths never cross again." Another pause. "But I guess that would be asking too much."

It was early evening in Buenos Aires. Janos Mink sat alone at a local bar. He closed the phone and placed it on the countertop. A bartender wiped the slick, dark wood in a slow circular motion, not paying attention to the phone left behind.

The bar was crowded and the noise was beginning to rise like the temperature on a California summer day. Janos Mink reflected on his last life, the life in America. Learning a new language was easy when you're young. It was ridding yourself of the accent that showed your talent. He was good at that. He did it well when he took on the identity of Alvin Cooper. Now it was time to learn another language a world away.

He turned around and watched the patrons, studying their faces, their body language. It was a new place for a new look. He scanned the area for a new target.

George Fong spent twenty-seven years as a special agent with the Federal Bureau of Investigation, investigating all facets of violent crimes, including kidnapping, extortion, serial killings, crimes against children, bank robbery, drug trafficking, fugitives, and Asian gangs and was a member of the FBI's Evidence Response Team and a certified undercover agent. He is now the Director of Security for a world-wide sports television network.